Old Wrongs

Published 2023
Askance Publishing

ISBN 978-1-909009-38-7

British Library Cataloguing in Publication Data
A catalogue record for this book is available from the British Library

Set in Sabon by Askance Publishing

Cover image courtesy of Viktor Forgacs on Unsplash

Old Wrongs

DJ Wiseman

For Joseph

Stoppes of St James

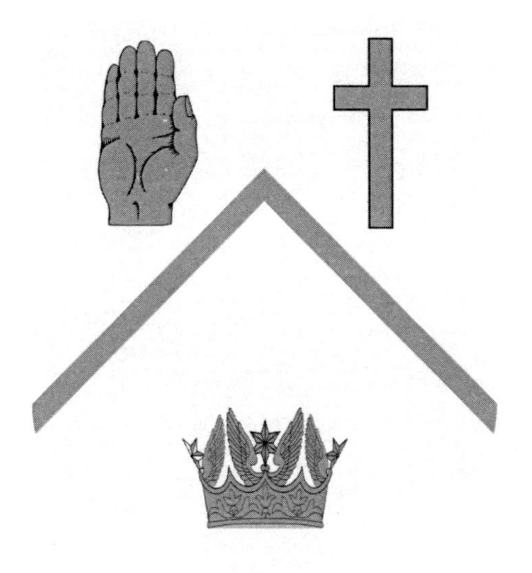

Sir Clarence Charles Tremain Stoppes
1st Baronet 1819 – 1898

Sir Edwin Tremain Stoppes
2nd Baronet 1861 – 1928

Sir George Melville Stoppes
3rd Baronet 1899 – 1972

Sir Charles Melville Stoppes
4th Baronet 1933 – 2005

Sir Christopher Melville Stoppes
5th Baronet 1959 – 2022

1

They'd barely settled at the table before Derek Ballard said, "Lydia, I'm sure you'll ask about my uncle Robert." He paused a fraction, just enough to signal the news he was about to deliver. "I must tell you that he died a few weeks ago."

"Ooh, I'm really sorry to hear that," Lydia said, and she meant it. Robert Ballard had been a gracious, old-world gentleman on the one occasion she'd met him, someone who, if she'd thought about it, she'd have hoped she might know for longer than a few months. But then friendships are never started on that basis, that they should be made the most of in case one or other party dies before it's really got going.

"It shouldn't have been a surprise at his age, but it was. We thought he'd go on for ever," his nephew said with affection. "He thought well of you, too, he often spoke of you, called you 'impressive' more than once. The indications are that he went peacefully in his sleep."

For a few moments they sat quietly, savouring fond recollections of the old man. Around them the slow business of the river, the sparkling ripples of the mill pond, gave a calm space for their thoughts. Derek brought them back to the present and to their reason for sharing wine at The Mill on a brilliant May afternoon.

"I know you're not long back from your travels and you'll have things to catch up on, but I wonder if you have much on at the moment?"

"You mean a project, like Freddie and the medals?"

"Yes," Derek nodded.

Lydia might've guessed he'd have something in mind for

her. Much as she enjoyed his company, their friendship wasn't quite deep enough for a lunch invitation without there being an ulterior motive.

"Well, yes and no," Lydia said cautiously, "I do have something I'd love to spend some time on, and I've no idea where it might lead or what it'll involve, and I've given it a lot of thought, tinkering with ideas, but I haven't actually started the real work and it might be something, or nothing at all. And you're right, I've only been been back a week and I have a lot of catching up to do, and Stephen will be home at the weekend for three weeks. But otherwise, no projects."

"That's good, I think," he said, pausing before continuing tentatively, "I have something that I hope might interest you, something I thought you'd be well suited to. There are specialists in London who we could use, they call themselves heir hunters of one kind or another, but I'd rather not, unless there's no alternative."

"It's kind of you to think of me, but I'm not sure I'm in that league. Family Bibles and old photo albums are more my level. It must be a large estate if you're thinking of hiring professionals."

"Yes, it is," Derek nodded, "but it's not simply the estate, there's a title involved too, and we already have obvious beneficiaries. It's an odd one, unique perhaps. Can I tell you about it, in confidence of course, then you can see what you think?"

"Now I'm too curious to say no, as I'm sure you hoped. Yes, tell me everything, if I can help, I will."

"Right. I have some papers with me, something for you to take away, but I'll give you the outline as best I can. Do you know of the Stoppes family?"

Lydia shook her head.

"No reason you should. They have a fine manor house a few miles from here, at Wheadon St James. Sir Christopher Stoppes was the fifth baronet, and also an architect of some repute. He died a few weeks ago, coincidentally on the same day as my uncle. His wife Georgina, Lady Stoppes, and two daughters, Felicity and Amanda, survive him. So far, so easy, we have those obvious beneficiaries. There are personal belongings, some investments and bank accounts which will pass to them through Sir Christopher's will. They're well catered for."

"But ..." Lydia prompted as the solicitor took a sip of Chardonnay.

"There are two buts. First and perhaps the simplest is the baronetcy. So far as we are aware, the title, the Baronetcy of St James, will become extinct as there is no known heir. And really, if it were just the title, it wouldn't be our job to find them, even if it might be an interesting exercise. Sir Christopher's daughters, being female, are barred from succeeding their father."

"And such things are still allowed, even today?"

"Regrettably, yes, such things are not only allowed, they are practically written in stone. Or at least, on very old vellum. So far as I know, baronetcies passing through the female line are extremely rare things."

"And the second but?"

"The second but is the big but. The manor house, the estate, the flat in London, plus substantial equities and bonds, all these are held in a family trust, none of this property was Sir Christopher's for him to include in his will. With no male heir to become the sixth baronet the trust will be wound up and all assets distributed equally between the two daughters."

"So it's more a case of making sure there's nobody to find than finding a lost cousin. I seem to remember that proving a negative is notoriously difficult."

"You're as quick as ever, Lydia."

"Maybe. What if there were a sixth, what did you say, baronet? Would they gain anything apart from the title? And what is a baronet anyway? Some kind of junior baron?"

"Exactly so. The lowest rung on the aristocracy ladder. Or the highest of the commoners. And if there were a sixth baronet then the trust would continue and the successor would be entitled to enjoy the use of the manor house and the London flat. He and his family would benefit from the trust exactly as Sir Christopher's family has done and as his father did before him. Note I said the use of the manor, not the ownership. The trust would remain the owner."

"And you're a trustee?"

"Yes, because I'm the senior partner, but really it's the firm that's the trustee. We've looked after the Stoppes affairs since the 1940s, maybe longer."

"I know nothing at all about trusts and baronets, which makes it all the more tempting, although it might be a very short project. Are there family records?"

"Yes, quite a lot I think. There's no particular time scale, we're not in a rush."

"I'm sure you want to do it all by the book, but is there another reason to look? I mean, is someone suspicious of something, some skeleton in a closet nobody's opened for a hundred years?"

"I don't think so, no. The terms of the trust are the key thing here, they state that before the trust is wound up, the trustees must be completely satisfied there's no heir to the title. Of course, there's no such thing as complete satisfaction, not that I've ever come across, but I certainly don't want somebody appearing ten years from now claiming he's the rightful heir and with proof-positive in his pocket."

Lydia nodded, half smiling, "No, especially after what your dear uncle Robert and his father went through with the Durham business."

"Precisely. So, what do you think? Interested?"

"Yes, definitely, but I'd need a little more. You said you have some papers?"

"Right here." He pulled an envelope from his briefcase and

slid it across the table. "But there's something else. I wouldn't be asking you to do this without offering to pay for your services. And I'd want it to be for your time, not for the results, whatever they turned out to be."

"Thank you. I'm flattered. But let me look at what you've got, see how big a project this might be. It sounds straightforward, which makes me horribly suspicious. Have you told the family what you're proposing?"

"Yes, even though I don't have to. As trustees we have to act independently of the family. But in this case we need their cooperation, in fact it's essential. When I discussed it with them they were keen on something low-key, something private, they didn't want strangers rummaging through the house."

"Wouldn't I be a stranger?"

"Well, yes, but not completely. I know you, and the family liked that. We have some details in the office but the family papers are kept at the manor house. I'm sure it'll mean spending some time there, although I'll leave what you do and where you do it entirely up to you."

Lydia looked across the mill pond, green and glittering under the infinite sky. All was tranquility, the perfect start to the best an English summer can be. Once, the idea of being paid to do what she enjoyed so much would have seemed ridiculous, so ridiculous that she'd have declined immediately for fear of being discovered as a fraud. But then once, the idea of even having the discussion, the idea of her whole life as it now was, would have seemed incredible. Slowly she was becoming accustomed to it, accustomed to small successes, accustomed to being valued, accustomed to saying yes instead of no.

"I'll have a look at the papers," Lydia said, patting the envelope, "then I'll let you know. But probably, yes."

ooo

If ever there was a time to savour The Old Rectory it was surely mid-May, in the late afternoon of a glorious day when the pulse of spring was palpable and the prospect of an endless summer stretched to the horizon. And appreciate it Lydia certainly did, even if calling it home still didn't come naturally. Since letting her friends Gloria and Eddie have the use of her own house in Osney, she'd hardly stayed anywhere long enough to think of it as anything more than a bedroom and a place to park the suitcase. And being at The Old Rectory while Stephen was away still felt awkward, still felt like borrowing a friend's house, not at all like the home Stephen insisted it should be. He was right of course, if they were together, despite all their time spent so far apart, then it was her home as much as his. But she knew deep down no matter how long she lived there it would always be several decades less than Stephen had done. She would always be living in his home, he would never be living in hers.

These, and a few other thoughts circulated through Lydia's mind as she settled with a glass of wine on the terrace by the drawing room while her evening meal defrosted. Stephen's housekeeper – she could never think of Mrs Webb as her housekeeper – had taken advantage of his absence to sun herself, presumably with Mr Webb, somewhere in the Mediterranean. A good thing, Lydia thought, it gave her a chance to be truly alone in the house with no danger of interruption. What better time could there be to get some research done?

Derek Ballard's envelope of papers lay beside her on the table, as tempting a proposition as anything she'd tackled before. And neatly wrapped and defined for her, not something she had to discover for herself, not the usual family scrapbook, nor the lost cousin desperately seeking a return to the family fold. But it all seemed a bit too soon, she'd only just stepped off the plane and she hadn't seen Stephen for a month, and then only for a few snatched days in Cancun. She wanted a chance to draw breath and when she'd done so, there was a painting that had been waiting far too long to be united with the Victorian sitter's living, breathing descendant. It was an insignificant little watercolour, faintly inscribed on the back with the sitter's name and date: *Mistress Prudence Mallingford 1842*. The artist's name appeared to follow those words but she had never deciphered it. That was the project she'd hinted at to Derek, although if she were honest with herself, she'd also mentioned it so she'd have a truthful excuse to decline his commission.

After a second glass she slid the papers out. A few typed sheets with bare facts: property addresses, full names and dates of birth of the deceased fifth baronet, his wife and daughters, and their occupations; a list of the four previous title holders along with their children and dates; brief notes on the original 1874 Grant of the Baronetcy of St James and a summary of the conditions for terminating the trust. All very matter-of-fact with no suggestion of anything to fire the imagination. Lydia was fairly sure that all those births and deaths would have been properly registered, the marriages would have been correctly recorded, the wills would all have been perfectly drawn up and meticulously executed. There wouldn't be so much as a twig out of place in the Stoppes family tree and no hint of a misdemeanour to sully the family name.

Finding the records would surely be simplicity itself, finding what was not recorded might be impossible. But, she had to remind herself, those records were only as good as the information given, only one view of events, one version of the truth. It was not unknown for the record to be made purely to obscure the truth. Despite risking prosecution, many a groom had sworn they'd never been previously married, many a desperate mother had falsely named a child's father, many a pseudonym had been carefully entered in a register.

The records were not always true and even if they were, they rarely told the whole story.

Even as Lydia considered the prospect, the idea of discovering some blemish in the immaculate Stoppes history grew more appealing. But her life was no longer entirely her own, she had the duties and cares of love and friendship to consider. And the timing was not exactly convenient. She'd very much like to be with Stephen as much as possible while he was home. Two or three weeks he'd said, and he would surely need the break from his gruesome work exhuming bodies from a mass grave in Cuba.

The terrace, the seat she sat in, the private luxury of the gardens, it would all forever remind her of that first visit, already years ago and now, as she recalled it, already from a different life. Looking back, she wondered how on earth she'd ever found the courage to accept Stephen's invitation, she who'd deserved nothing and doubted her own sanity more than once. Yet meeting Stephen had started her on a journey, not always direct, never straightforward, but a journey that had brought her from her closed, tentative world to where she was now. Was this her final destination – world traveller, paid investigator, solver of mysteries, woman of means and partner of a renowned academic? The very idea made her smile. No, it didn't feel as though the journey was over yet, there were lessons still to be learned, adventures still to be shared. And, as she knew all too well, her demons of doubt and depression still lurked in the darker recesses.

ooo

Instead of heading straight to her house and the reunion with Gloria, Lydia parked a little distance away in South Street. It gave her a minute or two to walk and pause at the corner where, through the railings, she could catch sight and smell of her beloved Thames. It was instantly familiar: curling sluggishly green, earthy and heavy, before the stream rejoined the main channel down by the lock. The river was the draw, it wouldn't bring her back to Oxford on its own, but it called to her. And if Gloria wanted to end their arrangement then Lydia would have no choice but to come back, if not full time then at least part time, she couldn't leave the house empty. Selling it or letting it out to a stranger would be projects in themselves, something she could do without until ... until when?

At her door she paused: she had a key, she could've walked right in, but instead she banged loudly on the knocker. A beaming Gloria opened it almost immediately, pulled Lydia across the step and enveloped her in a trademark hug. Whatever Lydia had been expecting, Gloria's joyous welcome confirmed their friendship, confirmed too that it had survived a few months in the roles of landlord and tenant.

After a long embrace Gloria held Lydia at arm's length and said urgently, "Sorry, can't wait for the niceties. Do you want the house back?"

"No, I don't think so, unless you want to leave. I thought we should see what suited us both."

"Oh thank God for that," she sighed, deflating as if all the air had left her body, then coming back to renew the hug even more tightly. "That's such a relief, thank you."

Standing there in the narrow hallway with scarcely room to turn round, Gloria's and Eddie's coats and scarves hanging where hers once hung, the smell of the house still recognizable but subtly different, told Lydia all she needed to know about ever returning to live in West Street. She never would, it was over, that part of her life had slipped into the past. There were plenty of good memories, it had been her safe space, her fortress, for years. But it had also been her retreat from life, a place to lick her wounds. In that brief moment holding Gloria and instinctively saying no, she didn't want the house, one of her dilemmas was resolved.

Gloria had wine cooled, pizza poised for cooking and two

chairs out in the little back garden. They sat while Lydia answered all the questions about her travels in Canada and Mexico, how the journey had extended from simply Vancouver to slowly crossing the continent by train and an extra visit to Mexico to spend a few days with Stephen on leave from his duties in Cuba.

"And how is Lord Snooty, when's he back in Cambridge?"

"Soon, Saturday was the last I heard. And he's not like that, really he isn't."

"I know, don't mind me, I still can't quite believe it. Sounds like everything's OK in that department?"

"Yes, we're OK. You and Eddie?"

"Great, thanks to you. It's been really good, living here's been perfect. I think we might even try for a wedding again in the autumn. Don't double-book me this time."

"No, I won't," Lydia said quietly.

They ate pizza and drank a little more wine while talking of houses and reminiscing about past times, which brought Gloria to a sudden realization.

"Oh! You don't know! I'm temping. Guess where."

"Not at the old office, not out at Cowley?"

"No, but you're close. At County Hall!"

"I thought the deal was we'd never be re-employed, never darken their door again?"

"Apparently being a three-days-a-week temp doesn't count."

"Good for you," Lydia said, and meant it, but her heart sank at the idea that she might ever resume her old life of office drudge. That too belonged in a different world, the world of cramped and oppressive Osney, of safe retreats and licked wounds. "I might have a job too," she said, to look forward instead of back. "Well, not a job exactly, but I might get paid to do what I do, researching a family to see if there are any skeletons in their cupboards. There's a family trust that's getting wound up and they want to be sure who to give the money to."

"Sounds right up your street. Need any help?"

Such an idea had never occurred to Lydia. Her researches – her pleasurable hobby really – was something for her and her alone, even if she did sometimes enlist Stephen's help.

"I never thought of that. I don't know if there'll be enough to do. But I'll think about it. Anyway I haven't said yes yet."

"Yeah, but you will."

ooo

Town's End Cottage was everything the name suggested, the last in the village before the flat farmland stretches away to the east, past Cambridge to Suffolk and the coast. Lydia had been to the house once before when she met Derek Ballard's uncle, Robert. As she approached she saw Derek's car already parked. He was clearing out his uncle's house and had invited her to meet him there, ostensibly to choose a book or two that she might like, although it would be the Stoppes trust he'd want to talk about, to have an answer from her.

He met her at the gate, a slightly stooping figure, his sunhat raised in old-world charm. With his uncle's passing he seemed to have taken on something of the old man's gestures. Perhaps it was finding himself playing host to her at his uncle's cottage.

"Welcome back, Lydia. Thank you for coming. I can almost see my uncle Robert smiling with approval." To her slight surprise he drew her closer to him and pecked her cheek. Perhaps he was truly off duty. "Come in, I've been sitting in the garden reading some paperwork, hardly started downstairs yet."

Lydia followed him through the French doors into the sitting room. It was all as she remembered, comfortably furnished and as neat and uncluttered as she would expect from a retired solicitor. A few pictures hung on the walls and when Lydia went closer to examine one, she saw it was an engraving, gilt-framed, beautifully coloured and, to her mind, was certainly an original. It was a Wheatley, *The Orange Seller*, printed in Pall Mall, 1794.

"You like that, Lydia?"

"Very much. Might it be for sale?" She was the very opposite of an impulse buyer, but she was immediately drawn to it.

"Possibly, I can let you know. There's another like it somewhere."

Derek showed her into a room she'd not previously seen, half study, half library, where a polished writing desk stood beside another set of French doors. It was easy to see why the previous occupant had chosen that place to sit at his desk: the cottage garden could be seen at its best and beyond the low fence, green fields ran to the horizon. Despite the bookshelves on every wall, the room was light and airy. It was, she thought, a perfect room for research, for reading, perhaps for writing too.

"This is lovely, what a room to work in," she said.

"Yes, isn't it. To be honest, I've always been a little jealous of this room myself, always thought that one day I might have such a room." For a few moments they stood taking in the simple pleasure of the space, its welcome, its quiet solitude. "There are a few more books around the house, I haven't collected them all up yet, but as you can see there are a good few in here. I'd very much like you to look over them, see if there are any you'd like to have. Can I leave you to it? Call upstairs if you need me. When you're ready we'll have tea in the sunshine."

As soon as he'd left, Lydia sat in the chair at the desk. It was impossible not to do so, impossible not to sample that garden view from where Robert Ballard had chosen to sit. Not that she wanted to snoop into his life or go through the drawers, but she did want a fuller picture of how he used the room. What had Robert Ballard done with his time in that chair? Written a memoir, a diary – hadn't he once spoken of consulting his diaries when he and Derek and Lydia had sat so comfortably together discussing the Durham affair?

As she might have expected, the shelves were all carefully arranged according to the type of books they held and within each section alphabetically by author. Law volumes occupied at least a third of the space and she was about to pass them by with no more than a glance when she noticed several of John Mortimer's *Rumpole of The Bailey* novels in the middle of the section. They were certainly law volumes, but not quite how you'd expect them to be arranged. It made her look harder at what was there but nothing else brought the same smile. There was a lot of history too, from pre-history through the Roman Empire to Churchill's *History of the English Speaking Peoples*, plus geography and local history.

Place Names of Bedfordshire and Huntingdonshire might have been predictable but *Tracing Ancestors in Bedfordshire* was less so. Had he an interest in family history? Surely he'd have mentioned it when they'd met? Then *Prominent Bedfordshire Families* jumped out at her. She turned to the index and there, sure enough, were the Stoppes. The book fell open easily to their page, marked as it was by a small piece of card. Why would Derek's uncle have left a marker right there? She might never know, but if nothing else the entry would provide an interesting cross-reference with whatever else she found – if she took the job. Maybe a visit to the manor was called for before she finally decided.

On a shelf to itself were a collection of art books, not just big coffee-table books with beautiful images of famous works, but studies of more obscure artists and styles. One, *Before The Camera Changed Everything* caught her attention. It was a study of the British art world as it stood on the verge of the photographic revolution in the 1840s. She wondered if Mistress Mallingford or her painter knew anything of photography as she sat for her portrait.

Lydia took her four books and sat back at the desk, intending to browse through them but they remained unopened. Instead, her head filled once again with how to balance her time with Stephen and the other calls she felt so strongly. He would see no conflict, he would tell her to do both, tell her she was a free agent, free to be what she wanted. He'd say if it drove her then be driven.

"How are you getting on?" Derek was in the doorway, half in the room, half out, leaning round the door. "Ah, a collection started, excellent. Tea or something stronger?"

Lydia took her books to the garden with the tea and cake and explained her first three choices.

"And the fourth? It looks interesting but a narrow field of study, so my guess is either it's a special interest of yours or it has bearing on a project. Didn't you say you had a painting that needed to be found a home?"

"Yes, exactly so. And I know you're keen to have my answer on the Stoppes family. Did your uncle work on anything for them?"

"Probably, I've no idea what. Why do you ask?"

Lydia opened to the Stoppes page and showed him the marker. "I wonder why this page and no other. Could you look through the index and see if any other families listed ring a bell as being clients of Ballard, Edwards & Joyce?"

"So, have you started already?" he asked hopefully.

"No, but just in case I do, it might be helpful."

"I will, but I'll get someone in the office to look through the files."

"And another thought occurred to me while I was sitting at your uncle's desk. When we were here before, talking about the other business, I think he said he'd been looking through his diaries to remind himself about William Durham. I wondered if he might have made notes about his clients too, might have some observations about the Stoppes. If so, I thought maybe you could take a look and let me know."

"Yes, of course, I'll help in any way I can. And let me say I really do hope you take it on, I think I'd really enjoy working with you." For a moment he stretched out his hand towards her across the table as if he was about to hold hers but then thought better of the idea and drew back.

"Thank you, Derek. I know you need an answer. Nothing's changed since you asked me, Stephen will be back at the weekend and that's important to me. Could you arrange a visit for me to meet the family and see what their archive looks like, see if they'll be happy to work with me? Then I promise you I'll give you an answer, but I probably wont be able to start for a week or two."

ooo

Friday afternoon Lydia received the message she'd been waiting for: *hav/paris overnight fri/sat then af1280 lhr 16.25 sun*. So, a Sunday return not Saturday, and Paris first. Paris almost certainly meant a working stopover, hadn't 'Paris' become their shorthand for everything concerned with his assignment in Cuba? Was he giving her the chance to pick him up from the airport, not asking but hinting? The least she could do was offer: *Need a pickup at heathrow*? But there was no reply.

Two more nights alone at The Old Rectory, two more nights to make it hers, or more hers. Not that she'd do anything radical, not that she'd move a single item from its place. But she did want to belong and the visit to Robert Ballard's cottage had set her thinking about a place to work. No wonder Derek was jealous of that space, she'd very much like it for herself. How could she ever have been happy to work at her little table at the back of the house in West Street? The short answer was because it was all she had and all she knew.

But now she knew different things, now she could share that jealousy for such a chair at such a desk in such a room. She could probably afford to buy the whole cottage. No sooner had that subversive thought winked into her head than she pushed it straight back out again. The Old Rectory was her home, her life with Stephen was there, they hadn't committed to forever but they had committed to giving it a proper trial, not just a few months while they were both out of the country.

The study at Town's End Cottage had planted a seed, one that Lydia allowed to grow as she slowly toured The Old Rectory, standing on the threshold of each of its many rooms, taking in the space within and squinting to see if she could see a place for herself. Old rectories were built with the idea of only one private study being required, whoever heard of the rector's wife needing such a thing? Stephen's study, surely once the rector's study, was a good room and well used. It was certainly where many sermons and lectures had been prepared over the two centuries of its existence. But it was not a room for two people. And besides, sharing his life was one thing, sharing his study might be a step too far.

The tour over, she sat on the terrace with wine and considered the options. One of the bedrooms, perhaps once a nursery, might be suitable although it was north facing and held no great attraction. Of the main floor, everything was too big, although she could imagine a good desk in a corner of the summer sitting room. In a house that big she really ought to be able to find a corner for herself.

With Saturday unexpectedly free she contrived to waste it, frittering the day away picking at first one thing then another with little to show for any of it. It made her realize how much she'd been waiting for Stephen's return, how the extra day's delay had thrown her. Late in the evening he texted *thanks no - transport arranged,* leaving Sunday's prospects little better.

As the parish church finished its midday chime on Sunday, *early flight home by 4*, lifted her spirits immeasurably and she set about preparing a little homecoming.

Nervous and excited in equal measure, she was round to the front of the house the moment she heard the swish of gravel. A pause while some exchange within the car was completed, then he was out, turning and smiling, arms open to embrace her. It was hardly a public place, but their affection was usually muted anywhere but in private and this display caught them both a little by surprise. So much so that they drew back and still holding hands, laughed joyously at themselves.

"That's a fine welcome home," he said.

"It gets better," she said. "Come, follow me."

She took him to the terrace where a bottle of Prosecco was cooling, then directed him to take his suitcase upstairs and return to the terrace for smoked salmon and bread still warm from the oven.

When he sat again she filled their glasses.

"Do you remember the first time?" she said.

"The first time we sat here? Oh yes, I remember."

"It seems incredible now, so much has happened and yet it could be yesterday."

"A feature of growing older, I've found."

"How long have we got?" she asked, keen to get the shape of their time together fixed in her mind.

"Not as long as I'd hoped. And I have work to do while I'm here. I know we spoke of getting away for a few days but really, I'd rather stay here."

"Me too."

"I'm booked for two weeks today. Back through Paris again. But you never know."

Two weeks was a lot better than two days, which is what Lydia had feared when he first spoke.

"Will you work here?"

"Yes mainly, but I'll be in college tomorrow and Tuesday, then it should be easier for a few days."

"That's not too bad, not much of a break for you though. I've got something on Tuesday, too. Might be a new project. Do you know the name Stoppes, Sir Christopher Stoppes?"

"Vaguely I think, is that the architect?"

"Past tense. Was the architect."

They dawdled over their wine while Lydia told him why Derek Ballard was trying to recruit her, how she'd agreed to visit the Stoppes home with him, how the rest of Stephen's stay was sacrosanct, she'd already made that a condition.

When it grew too cool to sit longer and the exhaustion of travel began to overtake him, they went inside, Lydia tidying the few bits in the kitchen while Stephen showered. By the time she went to find him he was already in bed. Seeing him lying in there, his face relaxed in sleep, Lydia was struck by how drawn and grey he was beneath the effects of the sun. When she crawled in beside him and let her hand rest across him it seemed that the lean and lithe of a few weeks previously had become bony and undernourished.

2

The satellite image had told Lydia how to find the St James Manor House at Wheadon St James and Wikipedia had given her a potted history of the house and the estate, but neither had quite prepared her for that first view as she turned through the gate: to her right a broad lawn ended in a row of magnificent horse chestnuts in full bloom; ahead, the drive gently curved a hundred metres or so to a three-storey house of grey stone half covered in manicured ivy. In style it reminded her of The Old Rectory, but in scale it was perhaps four or five times larger.

She was reassured to see Derek Ballard's car parked by the front entrance, meeting the Stoppes family on her own would surely have tested her newly acquired self-confidence to the limit. As it was, she was relying on Derek's endorsement to see her through.

Before Lydia could ring the bell, the door opened. For a moment she feared it would be a butler or housemaid but it was Derek, smiling and welcoming. He ushered her through to a huge room near the back of the house where three women waited. The younger two were slim, a little shorter than Lydia, their dark hair cut to the jawline. Both were clearly their mother's daughters in height and wiry build, but the mother's hair was steel grey, cut boyishly short. She had a sharp look about her, attentive and perceptive. At her throat was a thin string of pearls, luminescent against tanned skin.

"Miss Silverstream, welcome to The Manor," said the new widow, extending her hand. Lydia thought she looked many years younger than the sixty-plus she knew her to be. Wasn't it always true that the wealthy aged so much better than the poor?

Lydia took her hand before stumbling over, "Pleased to meet you, Lady ..." quite forgetting the protocol of addressing a baronet's widow that Derek had mentioned.

"We're not keen on titles here," she smiled. "May I call you Lydia? If so then Georgina will be fine. I dread to think you'll find the next baronet, because if you do, I think it'll make me the Dowager Lady Stoppes. Appalling. Meet the girls. Felicity, who hates the name and goes by Flicky and Amanda, who hates most other things but has stuck with her name."

Lady Stoppes' two daughters shared their mother's youthful looks – neither looked much over thirty although Lydia knew them to be closer to forty. The elder of the two, Flicky, smiled warmly enough but Amanda was all business-like. "Take no notice of my mother," she said, "with whom I disagree about most things. But I can tell you now, Miss Silverstream, I agree with her about not finding an heir. I hope you don't and this nonsense of hereditary titles can have one less family to continue it. The sooner they all die out the better."

"Mandy, why must you be so confrontational all the time? Give her a chance," Felicity said, with all the weariness of an older sister who's suffered the tantrums of a younger sibling longer than she would wish.

"And you, why must you be so passive, so compliant all the time? Don't you have any views of your own?" Amanda snapped back.

Lydia looked first to Derek for some support, then to the squabbling daughters' mother. In return she had looks of resignation from them both.

"Well," she ventured, "if I take on this project I'll do my best, that's all I can say. If there's something, or somebody, to find then I'll do my best to find them, or at least identify them. But I hope you'll all help me as much as you can."

"Yes, of course we will," said Georgina Stoppes, "take no notice of these two, they're really quite lovely. Now, Lydia, what can we show you, what would you like to see? Or shall I just give you the tour?"

The tour took a while. They started at the top of the house, the old servants' rooms, now disused and mainly empty save for a few boxes and trunks from childhood. On the first floor most, but not all, of the bedrooms were filled with antique furniture, all beautifully kept after more than two centuries of use. The daughters had their own rooms, not guest rooms – "they stay quite often, it's still their home after all" – and besides the bedrooms and nursery there was an upstairs reading room and a sitting room that looked out over the lawns to the horse chestnuts. Despite the obvious luxury, the sense of understated wealth, it was clearly a family house. Or it had been, and the current Lady Stoppes seemed set on keeping it so. Lydia wondered about grandchildren but kept her wonderings to herself.

In Sir Christopher Stoppes' office, a huge room at the rear of the house, were two desks and his drawing table still covered with pencil drawings of architectural details.

"I'm sorry for your loss, I should have said so when I arrived. May I ask if Sir Christopher died suddenly? It's just that seeing his work still here ..."

"Thank you. Yes, quite suddenly. Here, actually. His heart. Very quick. Very quiet. I was in the garden, never heard a sound." She spoke flatly, but precisely, concentrating on the words to cover her lingering grief.

"A terrible shock, I'm so sorry," Lydia said, and meant it.

The two stood silently for a few moments, Lydia reaching out to feel if some trace of the man remained while Georgina briefly relived the moment of discovery.

"Is it all business in here, all Sir Christopher's working papers and so on?" Lydia asked.

"Yes, I think so. I've asked one of the partners to come over and clear it out. There might be something important, otherwise I'd do it myself. The family papers are in the study and there's a section in the library too, more of an archive I think."

At the study, Georgina stood in the doorway while Lydia took a few tentative steps inside, nervous of touching anything. It was a fine room on the north end of the house. Beyond the French doors, a small terrace gave on to a stretch of lawn on the far side of which was a grass tennis court, immaculate in every detail, missing only the players and the thwack of racket on ball.

"If I were working here at the house could I use this room?"

"We thought this and the library. There's a good reading table in there and if you wanted to look through the family archive it would save you carting it through into here."

It had all been thought through, Derek Ballard must have given the family an idea of what might be involved. But did they realize she'd be exploring their immediate history, not just the distant ancestors but the recently deceased too?

"Georgina," Lydia began, still uncomfortable with the familiarity, "I wonder if Derek has explained that I may need to dig into the family's past and maybe into its secrets, if it has any? How would you feel about me finding something that might not reflect well on the family or even Sir Christopher?"

"Some secret, some deception you mean?"

"It sounds trite, but family history can get very personal. It can all seem clear-cut, well documented, then you just lift up one piece to see what's underneath and the whole thing can unravel. If I take on this project I'd like to know that you're supporting me, whatever I find."

"Yes, I will," Georgina said. "But, oh, yes, now I understand what you're hinting at and I would ask you for just one thing. If you find something about my dear Chris, something that would make me sad, then you'll tell me before anyone else and show me what you've found. Will you do that for me?"

"Yes," Lydia answered. "That's an easy promise."

In the library there were six shelves of files, a dozen or so photo albums, boxes of memorabilia, diaries and paperwork of all kinds. Selecting at random Lydia first hit on the estate accounts for 1923, in the second, 'house correspondence' for 1931, a third contained the inventories for the flat in London 1950-1959. It appeared as if everything she might struggle to find for any ordinary family was already neatly ordered and indexed, simply waiting for her inspection and approval. Somehow she doubted there'd be any blemish on the Stoppes family history, there'd be no sadness for Sir Christopher's widow to endure.

ooo

It was all very well making the world, or at least the St James Trust, wait for her to decide whether or not she'd accept the commission, but it occurred to Lydia that if she were to accept – and surely she would – then it might be as well to have some plan as to how she should go about the task. She was happy enough to work with the family, and she hoped they felt the same, but that remained to be seen. In the meantime, it really couldn't do any harm to start planning. Derek Ballard deserved to have an idea of those plans too.

In essence it was simple: she was looking for a male line from any of the five baronets, a boy child not otherwise recorded or acknowledged and who had a living male descendant through a male line. In modern times British descendants weren't too difficult to find, especially as the family had documents there for the reading: it was the unrecorded and unacknowledged that presented the difficulty.

She reasoned that her first priority should be to take all the family records about who begat whom and compare them to the official record. That at least would give her a firm foundation to build on. Second, for each of the five generations she should search in all the usual places for any child not present in the official family tree. Whether or not that process revealed anything noteworthy, she should also go through all the diaries, all the correspondence, all the photo albums, for anything which might suggest another child. Titled 'gentlemen' being fathers of illegitimate children might be a cliché, but statistics didn't lie and there was no reason to think the male Stoppes were any more or less 'gentlemanly' than anyone else.

But she had to remind herself that the first rule of research was to always talk to the living, and that she would do. She must tease out any family stories that might touch on rumour or scandal, however unlikely. And she should ask the unaskable about Sir Christopher, ask it of his widow despite their earlier conversation. And who else might there be? Did the late baronet have sisters, cousins, friends who might throw light where his widow could not?

She could make a small start in the hour before Stephen returned from college. Sitting with her laptop at the table in the conservatory, she opened Derek Ballard's envelope and leafed through the pages. There was her new friend Georgina Stoppes, born Georgina Pygot, 1960 in Reigate, just below the bare details of her husband, Christopher Melville Stoppes, born a year earlier in Bedford. Felicity and Amanda followed in 1983 and 1985. It wasn't given, but Lydia guessed at a 1982 marriage in Reigate. Where did Christopher and Georgina meet? Not at the local dance in the village hall, for sure, more likely university.

Their births were easily confirmed, and having done so,

their marriage was just as easily found, but her guess was wrong, both in year and location: not Reigate but Bedford, 1979. And it was hardly likely to be a mistake since there were so few records for the Stoppes name. Even when topped up with a few Stops and Stapps and a solitary Stappes-Crenshaw, the results of her searches were extremely few. There'd be no endless hours spent pouring over the details of unconnected people scattered from Taunton to Tynemouth in tracking this family. There might not even be enough work in the project to bother charging the trustees for her time.

If it was this simple then she'd better start making a few notes. On the sheet with the family's details she added the additional information from her searches, noting the references and sources. She'd make one of her spreadsheets to hold all the Stoppes information another time, today was no more than a preliminary excursion. But preliminary or not, experience had taught her to be thorough and keep notes, so Felicity and Amanda were next. Again, all present and correct, with their births recorded in Cambridge. And while she was looking at those two, she really should do the simple thing and check for all children with a father named Christopher Melville Stoppes.

Felicity May, Amanda Jean and Charles Alfred. The last of whom left Lydia wide-eyed, staring at the screen. She clicked on the details and there, sure enough, was Georgina listed as the mother. Charles Alfred Stoppes, born December 1979. It hardly qualified as a secret since it was a public record open to anyone who chose to look, but it was certainly an omission from the details Derek had given her.

There would be a reason, almost certainly a sad reason, for Charles' absence. Searching the death register was a matter of a few clicks, but Lydia hesitated. These were the moments in her research when the impersonal record became painfully personal, moments when the simple enquiry became an intrusion into private lives. Charles was more than an abstract idea, he was a real child, Lydia had met his mother only hours ago.

A few seconds later she had the record and with it the shape of the tragedy. The boy had died within days of his birth in Bedford. That fact alone said something of the anguish his parents must have suffered. Lydia couldn't stop herself from wondering whether Christopher and Georgina would have married in the July, or even at all, if that poor baby had not already been conceived. Such a small life, yet who knew what impact he'd made. Not only that, but had he survived he would be the sixth baronet and Lydia would not be looking for him in the records, she would not have visited St James Manor nor met the family, Derek Ballard would've had no excuse to invite Lydia to lunch.

Lydia's phone buzzed: Derek, as if summoned by thought. He'd want an answer.

"What did you think of the manor? Isn't it a gorgeous place? Do you think you could work there for a while?"

"Oh yes, quite beautiful."

"And the family, what do you think?"

"Lady Stoppes was very kind, I think she'd help with anything I needed. Did you speak to her about having me there, burrowing into their secrets?"

"Yes, she said you'd had a talk about things and come to an agreement. She didn't say what about. I think she liked you, if that counts for anything."

"I don't know if it does or not. I liked her too, no airs and graces, very straightforward, said what she thought."

There was a pause, which Lydia well knew was the solicitor not asking whether she was going to take on the project. Slightly to her own surprise she mischievously let him wait a few extra seconds before saying, "If you still want me, Derek, I'll see what I can find for you, but there's no guarantees. I might find nothing and still be wrong, the sixth baronet might walk through your door the very next day."

"Thank you Lydia, I'll take that risk. I'm delighted, that's excellent news. I'll draw up something about fees and expenses and what you'll do by way of a report when it's all done. I think it'll be important to record all the places you've searched and not found anything. Probably the opposite of what you're used to."

"True. Don't forget, I'm not starting properly until Stephen's gone away again."

"Understood."

"Did you find anything in Robert's diaries? Or from the Bedfordshire families book?"

"No, but I haven't forgotten."

Lydia fiddled at a few things but couldn't concentrate on anything until, a little after five, she heard Stephen in the house. He called out for her then came into the conservatory smiling. Welcoming him home certainly made The Old Rectory feel more like Lydia's own home. Behind his smile she could see that he was still grey, his skin stretched a little more tightly across his cheeks than looked healthy. There was no doubt in her mind that the Cuban days were taking their toll.

"How did it go? Was it a college day or a Cuba day?" she asked, expecting only the vaguest of answers.

"College. And it was a good day. College days are generally good days. It's easy to forget that and good to be reminded. Yours?"

"Also good. I've told Derek Ballard I'll do the job, but not do much before you go back."

They dawdled over their meal in the evening light, talking little and all the closer for it. When the light faded, cool air drove them inside a little too early for bed, and yet neither could settle to anything. Lydia played without purpose at Stoppes searches, while Stephen sat, still jet-lagged, with a magazine unread on his lap.

"Early night," Lydia announced after a while and he made no complaint.

Instead of settling down to instant sleep as she'd expected, he sat up in bed, his light still on, some slight renewal of energy apparent in him.

"Will you tell me what you can of what's happening in Cuba?" she said when she climbed in close beside him. He was always discreet, sometimes to the point of secrecy, but Lydia couldn't help but connect his gaunt appearance to his work. Unravelling the secrets of a mass grave must surely be an awful task, no matter how professional and detached you might be. But not only did she want to know more, she wanted Stephen to speak of it, if not the facts then certainly the feelings. He'd said nothing when they'd met in Cancun, declining her questions with a silent finger raised to his lips.

He looked doubtful.

"It's only you and me, Stephen. No one's listening."

"Yes, I should tell you some of it," he said, without adding to the simple statement. After a minute or two he collected his thoughts and started, academically at first as if he might be addressing his students. "We seem to be dealing with four burial periods, the first most likely from the 1890s, the period of the Spanish-American war. It's possible that gave the place a reputation as somewhere to dispose of bodies, because it looks as if it was used again, twice, in the fifties, possibly first by the old Batista regime and then again later by Castro's rebels. Then there's the most recent we've found so far, not so many, maybe individuals rather than a number at one time. It all reinforces the idea that this place has been used for years, certainly more than a century."

"I want to ask how many, even though I know the numbers don't really matter."

"I don't know, when it's all done we may have a hundred, we may have more. The search area's being extended slightly. But you're right, the number is both important and irrelevant.

Each of the remains was a person, and more than likely they didn't die from old age."

Now she had him started, she wanted him to continue. "Tell me about the process, how it works."

"One trench across the site, layer by layer with immense care. That gave us the idea of four different phases. Then inch by inch we are taking off the top layer. Each set of remains is excavated individually. It's painstaking work. That's my part of it, supervising, directing the excavation, making sure nothing's missed, understanding the physical context. Then the other specialists get to work, taking samples, looking at teeth, height, likely weight, likely cause of death. Even when it looks obvious. And gender of course."

"Are there women buried there too?"

"So far only two out of fifteen. No children yet."

The numbers suddenly struck her. "Fifteen? Out of a hundred?"

"Yes, we're getting quicker, but it's slow work and I'm going to be on this a long time. They're giving us more resources, but even so."

"So, you end up with a detail record of everything you can find about each person."

"Yes, and their location in the whole site, who they were buried next to."

She said nothing, hoping he would continue. They were both staring at the foot of the bed rather than looking at each other but some extra sense made Lydia turn her head. She had never before seen tears on Stephen's face but they rolled down his cheek and dripped off his chin. She took his hand and lifted it to her lips, pressing a kiss into his palm.

"Tell me," she said.

"There was one," he said after a few moments, "the first female, when we uncovered her, it seemed she was holding hands with the person next to her. It may have been nothing, simply how she was buried. Several of the team shed a few tears that day."

"But not you."

"No, not until now. Funny how things catch up with you. After all these years and all I've seen. I must be getting sentimental in my old age."

ooo

By the end of the week, Stephen appeared a little recovered and certainly more inclined to enjoy his time at home. He'd never contributed in a practical way to the maintenance of The Old Rectory, never been a gardener or a painter, but he cared very much for the place and still took pleasure in all aspects of it. He was also keen that Lydia should share those pleasures.

When they spoke about her having a desk and a place to use it, he said, "Of course! I should have thought of that. There's the study, we could put another desk in there, or you can use mine," but he said it without much enthusiasm. "Have you any ideas?"

She didn't really, none of the places she'd considered appealed much. Remembering the lack of space at her house in Osney, she thought perhaps she was spoilt for choice and being a little too picky.

"What about the summerhouse?" Stephen said suddenly, then seeing her doubts, "For now, for summer, while I'm away."

"Isn't it full of garden stuff?"

"Not sure, let's go and see. Even if it is we can empty it."

The summerhouse was a solid wooden structure with an angled roof overhanging the windows to make a kind of verandah at the front. It overlooked the lawn, while behind it was the orchard. Disintegrating net curtains hung limply across the windows, the once-smart green paint now dull and peeling. There was indeed plenty of garden stuff: two floral armchairs too dusty to try out, folding lawn chairs and tables, a couple of sun shades rolled and leaning in a corner, an old push mower, a croquet set, the tiny desiccated remains of a long-trapped bird, and spiders by the dozen. But as unpromising as it at first appeared, it did have enough space, even without being cleared out, and it had electricity. She tried the light but it did not illuminate.

"We can fix that, it's probably turned off at the house," Stephen said. "I never thought of working out here, do you think you could?"

"I could try."

Garden sheds and summerhouses acquire a distinctive and not unpleasant smell as they are successively heated and cooled over the years, the more so if they are kept dry and shut up. Less pleasantly if they leak, but everything in Lydia's new office was bone-dry.

"It's perfect," Lydia said after a few minutes of poking around. "Or it could be, will you help me?"

By late afternoon they had everything, apart from the easy chairs, out on the lawn, opened up and hosed down to dry in the sun. The chair covers were carefully removed, shaken out and were on their second wash. The chairs themselves were sound and free of infestation, and although they'd need some better cushions to be used regularly, for now they'd serve their purpose. Power was a matter of throwing a switch – and then finding the fuse box and throwing another. The tattered curtains were disposed of and the dust of ages was vacuumed out.

Lydia let Stephen clean the windows of their coating of dirt and webs. While he did so, she stood by the door looking alternately at him and across the lawn to the house. There was new life in him, new vigour in the movement of his body. What better distraction from the horrors of death and decay than to be cleaning windows; what better therapy than to be sharing the rejuvenation of the summerhouse.

Over dinner at Le Chat Noir that night they talked easily about many subjects, both pleased with their day's work. It was already hers, but she would add a rug or two over the old lino and maybe a desk, although she'd try out the folding tables to start with.

"Did you ever use it for anything other than a place to store the garden furniture? I mean, did anyone ever use it?" she asked, self-conscious and clumsy in alluding to Stephen's late wife, Elspeth.

He studied her briefly, before saying gently, "Lydia, you may say her name, but thank you for being considerate. We were very happy, but that was then, and now, well, we are now. I must be free to speak of her without feeling she's a taboo subject, and you should too."

As direct as ever, Lydia thought. How much simpler it made life.

"I don't always have the confidence, but yes, I should."

"So, to answer the question, no, not that I recall. Jacqueline used it when she was a child, more as an oversized Wendy house than anything else."

"Have you heard from her lately?"

"Yes, just little updates. Still in New York, but soon San Francisco. She seems to be all right."

"Good. What would you think if I invited Gloria to come for a day or two while you're away? Maybe Gloria and Eddie? I wondered about my brother and his family too, what do you think?"

"I'd be very pleased. I'd think you were starting to feel at home."

"I think I am, I really enjoyed today, doing all that together. Did I ever show you my little portrait, the watercolour of Prudence Mallingford, it's about so big." She held up her napkin to illustrate the size.

"Yes, I think so. The artist's name is just a pencil squiggle?

A woman in a blue dress standing a little stiffly? And not really a great work of art, right?"

"Yes, that's it. I think before I get properly started with the Stoppes, I'm going to see if I can finally find a living Mallingford who might like it. I like the idea of doing that while you're still here, it'll be something of my own that I can pick up or put down according to what we're doing. Or you might even help me with it."

"I might. It could've been painted because she was ill and it was thought she might not survive."

"I hadn't thought of it, but you could be right."

"Didn't you have an album of old letters and one of the people was dying of TB and she sat for a portrait? What did they call it?"

"A likeness," Lydia said, "She sat for her likeness. I'd forgotten that, and only a year or two different from my Mistress Mallingford. But I think having a portrait done was too expensive for most people."

"Do you know of *memento mori*? It's a very old idea, the reminder that death is inevitable, but in Victorian times it took on a new life after photography became affordable. There was a whole sector of the death business that specialized in taking pictures of the dead, especially children, sometimes propped up against the living. They would even paint eyes onto the closed eyelids to make it appear they were alive. It might be all that a grieving family would have to remember a child by. Absolutely ghoulish idea now, but they were different times."

"Did you know there are digital services now that take old photos and produce a moving image from them, so you can see your great-grandfather smile again? Just as ghoulish, in its different way in these different times."

"No, I didn't. Imagine taking one of those posed *memento mori* and animating it. I wonder if it could be done from a painting? It might be interesting to see."

They fell silent for a moment, each considering the idea of animating the dead, not as some curiosity to see great-grandmother's smile forced from her Victorian sternness, but wondering if it might be a way of restoring some dignity to the anonymous victims of countless crimes in countless unmarked graves.

ooo

"I'm not at all sure about the fees," Lydia said, shaking her head. "It seems wrong, it's way too much."

Derek Ballard had anticipated just such a reaction. "Well, if it makes you feel any better, I've done some research, not for your benefit, but for the trust. I have a duty to be sure that the fee is reasonable for the service. I could never authorize the trust to make a payment that wasn't justified. And I can assure you that this is. It would be quite wrong for the trust to pay anything more or anything less."

Which rather put an end to Lydia's objections. Still unhappy, but mollified, she signed the agreement, slipping her copy into her bag.

"So, you'll start on Monday? I'll let Lady Stoppes know. From then on you and she can make your own arrangements."

"Could you ask her to write a letter of introduction for me, something I can use if I want to talk to any relatives or friends or work colleagues? Something similar from you might be handy too, you'd be better at wording it than I would."

"Yes, we can do that. Do you have somebody in mind?"

"I do actually," she said sheepishly. "I've done a little preliminary exploration and the late Sir Christopher's aunt and a cousin are still alive. I hope she'll have memories and stories of the family, her father was the third baronet, her brother the fourth and her nephew the fifth. You can't beat an eyewitness account. I thought I should talk to them, get another view of the family apart from Lady Stoppes'. But I didn't think I should just go barging in."

She was tempted to also mention her discovering the birth and premature death of Charles Alfred, as though it might somehow verify her diligence, but she stopped short. It could have no relevance to the enquiry, no bearing on the outcome.

"It's no problem, I'll get it done. Now, I have something for you, Lydia." Derek Ballard slid *Prominent Bedfordshire Families* across the table towards her. "My uncle's book, I've had someone go through it and compare the names to our files. Apart from the Stoppes there are three other families who we have as clients, or rather two, the third was a long time ago. I've put a marker on those families' pages in the book, along with a note of what kind of work we've done, which partner and the date of the last work. The one who we haven't done anything for many years, the Claptons, were clients of my uncle. The two others for whom we still work were never his clients, although over the years he'd certainly have known about them."

"That's great, thank you. But the question remains: why did your uncle put a marker against the Stoppes?"

"I haven't been through his diaries yet, there may be a clue in there, or perhaps in the firm's files."

"They would be for you to look at rather than me, I assume."

"Yes, I'm sure you'll find copies of most of it at the manor, and better you see it there than in the files here. But I think I can trust you with my uncle's papers and diaries. It's more work, but you'll know what you're looking for better than me."

Lydia thought it would be nice to think so, but said nothing.

"Would you like a second look at Town's End Cottage, to see if there's anything else you'd like to have?"

"I could pick up the diaries one day next week if you like."

"Yes," the solicitor said, as if about to add something before changing his mind. He sat for a moment, considering, pressing his fingers together as if in prayer, pursing his lips in concentration. It was exactly as he'd sat during Lydia's first visit to the office, when she'd manoeuvred her way into seeing him. His uncle Robert had sat in the same pose while she'd recited the Durham case to him.

"How is Stephen?" Derek said suddenly.

"Oh, he's fine," Lydia said, somewhat surprised by the change of subject. "Off again at the weekend unfortunately. Hence my start on Monday."

"Yes, yes of course. The next time he's home you should bring him over to the house one day, lunch or supper or something. Or maybe at the club, the food's probably better there."

That evening while Lydia and Stephen sat together after their meal, Lydia mentioned Derek asking after him. "It's funny to get a glimpse of how others see you. Derek Ballard sees us as a couple and I've only just got used to feeling that way myself. I'd never really imagined how others see us. Apart from Gloria, and she's an open book. Do any of your colleagues ask after me like that?"

"Sorry, no, not that I recall."

"You know, Stephen, I'm beginning to think that the Stoppes affair is going to take a very long time. There's almost no end of records and places I could investigate just in case there was something to be found. I don't know how I'll call a stop to it and say, enough, there is no sixth baronet. I'm not even sure I'll know if I do find someone, how I'll be able to say anything with certainty without any records to back it up."

"DNA, I suppose."

"Are you using it to identify your victims?"

"Yes, but not so much identify an individual, that's extremely unlikely, rather more to identify the person's background, American, European, African, that kind of thing. That can tell us a lot, especially when there might be a little clothing, a buckle, a shoe or another artifact like a rosary. It's not any one thing, it's building a picture. Oh, and with teeth and bones there is a way of working out where a person is likely to have lived, especially in younger life. There's an element that's incorporated into teeth from food and water. It's a strontium isotope. But, like everything else, it's a contributor to the picture, not an absolute. And of course if the individual has such-and-such strontium then you need a comparison marker to work out anything."

"At the end of it all, what's the best you can possibly hope for, for the people you're exhuming?"

"For me that's easy. That we have discovered everything about them and their manner of dying as is possible to discover with the resources we have. We cannot bring them back, but if we can tell their stories, even part of their stories, that will be something."

ooo

At precisely two in the afternoon, the car arrived at The Old Rectory. They were both listening and watching for it, its imminent arrival blighting their conversation, inhibiting action.

"I'm sorry we didn't get very far with Mistress Mallingford," Stephen said.

"I don't know where to take it from here, we don't even have a starting point. My guess is that she was either never on the census or the transcript has her recorded under something quite different."

Talking of the Mallingford portrait was a distraction, it was something for them to focus on for a few moments, something to delay the parting words. His case was packed and ready, had been since they'd risen at ten, luxuriously late for them, after a breakfast in bed. A grey and drizzly day had kept them indoors, finding little jobs to do, reminding each other of items to be attended to in the coming weeks. She could visit him whenever she wished, they could take a break in Cancun or Nassau or Kingston or any of a dozen other Caribbean resorts, and they might yet, but they were both expecting that the next time they would meet would be his next planned leave in ten weeks' time, right where they were.

"If you need me, need someone to talk to, just say and I'll come. I can drop the Stoppes thing, I can drop anything," Lydia said, her words muffled in his goodbye cuddle.

"Thank you, we'll talk soon. I'll be OK. I've got a perspective on it now, thank you."

"I will miss you very much, more than I could have ever thought," she said, pushing him away slightly to make room for the final kiss.

"Yes, me too," he said.

Then he was turning away and out into the rain, the car door held open for him, his bags already loaded. "Look after the old place," he said, and moments later the wheels crunched the gravel and he was gone.

It is always easier for the leaver than the one left, or so it is said. It was certainly how Lydia felt as she stood alone at the door, the big house silent around her. She had plenty to look forward to, she had her passion, her family history sleuthing, but she had nothing right at that moment except the space where he had been. He was already being whisked to Heathrow and from there to Paris and important conversations with important people. He would barely be out of the village and yet she was sure he'd have his papers out, the first call of his journey would already be ringing on a phone in London or Paris or New York.

She wasn't short of practice at being alone, it had been her way of life for years. But she'd taken to sharing life with Stephen, tentatively at first, but with growing pleasure. Now she must once again dust down the old ways and relearn them.

Between the moment he left and Monday morning she must make a plan of all she intended to do at St James Manor. Above all she should have a methodical process, in her mind at least, as to how to tackle the sheer volume of the family's records. She should also get her workspace in the summerhouse organized and comfortable. But even as she considered it, the wind rose and the drizzle hardened into proper rain. For today it would have to be Stephen's desk. The prospect, once a little daunting, was suddenly welcome.

3

The last of the rain cleared as Lydia drove west from Grantchester toward Wheadon St James and her first official day on the Stoppes project – in fact, her first day of paid work since redundancy a lifetime ago in Oxford. It was a peculiar thing, the idea of being paid to do what she loved doing, and it would have her working to a different beat. It might be a good thing, she thought, as she turned down Manor Lane from the centre of the village, it might concentrate her effort when all too often she could waste endless hours sitting and dreaming of solutions to her puzzles.

Immediately to her right was the parish church of St James with its graveyard, flanked by the more modern burial ground. After that, hiding behind tall hedges, were a couple of newer houses, from the sixties or seventies Lydia guessed. Beyond them it was open farmland. On her left the walled grounds of the manor house ran the length of the lane, ending in the gated farmyard of Manor Farm, which was also part of the trust's holdings. Slowing to turn through the main gate of the manor itself, she was again taken by the beautiful prospect it presented, the huge expanse of close-cropped lawn freshened to perfection by the weekend rain, the house itself solid and reliable, and above the whole scene the perfect clarity of blue sky and white clouds after a clearing shower.

Georgina Stoppes must have been looking out for her because no sooner had Lydia stopped by the main door than it opened, the lady of the house beaming a welcoming smile.

"Right," she said once Lydia was inside. "Let's get the ground rules established. First, come and go as you please, here's a key to the side door. Park by the stables and come in that way. If you want coffee or anything I usually have some brewing, if not please make it for yourself. I haven't been going out much lately so I'm usually home, but we'll make sure we know what each of us is doing a couple of days ahead. If I'm home we'll have lunch together, I should say if you'd like. I know I would like that, I'll enjoy the company to tell you the truth. What else?"

"That's really very kind, thank you. I was going to try and be invisible, even if that sounds odd. I don't want to disturb you. I know you're adjusting to a different way of living. It can't be easy."

"No, thank you, but you're an excellent distraction. Where do you want to start?"

"In Sir Christopher's study if that's all right with you. I want to go through everything there before starting on the library. Actually the amount of work in the library is really quite daunting. Ah, but I forget myself. There is one thing in the library that I want to look at before anything else. I saw a family Bible in there when I was here last. That's my starting point. Oh, and if we're having lunch together, do you think you'd mind just talking about the family, I mean Sir Christopher's family, nothing in particular, just chatting really."

"I don't mind chatting, what are you looking for?"

"I have no idea. Hopefully it will reveal itself to me at the vital moment."

They both laughed, Georgina putting her hand loosely on Lydia's arm as they did so, as if they were the oldest of friends.

The Bible was where Lydia remembered it, the first volume on the topmost of the three lower shelves of family records. As she expected, it was hefty, its corners brass bound and the whole volume fastened by brass clasps. With luck, it would contain a record of the Stoppes births, deaths and marriages from the early years to modern times.

Lydia laid it on the library table, undid the clasps, then opened it gingerly in case the binding might be damaged. It was a beautiful object, illustrated with coloured engravings to show off all that was best in British printing and publishing in the 1850s. Close to the front were the pages where the family and successive generations could enter their names and their children's names. This was a Bible intended, and expected, to last.

Georgina Stoppes stood at Lydia's shoulder as they examined the first entries: Clarence Charles Tremain Stoppes and Evelyn Mary Battams, married in 1857, their first child, Mary Eloise, born in 1859. The handwriting suggested that the three entries were made at the same time, perhaps new parents proudly recording their new daughter, the first of those many hoped-for generations to follow. Edwin Tremain was shown in a different ink, but the same firm hand, for 1861, Sarah Lucy in a more looping style for 1863.

"Clarence Stoppes was the first baronet, I think," Lydia said, knowing very well that he was but not wanting to appear more knowledgeable in family matters than her host.

"I've never looked at this before, not in all the years I've lived here."

Marriages for the two daughters followed, Mary in 1880 and Sarah in 1886. Each union produced children, Diana and Valentine to Mary and a son, Albert, to Sarah. Edwin's marriage to Henrietta Jane Mathers was twelve years later with no children recorded. In fact, Edwin's marriage was the last entry, neither he nor any of the subsequent baronets had seen fit to record their marriages or their children, it was a family tree apparently cut off in its prime. A lack of interest? Or something that couldn't be recorded? Certainly not lack of opportunity.

"That's disappointing," Lydia said, as much surprised as disappointed. "Even so, I'll photograph these pages, then cross-check them to the registers and anything else I find.

And, since I must start as I mean to go on, I'll make my first record of what I found and where. I was really expecting nothing at all, or the whole family all the way down to you, Felicity and Amanda."

"Felicity has two of her own, Matthew and Catherine," Georgina said proudly.

"I expect you enjoy them."

Lydia leafed through a few more pages of the Bible, looking for any document that might have been placed there, before closing it up and replacing it on the shelf.

"Lydia, I'm going to let you get on. Find me if you need anything, coffee in an hour or so."

In the study Lydia settled herself in Sir Christopher's chair at his desk and took stock of what the room contained. More bookshelves, inevitably, but not crammed full like Robert's cottage. A quick scan of the titles showed many concerned architecture. Two easy chairs faced the window, a coffee table between them. There was art on the walls, unframed and painted in a modern style. To Lydia's untrained eye it had a certain quality to it, which suggested that the owner had known something about art.

The desk had seven drawers plus a wide drawer across the middle. Somewhat predictably the wide drawer contained all the unclassifiable bits and pieces that all such drawers collect over the years. It was dozens of things but it was devoid of information. Four more held much of the same, old phones and chargers, cables with no function. The fifth was more promising, a file of recent bills, credit card statements for the previous few months, a tax assessment for the manor which took Lydia's breath away and then made her wonder why it wasn't with Derek Ballard since surely the trust would pay the house taxes? But there was nothing of immediate interest. The sixth held the office hardware: stapler, hole punch, rulers, a dozen pens. The seventh, the double height drawer on the bottom right held files all neatly labelled. Despite the labels, if she were looking for something hidden shouldn't she look in *Volvo Service Info* and *Guarantees & Warranties* just as diligently as in *Children's Trusts*?

Diligence being one of Lydia's virtues, and, she supposed, one reason that Derek Ballard had employed her, she dutifully leafed through every page of every file. Of them all, the information on Felicity and Amanda's trust was the nearest thing to be relevant, but there was no shock mention of a third child. A picture was emerging of Sir Christopher Stoppes as a steady man, a careful man, he might even have been a slightly boring man, although as soon as she thought it Lydia took it back, at least until she'd seen something of the buildings he'd designed. And besides, couldn't the same be said of Stephen, wasn't he a steady man, a careful man, yet very far from boring?

She wearily recorded her searches, each of the files examined, the lack of any discovery. As she finished the last entry it suddenly struck her that this was how the whole project would be. Finding nothing was the project, it was the purpose of it all, it was the expected outcome. More than expected, it was the highly likely outcome. She could talk all she wanted, open a thousand files, check a hundred diaries but when it was all done, there'd be nothing to show for it. Derek Ballard could save everyone a lot of time and trouble and declare himself 'completely satisfied' immediately.

Over lunch in the kitchen – crusty French bread and Camembert washed down with chilled Sauvignon – Lydia asked Georgina for all the dates of all the events she could recall for her husband and his family. She could do the simple research, it would hardly be difficult, but in asking Georgina she began the process of discovering the Stoppes through memories and stories. Talking of someone's birth date can so easily lead on to memories of those birthday parties.

"Everything has always revolved around this place, around the manor, we never seemed to go anywhere else. People came to the manor. No surprise really, it's a wonderful place."

"Did you live here after you were married?"

"Yes, we did. And that might not be a good thing for many people, but it worked for us. Of course, there was the flat in town, we used that quite a lot, like Amanda does now."

"That was a long time, thirty or forty years you shared the house with Sir Christopher's parents."

"It does make you lazy," Georgina said with a smile. "Oh, and when we were first married, Chris's Aunt Elizabeth was here with her husband Richard and their daughter Ann, Chris's cousin. They were fond of each other, more like brother and sister really. I think the children of the family have always lived here with their parents, maybe their grandparents too, but I never knew Chris's grandparents."

"So, there was Sir Christopher, his parents and his Aunt Elizabeth's family. Was there ever any mention of other siblings?"

"I suppose that's the big question, that's why you're here. No, not that I ever knew of."

Lydia was enjoying the lunch and the company, in a very short time she'd felt comfortable with Georgina Stoppes, although she hesitated over the question she most wanted to ask. But a fine lunch or not, she was supposedly working, not socializing.

"Yes, that's why I'm here," she said slowly. "Do you think it's even possible that there's a sixth baronet waiting in the wings, from what you know of the family? From what you know of Sir Christopher?"

"I don't. And by that I mean I don't think he had a long-lost brother and I don't think Chris had another son by someone else. Did you know we had a son ourselves? Our first baby. He died after four days. We don't know why."

"That's so sad," Lydia said, avoiding Georgina's eyes and forcing herself to think it was the first she knew of it.

"Yes, it still is, even though it was a very long time ago. Do you have any children Lydia?" Georgina asked, gently enough to overcome any pain she might invoke by asking.

"No, I don't. I was married, once, although that seems a very long time ago too. Nothing dramatic, it kind of petered out."

"Divorced?"

"Yes."

"Then tell me, when that happened, did you know something was wrong, did your husband have an affair?"

"Yes, he did. And no, I didn't so much know, it was more that I just wasn't surprised."

"Well, I was lucky. Just as you weren't surprised, I will be absolutely astonished if you find something. Chris wasn't a man who'd have ignored a son."

Which Lydia thought was as good a yardstick by which to judge Sir Christopher as any she could imagine. The file marked *Children's Trusts* would surely have been the place for a reference to a son if there were any to be found.

"Georgina, were there any surprises in Sir Christopher's will? A bequest to someone you didn't really know?"

"None at all. A few local charities, something for his cousin Ann, otherwise just Felicity, Amanda and myself. Chris and I drew up our wills together, and the girls' trust, twenty years ago when his father came close to dying without making one. We didn't want that last-minute fuss, or worse, to happen to us."

ooo

Tuesday afternoon saw Lydia once again calling at Town's End Cottage. She'd spent the morning finding Stoppes in the birth, marriage and death registers, finding Stoppes in censuses and electoral rolls, finding Stoppes occasionally at the West End flat, but, almost always when something was to be recorded, finding Stoppes at St James Manor. But what she did not find was any stray Stoppes who was not otherwise accounted for.

"Here's that letter of introduction you asked for. Three copies," Derek said, handing her the envelope, hesitating before he added, "I know it's only day two, but how's it going?"

"I think it's going just how it's going to go until we say, enough. It's fine, nothing whatsoever out of the ordinary, and sadly nothing to put the smallest gleam in my eye. I was at the manor all day yesterday, going through files and papers. I need a break from that, so tomorrow Georgina, Lady Stoppes, is going to talk me through the photo albums. I don't suppose you know her much, but she's a very nice person. And we've discovered an archive of correspondence, every letter ever received at the manor I think."

"Marvellous. I knew you'd be right for this."

"Thank you Derek, but let's wait and see."

"I'll get you my uncle's diaries in a minute, but is there anything else I can do for you?"

"I'd like a copy of the whole trust document, if that's possible. And what about the baronetcy itself, are there some documents, warrants or something like that, from when it was created? Are they something you'd have or should they be at the manor somewhere?"

"Not with us, at the manor, I'd say. But before we look at the diaries, would you like a proper look round? There might be something else you'd like, besides those few books you have."

Curiosity made Lydia agree. The cottage was entirely in keeping with all that she knew of Robert Ballard, above all it was well ordered. His nephew had emptied cupboards and wardrobes of linen and clothing, some of the books were packed into boxes ready for donation, but the owner's stamp was still on the house.

On the upstairs landing, beside the door to the bathroom,

Lydia stopped, her eye caught by a painting. The style and subject, the size and the choice of colours were strongly reminiscent of the Mallingford portrait. The painting she saw now was behind glass in a modest frame that somehow suggested a family connection rather than purchased art.

"You like that?" Derek asked, close behind her in the narrow space.

"It's not that I like it so much, it's that it reminds me of a painting I have, the one that might have been my project if you hadn't sent me down a different road. Do you know anything about it?"

"Not a thing. Let me take it off the wall and see if it can tell us anything."

He eased it off its hook and flipped it over. The back was a plain black board, tacked in place. It had no labels or identifying marks, again suggesting that it was a family item.

"I could take it out of the frame," Derek suggested a little doubtfully.

"It might be fragile," Lydia said, "and the glass might be old and thin, perhaps original. I should hate it to break, it could scar the painting. But I will take a photo if you don't mind."

"I wonder if it was my aunt's, she died twenty years ago. I never knew anything of her family. Actually, come to think of it, I hardly know anything of my own family, not back to the 1800s."

"One project at a time," Lydia said, looking sideways at her employer.

"Yes, quite right. Let's look at the diaries."

The tour completed, they returned to the study where Derek presented Lydia with two boxes of diaries, nearly sixty in all.

"Sixty?" she said, eyes wide. "That is a little more than I was expecting."

"I think it's everything. I arranged them in order and so far as I can see there is only one year missing, 1955. If I find it I'll let you know. I think he must have stopped writing about six years ago. I don't know why he would stop after so many years."

"Have you looked at them?"

"Here and there. I think it's fairly dry stuff, not really very personal, which would have been more interesting to me. But it's probably better for what you might be looking for."

Over coffee they talked a little more about Georgina Stoppes and her daughters, about the manor house and how it was a very large house for one person, no matter how often a grown-up child might come to stay.

"Are you still living in Oxford?" the solicitor asked casually.

"No, I've let my friend have my house for a while. She had trouble getting a place and, well, it's a long story."

"So you're in Cambridge now?"

"Grantchester, nearly Cambridge."

He nodded, weighing his next question before taking the plunge. "Might Town's End Cottage be of interest to you? It'll go on the market in a couple of weeks."

Once, it could have been of interest, but that would have been in the surprisingly few weeks – or was it only days – between having enough money to think of such a thing and deciding to live with Stephen at The Old Rectory. True, the idea had drifted through her head more recently, but it hadn't lodged there.

"Oh, thank you, but no. I'm settled in Grantchester now," Lydia said, not lying but stretching the truth just a little. She certainly intended to be settled in Grantchester. "I could've seen myself here, it's a lovely spot, but it's not for me now."

"No, right, I understand," Derek said quickly, not quite hiding his disappointment, then covering it with, "I've been asking a few people, friends, cousins, you know."

ooo

As instructed, Lydia left her car by the old stables and went to the side door of the manor. To her surprise she found it locked, so used the key she'd been given. The alarm wasn't set, so she assumed that Georgina Stoppes was out on a brief errand, especially as she'd made no mention of being away.

It felt strange to be alone in the place, to have free run of someone's fine home after what was really only the slightest acquaintance. A friendship might grow between them, but a few coffees and a bread and cheese lunch were a very small start. Was it the connection to the family solicitor that made Lydia unquestioningly trusted, not just with knowledge but with the property itself?

Having called out a few times to be sure the house was deserted, Lydia took the opportunity to explore the stillness of each room, wandering slowly, pausing where she wished, examining what caught her eye. It was an opportunity to let the manor speak to her, if it had anything to tell.

It spoke of a family at ease with itself, of solid foundations, of love and respect. There was no tension about it, no jarring notes, nothing out of place and yet everything seemed touchable, movable, flexible. The lady of the house would not return and reposition a photo frame that Lydia had shifted a half-inch on the shelf. Photos, like everything else, could be picked up, examined and put back without fear of disturbing a precise arrangement.

In the entrance hallway, where the main staircase swept up to the first floor, there was no art, no massive portraits of baronets, no Victorian swords or armour proclaiming an exaggerated pedigree for the Stoppes. It was the library that held the portraits of the first and second baronets, modestly sized paintings of apparently modest men in their Victorian solemnity. *Sir Clarence Charles Tremain Stoppes of St James, Secretary to Her Majesty's Treasury, Bart.* hung to the left of the French doors while *Sir Edwin Tremain Stoppes of St James, 2nd Bart.*, painted when he was a little younger than his father, hung to the right. There was no grand image of the third, fourth or fifth baronets to be seen. Neither could Lydia recall seeing such paintings or photos anywhere else in the house.

Which made her think of the London flat. Perhaps those missing portraits were there, although you would expect them to be here at family headquarters. Even so, she should make arrangements to see the flat, see if it contained the slightest clue. She might go on her own, might even catch Amanda there to see if her view of her father was as adoring as her mother's.

"Lydia, are you in the house?" Georgina, calling as she headed for the library.

Before Lydia could answer, the door opened.

"I've been looking at these two," Lydia said, motioning to the paintings. "You might expect there to be at least two more, maybe three. Any idea why not? Or are they on a wall somewhere else?"

"Not so far as I know. And Chris would never have had anything formal like that done, not even a studio photograph so far as I'm aware."

"Is there anything that might be useful at the flat?"

"I doubt it, but there might be. I don't even know when it came into the family. I'm trying to think if there are any boxes or files in a cupboard or under a bed. I don't think there are."

"If you don't mind, I think I should go and see. Is Amanda there at the moment?"

"Yes, home on Friday for the weekend. If you're here you could fix something up with her."

Together they pulled out three photo albums plus an envelope of prints from the shelves in the library. The envelope held what they assumed were the earliest photographs, all mounted on card. They were intended to be durable, intended to be proud records of important people, not the ten-a-penny snaps of a century later. A couple were stamped with the photographer's details, a few had the dates and locations written on the back.

Slowly they looked through the twenty or so images, about half of which were of the first baronet, Sir Clarence Stoppes, or his wife Lady Evelyn, both in the stiff unsmiling poses of their time. In one, Sir Clarence appeared to be wearing a semi-military uniform that caught Lydia's attention, although it might have no significance in her quest. One for each of the couple's three children, Mary, Sarah and Edwin – later to become the second baronet – shown in their cribs lavishly surrounded by layers of lace. The remainder were of buildings, some she recognized without checking the inscriptions as being of the manor, a couple she guessed as being the neighbouring farm. Photos of the parish church and the manor house in 1872 completed the set. Lydia selected one each of the first baronet and his wife to take copies of, just to remind herself of who was who in the family tree.

The albums held more of the same, serious people in serious poses, a hand resting lightly on the back of a strategically-placed chair. Even the children could not be mistaken for enjoying themselves. Edwin, Mary and Sarah with their spouses, all aging as the century turned. The third baronet, George Melville Stoppes, duly appeared in another sea of lace.

Like most people's photo albums, Lydia reminded herself, these were the photos suitable for display, for the official family record, they were hardly likely to include anything but the complimentary and the heroic. Any other photos, anything that might reveal something unsuitable, had already been edited out. We, in the digital age might have made editing out into a whole new art form, but we are no different to our grandparents and their grandparents before them.

"I don't think this is going to take me anywhere," Lydia said, a little downcast.

"I'm quite enjoying it," Georgina said. "I'm wondering what else there is in here that I've never seen before. Now I think about it, everything in this library was always the family's, I never thought of it as mine, or even ours. For forty-odd years I've paid it hardly any attention. No, I tell a lie. There was a whole cookery section which I moved into the kitchen twenty years ago."

They pulled out the next three albums, each subtly illustrating the family's transition from Victorian dour to Edwardian gaiety. Suddenly everyone was seen doing enjoyable things, and even if smiles were still at a premium, extravagant hats were not. Yet, within the albums, the family and the manor continued to hold centre stage: Edwin, now Sir Edwin, second baronet, and his wife Henrietta, assorted sisters and their spouses, and the new pride and joy, George Melville in selected poses and outfits. As the boy grew he was accompanied a couple of times by a friend. Then the clouds of war brought uniforms to the third album. The first shown was Sir Edwin's nephew Albert Morrisey, his sister Sarah's son. Then Sir Edwin too, in an officer's uniform but also resting on a cane, a public statement of willingness to serve, along with the reason he could not. On the last page of the album were two young men, both in military uniform, one seated, the other standing, and also relying on a cane.

Lydia slipped the photo from its pocket. Written in a clear hand on the back was the inscription *George with William September 1917*. Lydia calculated that George would have been 18. For William she had no information, but some resemblance between the two young men suggested he might be a cousin. But which was which? The inscription gave no clues. To the writer and to whoever the writer thought might view the photo, it would have been obvious.

For another couple of hours they sat at the library table pouring over the family albums, remarking on some points of interest, some curiosities and also on some absences. Between the 1917 image of George and William and a rather dour picture of a bearded Sir George and his bride Miriam Forsyth in 1933, there was not a single photograph of the third baronet in the albums. Lydia wondered if perhaps the family had fallen on hard times, although it seemed unlikely. According to Lydia's family tree crib sheet, George's mother Lady Henrietta had died in 1922 and his father Sir Edwin in 1928. The Great War and the deaths of George's parents might have cast a shadow over those years or it might simply be that an album or two that once existed had been lost.

The 1930s fared little better, the wedding pose, the mandatory records of Charles and Elizabeth in their formative years, a couple of stiff family groups and then it was straight back to war. Lady Miriam appeared in her WAAF uniform in a photograph dated October 1939, then for the first time that Lydia could see, non-family photos began to fill the pages of two albums. They showed happy times, despite the war, photos of Miriam with friends in uniform, photos of RAF officers at ease in the manor grounds, and most surprisingly, photos of German prisoners of war working on a farm, presumably Manor Farm. The house itself appeared to be used in part as a billet for RAF officers, while the sumptuous main lawn was covered in a huge marquee.

"This is absolutely fascinating," Georgina said. "I don't know why I've never looked at any of this. It's making me wonder what else there is on these shelves."

"I'll let you know when I've finished, although I have a feeling the albums are the easiest part."

Post-war pictures were as scarce as the pre-war: while the rest of the world was busy snapping every smile and kiss, the Stoppes were not. There were a few exceptions, events that couldn't be ignored, such as the marriage of Charles' sister Elizabeth to Richard Wykham, followed by the future baronet's own marriage in 1956 to Catherine McIver. Then an explosion of glorious colour burst onto the pages: happy holiday photos, St James Manor hosting the village fête, young people proudly seated in Minis and MGs, sixties hairstyles and teenage sulks. Suddenly it was the awkward seventies and a few pages later Georgina herself made her first appearance, smiling uneasily beside her future husband, flanked by his mother and father.

"I was pregnant in that photo," she said flatly. "We'd just found out. A couple of months later we were married."

There were a dozen things Lydia might have said, but she said nothing. Even though she was curious about this family, about relationships and how their stories unfolded, how changing one small thing might change everything, ultimately it wasn't her business. Unless it had some bearing on her search, and she truly doubted that.

"We were so lucky, Chris and I, it could have been a miserable mistake, but we never looked back. Even when our baby died, even then."

Lydia paused, waiting for there to be a little distance between that reflection and what she would say next, even though the one clearly led to the other.

"I was planning to spend a few minutes in the churchyard after lunch. Do you go there, I mean go to church?"

"High days and holidays only. We're expected, I should say we *were* expected, to show support, even if it was only a token. Chris did his duty but without any enthusiasm."

"Is he buried there, are all the Stoppes buried there?"

"They are, but he's not. Cremated, as he wished. And scattered to the wind out on the farm. That'll be me too, when my time comes."

The parish church of Wheadon St James, medieval in origin, enlarged and embellished over the centuries, its tower visible for miles around, was a building that had outlived its purpose. Supported by a diminishing congregation, vastly expensive to maintain and locked for all but two Sundays a month, it was in danger of closing permanently.

"It'll be such a shame to lose it, but what can you do? The village wants to keep it of course, it's beautiful, but nobody wants to pay for it. They say they need more than a million for repairs."

"Someone looks after the churchyard."

"That's our contribution. Whenever the grass is cut at the manor, they come over here and keep this tidy too. Not the burial ground, the parish council does that."

Georgina Stoppes led the way round the ancient walls to a group of headstones near the south corner. The grass may have been well tended, but the older stones were weathered by age and disfigured by lichen. By instinct Lydia went to the least legible first where she began to feel out the unreadable letters. In a few minutes she had enough to write the whole of Sir Clarence Stoppes and his wife's memorial in her notebook. His son Edwin along with his wife Henrietta were next, made all the easier by knowing the names and dates from her notes, likewise for the third and fourth baronets. The four graves were arranged in a rectangle, two by two. Close by was another, not Stoppes but somehow too close to be unconnected. It was fairly modern, so still legible with a little squinting and feeling out of a few letters. Lydia added to her notes: *In Loving Memory of Elizabeth Calbain born 1878 and who left this world on 5th July 1952 A truly loyal and loving mother who rightly takes her eternal rest in this place.*

Some aspect of the memorial suggested to Lydia a deeper meaning not spelled out. The close proximity to two of the family graves, those of Edwin and George, the second and third baronets, might have been poor planning but could surely have been avoided simply enough.

"Do you know who Elizabeth Calbain was," Lydia asked.

"I can guess. I think she may have worked at the manor, as

a housekeeper or nanny. Years ago I remember Chris's father referring to someone as Nanny C. I'd say she was spoken of with affection."

"That would explain her being laid to rest so close to the family. I think we sometimes forget that long-serving family servants, especially nannies, often came close to being part of the family themselves. Perhaps we'll find her in the mountain of paper that I have as my next task."

ooo

Lydia had looked at many photos, read, or at least skimmed, hundreds of documents, and talked to Georgina Stoppes all week and her daughter Amanda for more than an hour. And yet the very best she could say for her endeavours was that there were now some things she knew she need not look at again. She'd spotted no clue hiding in the photo albums, unless she counted the absence of photos for long periods as being significant. Now, returning to The Old Rectory after her first week's work, she found a manila envelope from Derek Ballard waiting for her.

Her new space in the summerhouse had been unused all week and she'd looked forward to trying it out, but the evening light had been cut short by the rain that had followed her east from the manor. Instead, she settled in the familiar comfort of the sitting room with a glass of Bousval *pinot grise* and reminded herself that one of the summerhouse purchases she needed to make was a small fridge.

The envelope contained a copy of the trust deed. Not as long or complex as she imagined it would be, but in essence a list of property, possessions and money that the third baronet, Sir George, had transferred to the trust. The headline items were the manor house, the farm and a couple of cottages in the village and the flat in London. The furniture was included too, and Lydia wondered if that hadn't appreciated at least as much as the buildings and land, because some of the antiques in the manor would surely be extremely valuable.

The St James Trust had been created in 1953, earlier than Lydia had thought, and for its time, the amount of money was surprising: more than a million, which by Lydia's quick reckoning was more like twenty-five million in today's money.

As Derek's accompanying letter explained, there was little unusual in the trust's main provisions of providing for the descendants of the third baronet. It was a common practice for the wealthy to try and avoid taxes, especially death duty. It was also a way of preventing estates from being split up by being sold piecemeal to meet liabilities to the revenue. The unusual part of the trust was limited entirely to the winding-up provision:

> *In the event of there being no natural male heir to the Baronetcy of St James then the trustees will distribute the assets of the trust equally between any living children of the last deceased Baronet or those children's heirs and successors providing that the trustees have first completely satisfied themselves by diligent search and enquiry that no natural male heir exists.*

So why not continue the trust until there were no direct descendants at all? The tax and property advantages were not limited to there being a male heir, a trust could benefit every generation, just as the fifth baronet had set up for Felicity, Amanda and their children. It made Lydia, and according to his note, Derek Ballard too, wonder if there were another reason for the trust, as if the third baronet had perceived some other threat to his property and fortune.

The date of the trust would be at least an entry point for Lydia to examine Robert Ballard's diaries, rather than the chronological and slightly tedious process that she'd embarked on as her bedtime reading. Robert Ballard was a good diarist with an eye to the detail of his life and work, but with very little comment on anything remotely personal, his record brought sleep easily to tired eyes.

As she was considering her week and the small discoveries she'd made, Lydia's phone buzzed. To her surprise and delight it was Stephen.

"Hello!" she beamed at him. "You don't usually call at this time. Knocked off early for the weekend?"

"In a way. 'A procedural difficulty,' is the diplomatic way of expressing it. How has your week been?"

"I'm not going to ask you for details. Your smile says one thing but your eyes tell me another. I can guarantee my week has been better than yours. Very pleasant, no obstacles, a few little oddities but no skeletons ..." she started to say but cut herself short, blurting out, "I'm so sorry, I didn't mean that. That's awful."

Of all the things she might have said, surely nothing could have been more insensitive, more disrespectful of Stephen's ugly work of exhumation.

"It's OK," he said. "An association of ideas. It happens all the time. There's some very dark humour here sometimes. It's a way of coping."

They talked for a while over trivial things, the weather – that most talked about subject in long-distance relationships – arrangements for his laundry, the fridge, until Lydia thought again about the St James Trust.

"Do you know anything about trusts?"

"Not as much as I should. I've often wondered about setting something up for Jacqueline, but I never have. I should change my will now too."

In that moment Lydia sensed their stuttering living-together trial had become something more permanent, despite the distance between them. Without any discussion and certainly without the incentive of passion, Stephen had taken another step. What would so recently have been unsettling now sat comfortably with her.

"Thank you," she said without exactly knowing why, but it seemed right.

After looking at each other for a few moments he said, "What about trusts?"

"Yes, the Stoppes trust, the thing that got me into all this, has an unusual termination clause." She read him the relevant piece and outlined the likely value of the trust, mentioning too, Derek Ballard's comments. "I thought you might have some ideas. I'll let you think about it, it'll be light relief from your day, something to puzzle over as you go to sleep."

Her own puzzle as she went to sleep was how Elizabeth Calbain, buried almost, but not quite, in the family plot in St James' churchyard fitted, if at all, into the family jigsaw. According to Lydia's late-night searches – her birth in 1878 and death in 1952 having been confirmed by the record – Elizabeth lived in Lincolnshire with her parents until being recorded alone in New Street, St Neots in 1901, 1911 and 1921. But if this was the *loyal and loving mother* remembered at Wheadon St James, Lydia had so far found no trace of her children.

4

With the little wine-cooler fridge installed and a couple of rugs spread out, the summerhouse began to take on the feeling Lydia had hoped for: a space of her own, a wonderful outlook across the lawn and roses, and just enough comfort – although a better chair for her makeshift desk would help. Sunday was never meant to be a working day, Derek Ballard had made that clear, but if she chose to then she knew she'd certainly be paid for her efforts. This thought reminded her that she must record her first direct expense of the project: Elizabeth Calbain's death certificate.

The woman felt like an anomaly in the smooth history of the Stoppes. Not that Lydia had anything other than the location of her grave to suggest it. But a mother with no marriage and no children with her name in the record? That alone was enough to raise suspicion, and naturally it piqued her interest, regardless of any Stoppes connection. Having tried for the tenth time a variation on the search for Stoppes births, with or without Elizabeth Calbain as the mother, the answer remained stubbornly elusive. Calbain births were equally few and the couple she found needed no detail enquiry to reject them.

The telephone directories for the area revealed nothing, not a single Calbain listed as being a subscriber. But one source did answer one vital question: the Bedfordshire electoral roll. It showed Eliz. Calbain as registered to vote in 1932, giving her address as Manor Lane, Wheadon St James. She lived either at the farm or the manor and Lydia would have bet strongly on the latter. Now there was a physical connection,

Lydia would surely find mention of her somewhere in the family's archive.

With that clear purpose now in mind for her next stint at the manor, Lydia turned her attention to Robert Ballard's diaries. She'd completed 1941 and 1942 but now she skipped directly to 1953, hoping to find a reference to the St James Trust. It was right there in the second entry for the new year, January 6th, *Sir George S required a family trust to be established for his descendants*. Then, on the 20th, *Sir George S unhappy with the trust, required a particular clause. Needs the correct wording to be watertight. Unusual. Spoke with father*. Again, a week later, *Suggested to Sir George S that he take advice from a tax accountant, but he was set on it. He'd made a promise and would keep it.* He wrote again of his reservations on February 12th, *Sir George S in today to sign the new trust deeds. Refused any alteration or advice. Made a note in the file and had him sign it to protect the firm. Transfer of funds and property completed. A poor day's work.*

That last sentence was as close to a personal comment as Lydia had found in either of the two earlier diaries she'd read. She guessed Robert must have felt deeply that Sir George had chosen to ignore what he'd considered to be sound advice. And Lydia would've given a lot to know what promise Sir George had given and to whom. But the diary gave no further clue, in fact, skimming through the rest of 1953 she saw nothing related to the trust or even to the Stoppes family.

Even without any further commentary, Lydia reasoned that his promise would surely have been related to the special clause rather than the trust itself. In effect it was a promise to someone that before the Baronetcy of St James were allowed to become extinct, a careful effort would be made to find an heir. And more, that the considerable wealth entailed in the trust would be preserved for the benefit of any such heir before it was distributed between children of a generation as yet unborn. To Lydia's mind it could only mean that the third baronet thought there was at least a possibility of an heir through a different male line. The most obvious reason for such a thought would be that he had fathered a son other than with his wife Miriam. And to whom but that son's mother would he make such a promise?

Of all she had so far examined, it was the first suggestion that there might yet be a sixth baronet to be found. It was the trust itself and the peculiarity of the wording which suggested it, that and Robert Ballard's diary and his conscientious execution of his duties.

To better think, Lydia took herself on a slow walking tour of the garden, letting the Stoppes and their mysteries float as they wished through her head. What luxury to have a garden of such perfection to walk in, to have her own space within it and, on the grander scale, how fortunate she was to have such a life. Yet even in the midst of this recognition, self-doubt lurked in the shadows, ready to remind her how little she deserved her good fortune. Those pernicious thoughts were ever-present, even if lately she'd kept them at arm's length, more able to look at them squarely and see them for what they were. Like a migraine aura that hints at the crushing pain to come, she was slowly learning to recognize the onset and deal with it before it had time to take root.

Back in Oxford, in her Osney fortress, she would've headed to the river, been walking beside it in a matter of minutes, its sights and sounds, its smells and surprises filling her senses and driving out her demons. But here in Grantchester, the Cam seemed little more than a poor cousin to her precious Thames. Even so, the prospect of walking by water was irresistible.

Taking nothing but her phone and a sunhat she turned down the High Street, past The Red Lion, then out across The Meadows toward the river. Slow and clear, dark green fronds waving in the gentle stream, it immediately refreshed her spirits as she stood on the bank, letting herself settle into the unfamiliar surroundings. She'd been here just once before, an excursion on a grey day to find where the river was, to know where she could go if she needed. Now she headed north towards Cambridge, dawdling as she pleased, no destination or purpose in her mind.

Although it was easy going, the path along the bank was little used, there being a more direct route for the few who crossed The Meadows to commute to the city. So far as Lydia could see, she was completely alone, no cyclist or jogger on the path, no cows grazing, not a duck or swan to disturb as she strolled.

After a mile or so of her wanderings she came to a little sandy bay, a place scooped out of the natural bank to give cattle easy access to drink from the river. Grounded in the shallows was a punt with two young people sprawled on its cushions, their eyes closed, their clothes in revealing disarray. Lydia was jerked from her dreams abruptly. For a split-second she feared they might be dead – why else would they be in such poses? Some sound roused the young woman who opened her eyes. Seeing Lydia standing open-mouthed, she raised a single shushing finger to her lips, followed by a wide smile. It was, Lydia thought, a beautiful moment, something not quite defined yet shared between two women. The young man slept on, oblivious.

Lydia returned the smile, gave a little wave and stepped quietly away. She doubted that either of the lovers would question their moments of bliss as being undeserved. The very idea was comical, impossible, and being so, blew the last wisps of her black fog completely away.

ooo

Somehow the manor house managed to retain all its attraction even under Monday's grey skies and squally rain. Perversely, it seemed even more alluring as Lydia turned up the drive. Like a log fire that is never so welcoming as when a winter storm splatters sleet across the windows, so St James Manor offered its security, its constancy, shrugging off the purely temporary inconvenience of unseasonal weather.

Parking by the stables, Lydia saw that Amanda's car was gone, presumably back to the flat in London where they'd meet up later in the week. Georgina was ready to leave as Lydia went in through the back door.

"Help yourself, back for lunch, I think. Coffee's just made," she said as they passed in the kitchen. "If you need anything, call me, I'm only shopping."

With that she was gone, scuttling out into the rain.

Once again Lydia had the house to herself, but today there'd be more purpose to her endeavours. Before doing anything she sent Derek Ballard an email requesting information: how long had the Stoppes been clients of the firm, when was the flat in London purchased, and could she have copies of any and all Stoppes wills still on file. She might find her own answers but his corroboration wouldn't hurt.

She hoped to find Elizabeth Calbain mentioned somewhere, something to help understand how she was tied to the family. According to the census she'd been in St Neots in 1921 and eleven years later was registered as a voter living in Manor Lane. What happened in those eleven years? Lydia made a list of what she could be sure of: Lady Henrietta Stoppes had died in 1922, Sir Edwin in 1928 and, less directly connected, Sir Edwin's two brothers-in-law had died in 1927 and 1929. Could Elizabeth have come to the manor as a housekeeper when Lady Henrietta died? Or even as something more than a housekeeper? What was more than a housekeeper, other than a wife or lover? Not a wife, not one registered under that name for sure, so a lover? For a moment Lydia baulked at the idea of a lover in her mid-forties, surely lovers were young people who lay in a punt under the summer sun. But then what were she and Stephen, if not lovers? She pulled two fat box files from the archive shelves. *Household Correspondence 1921-1926* and the less specific *Correspondence 1920-1926*.

After more than an hour sifting through the first, Lydia knew a lot more about the wide range of people who serviced the house in the 1920s than she did previously. They were all there, the plumbers and stonemasons, the grass cutters and roofers, the electricians and the wine suppliers. She knew many of their names, some of their problems and often what a poor or good job they'd made of whatever they'd been asked to do. She also knew of the undertakers who'd taken care of the arrangements for Henrietta in 1922, and she knew which tradespeople had written with condolences. What she did not see was the name Calbain, nor anything approaching a personal exchange. Any of the people mentioned might have a relevance to her enquiries, but that relevance was not apparent from the file.

The second file was immediately more productive, not with Calbain but with a letter from Sir Edwin's son George. A letter from Canada. It was extremely short, to Lydia's mind short to the point of being terse, but she excused it for being of its time and not hers:

Brankota April 4th 1921

Father, you required assurances regarding progress with the Mary and I am able to give them. Work on the new passage continues despite adverse conditions. Production is steady and results in sufficient income to provide a small profit – made smaller lately by reduced demand. The whole venture is maintained by constant supervision. When convenient to your situation additional capital of £1000 to obtain improved equipment would benefit the previous investment.

Your affectionate son

George Melville Stoppes

The writing was scrappy, an irregular scrawl across the page, as if written with great difficulty by an uneducated hand, yet, once she'd deciphered it, the language was the opposite. Most likely George had received a good education, given his parents' social standing.

The future third baronet's absence from the photo albums was explained immediately. Not only that, but by 1921 he appeared to have been in Canada for a while. Perhaps he stayed there even longer. There would be other letters from him, other reports to fill in those years.

One thought, impossible to ignore given her whole reason for being at the manor, was the possibility that he might have fathered a son during his stay in the Dominion. Along with a note to herself regarding that search, Lydia added a few other questions that might be answered from censuses and registers, before continuing the file with renewed enthusiasm.

If she were looking for a word or sentence that might lead to revealing some great secret she must do more than scan each letter, she must read each one. Most were from family and friends: Sir Edwin's two sisters and their husbands; Henrietta's three sisters and her friends which were, not surprisingly, more gossipy than those sent to her husband; letters from the vicar on parish matters; two letters from what she assumed was Sir Edwin's old school – Snaresby College, somewhere in Essex; a second letter from George a year after the first and in much the same vein. In late 1922 the volume of letters was swelled by dozens of condolences when Lady Henrietta died after an accident. Not one of the letters referred to the exact nature of the accident – that might be something to discover from her death certificate or possibly the local newspaper.

Last among them was a third letter from George, his tone hardly softened at all by news of his mother's death:

Brankota December 3rd 1922

Father, your letter arrived only yesterday and was

a considerable shock. I write this with a heavy heart knowing that you will be in great distress. I trust the arrangements were all in order, and they were well-attended. I am confident you will be supported by all around you.

Your affectionate son

George Melville

PS The Mary is idle at present frozen solid in the bitter weather. Repairs to the boiler are under way.

There was that odd wording again, *The Mary*. A vessel of some kind? Curiosity wouldn't wait. *The Mary* returned a million hits with nothing of immediate interest. But *The Mary Brankota* gave her *Historic Sites of Manitoba: The Mary Mine* right away. And not only that, it gave her a location to anchor future searches for any child George Melville Stoppes might have fathered in that northern outpost.

That remote cold seemed to have crept into the writer too. Not a word in his letter that spoke directly of his mother, his heavy heart was apparently more for his father's loss than for his own. It was hard to judge a person at the distance of a century, a different time with different habits and certainly more repressed emotions. For all Lydia knew, that boy, barely a man at twenty-three, may have wept into his pillow. As it stood for the observer, his only concession to feeling or informality was to omit his surname when signing his letter.

A couple of hours later, as she pulled out the last few letters and thought of lunch, Lydia found a slim manila folder at the very bottom of the file. It was labelled Priory Villas. The name was familiar, yet for the moment she couldn't think why. The seven or eight letters it contained were all from a Bedford firm of solicitors concerning the sale of *Two dwellings known as nos. 1 and 2 Priory Villas, New Street, St Neots in the county of Huntingdonshire.* It was reading the town name that brought it back – Elizabeth Calbain had been recorded on three different censuses as being the only resident of 2 Priory Villas. Now it seemed that the family had owned that property. Lydia thumbed through the paperwork and found the reference she needed. Priory Villas had been purchased in September 1897. What prompted that acquisition and what now prompted their sale? Had the property come with Elizabeth as a tenant, is that how she came into the family's orbit, ending her days buried close beside them?

Lydia cut herself a chunk of bread and a couple of pieces of chicken, collected an apple from the bowl and returned to the library where, between mouthfuls, she carefully recorded all she'd looked at and what possible leads she'd uncovered. To her mind there was no doubt at all that George's time spent in Canada offered the greatest opportunity for creating another line of descendants. Whatever else she might find, this was surely the path with most potential. Wasn't it the third baronet himself who'd insisted on the special clause in the trust? Who better to know that such a line existed, or if not current, had once existed?

When she'd cleared away her lunch, Lydia surveyed the shelves. A targeted look at the archive had paid dividends. Where next should her enquiries focus? She pulled two more files from the shelf, *Household Correspondence 1927-1931* and *Correspondence 1927-1930* to cover the period surrounding the death of Sir Edwin Stoppes, second baronet, and his son George inheriting the title.

ooo

Lydia was at Stephen's desk, absentmindedly forking through her now-cold takeaway. She'd taken care to spread a cloth over the leather surface in case of escaping chow mien – and been glad she'd done so. She was vaguely considering how best to surmount the latest roadblock to progress. Her laptop displayed a page of Manitoba Vital Statistics where the search boxes remained unfilled. Researching births in Canada was a great deal more difficult than in the UK. First, such records as there were, were divided into provincial databases. And secondly the online index for many provinces was limited to births one hundred years and older. Manitoba was no different, there were simply no online records available for the years of interest. What was a public record in many countries was protected by privacy laws in Canada. Which left a whole avenue of enquiry closed. Even a personal visit would require that she should know who she was looking for, whereas what she really needed was to be able to trawl through the records with different filters to see what she might turn up. It was little different from how family history was researched before the internet and easy access to online databases. She'd done some of that herself, but for her Uncle Bill it had been the only method available, travelling the country from record office to record office, graveyard to graveyard, collecting and recording anything and everything that might be of interest. He'd made a fine, and most importantly, a largely accurate, family tree, but it had taken half a lifetime.

Relying on other peoples' research was fraught with obvious difficulties, but sometimes it could provide an insight or open up a new avenue of exploration. More in hope than expectation Lydia plugged in the Stoppes name to interrogate other researchers' family trees. Her instinct proved correct – not a single match, nothing even close. It was one thing to have a possibility of another line of descent from an imagined liaison in the wilds of Manitoba, but having no means by which to investigate it rather spoilt the pleasure of the chase.

Stephen's face appeared in the calling app on her screen, a welcome rescue from frustration and she told him so.

"Always available to rescue damsels in distress," he said.

"You've done it more than once. And this is the perfect moment. I'm so happy to see you. How's life in Guanito?"

"Much the same. We are back at work, our ... what did I call them, administrative difficulties? They've been overcome. It is all going on as before. The everyday horrors are just that – every day."

It was the nearest thing to expressing an opinion he'd ever come to on these calls. Perhaps horrors had no side, no political undertone unless they were attributed horrors.

"And your work, Lydia?"

"A poor ending to the day, as I've said, but otherwise productive. The mystery woman in the graveyard was a kind of housekeeper at the manor after 1927, there were letters addressed to her from various people which were all about housekeeper-ish things, nothing personal. Very few from the man in Canada, George Stoppes. And all very distant. He was a cold fish, even when his mother died.

"I think it must have been the housekeeper, Elizabeth, who wrote to him when his father died. You might have thought it would be one of his aunts, but by his letter back to her it looks like it was she who wrote with the news. His was a different letter, after what he'd written before it was unexpected, almost affectionate, more so than when he wrote to his father. It didn't take him long to wind things up in Manitoba and get himself back home."

"You say the family owned the mine?"

"I think so, or part of it. There are boxes of accounts to go through, I've rather been putting it off. There's so much stuff."

"What about Gloria, didn't you say she'd offered to help?"

"Yes! I'd forgotten that, she'd be perfect. Brilliant idea, thank you."

"Here's another one. I was thinking about your portrait. What about trying to identify the artist and then seeing if he has a descendant who'd like to have it? Not what you'd had in mind, I know, but a thought."

"I'll have to decide who he is, at the moment he's just a

squiggle, but it's an idea. And I might have another way into that. Derek Ballard has a painting very similar which I could take a closer look at."

"Busy lady. How's the summerhouse?"

"Very good. I love it but I might get a new chair. It's a miserable cold evening so that's why I'm in the study." As she said it she slid the remains of her meal away from the keyboard to avoid any risk it might be seen, then immediately regretted the impulse to deceive, even at the most trivial level.

ooo

Georgina Stoppes had just poured coffee when Derek Ballard called Lydia.

"Are you on to something?" he asked, with little in the way of greetings.

"No, definitely not," she said firmly.

"Right, I just thought you were asking some very specific questions."

"I'm trying to look at the whole picture, see where it's best to direct my energy. With a hundred and fifty years of family history to consider I could be here for ever."

"Fine, I was getting quite excited for a minute. I have someone looking for the Stoppes wills right now. If we have them I'll get copies for you. It looks like the firm, or its predecessor, was first involved in 1929. Although we have no files for that year, all we have is a kind of summary, just a line or two regarding what work was done for clients. We have no correspondence before 1939. I looked in the summary ledger for Stoppes and found a reference to the London property purchase, the flat at Whitecross Mansions, in 1933. All the papers for that will have been sent to the family at some point. What else was there?"

"The original Letters Patent or whatever they were called, the document awarding the baronetcy."

"No, nothing like that. Lady Stoppes may know. And I did

wonder if there might be a safety deposit box. Again, something for her."

"Thanks," Lydia said, hesitating before asking about the idea of Gloria working with her. Perhaps he was saying nothing because it was easier to ignore a question than say no. But, as the courage of her own convictions was her new best friend, she continued, "Did you think about my idea for Gloria Fitzgerald?"

Georgina Stoppes was hardly pretending to not listen to the conversation, she was, after all, intimately involved in the enquiry and its outcome. At the mention of a new name she looked up from her coffee questioningly.

"Yes, I did. Entirely up to you, so long as the pay is reasonable and I'm sure you don't need me to spell that out. Would it be at the manor? If so I think you should discuss it with Lady Stoppes, not exactly for approval, but certainly as a courtesy. You can do that?"

"Oh yes. And I haven't said anything to Gloria yet, it may not work out."

"Just let me know. Now, before I forget, the painting at the cottage. Why not drop in this evening when you're finished at the manor for the day? We'll take it out of its frame, carefully, and see what it can tell us. Or tell you, I won't know what I'm looking at."

Lydia made a quick note of what Derek had said, then turned to Georgina. "Don't worry, I won't really be here for ever. But there is a huge amount to go through and I daren't leave any stone unturned. Hence the mention of my friend Gloria."

She told her host how long she'd known her, how good a worker she was, how careful and accurate she could be and of course how discreet she'd proved in her years of working with personnel records. Slightly to Lydia's surprise it was a glowing CV she presented. It wasn't the right moment to mention Gloria's cigarette habit.

"So, I was thinking Gloria might come and help with some of the trawling through the files, especially the accounts. Do you know there are files going back to 1880? I've had a quick glance at one or two but they need a thorough look, line by line to see if some anomaly, some hint or suggestion is hiding there. If it's all right with you, I'd like to ask Gloria to come and help for a few days."

"Yes, of course, yes, why not? Will Gloria know what she's looking for?"

"As much as I do. No, I'll give her a briefing – if she can do it, I haven't asked her yet. By the way, have you ever heard of The Mary Mine?"

Georgina had not. Lydia told her what she had found, how the third baronet had spent years in Canada before his father died, how to Lydia's mind he must have returned more as a stranger than the prodigal son.

"You think this might be important?"

"Only because I can see it possible that a young man on his own in remote lands might have had the opportunity to ... what did they say back then? Sow a few wild oats. In fact he may have had more opportunity than any of the baronets before or after. He just seems like a person worthy of some attention."

Lydia had planned that closer attention to be a return to the correspondence files, earlier than the previous examination, looking for something to explain George Stoppes' presence in Canada. The last photo she had for that period was the one of George with an unknown William, September 1917, the last in the album. In the library she pulled *Correspondence 1915-1919* from the shelf and settled down to browse through every page.

It started badly with a letter from the second baronet's sister, Sarah, confirming the death of her son Albert, missing in action at Ypres since the previous November. She wrote,

Now all hope is gone. We are one amongst so many, but it is unbearable to us.

Letters from family and friends grew more sombre as the months passed, with scarcely one that didn't make reference to the war, especially the new terror of the Zeppelin raids. George's letters from school were irregular but Lydia thought they were a little warmer than the impersonal missives from Manitoba a few years later. The writing was different too. Lydia pulled out the file with those later letters to compare them. His writing from Snaresby College was schoolboy-neat, whereas the young man in Canada wrote with an awkward spidery scrawl. His "Dear Father and Mother" of 1915 had contracted to the abrupt "Father" just six years later. Did it speak of some family rupture or simply changing fortune as the youth became a man? No matter that she was holding the letters and sitting in the same space that they were received and first read, so much of those other lives could really only be guessed at.

Word of another death in the family came in 1917, from Sir Edwin's older sister, Mary. Her son Valentine had died in an accident with some machinery more than a month previously. Lydia checked the bare-bones family tree she'd created for the Stoppes and saw her note about not finding a death date for Valentine, yet here was his mother telling his uncle about it in 1917 when he would have been thirty-three. Another war casualty? She checked again for Valentine Charles Valence in her usual sources. No death recorded, not even among the dead of war. That, and the delay between his death and word being received suggested he died somewhere other than England.

A week later Mary wrote again, worried that *all would be lost with the mine* unless they could find a trusted agent or substitute for their poor Val. She wasn't even sure that he'd received *a decent Christian burial.* Was this the mine of *The Mary Mine*? It seemed a good bet. Lydia read on. Three weeks later Mary wrote once more, replying to a letter from her brother:

St Albans 4th August 17

My Dear Brother

It would be a great service to us if dear George were able to travel to Canada and attend to affairs there. We are most concerned that he should be well enough for the journey and for what he might encounter in Brankota. From what our dear Val previously told us it is a primitive life with few comforts. Noel would certainly take it on himself if it were not for his health, which is not improved. Indeed it is all the worse in these last few weeks for the news that they have brought us. I fear he may never fully recover.

Mary Valence went on to suggest how arrangements could be made, letters of introduction that would be needed and how her deceased son Valentine's affairs might be administered by the young George. It seemed that the family held a half share in The Mary Mine. It struck Lydia that at eighteen, George would have been taking on great responsibility for one so young. Then she remembered that at the same time thousands of young men hardly any older than George were already making life-and-death decisions on a daily basis.

Mary wrote again soon after, including in her letter:

It is a great comfort to us, and I'm sure to you and to Henrietta, that George will not be making the difficult journey alone. George and William are a fine pair, what one cannot do will be done by the other and vice versa. They can scarcely be in more peril than all the English sons in Flanders. They are spared that through no fault of their own.

Did George and William both have a disability of some kind? It was difficult to think of any other reason for the words Mary had used. But who was William and how did he fit into the family?

More exchanges followed over the next few weeks, all in respect of arrangements being made, the timing of incidental events. Lydia was left with the impression that George might return sooner than William, who could remain at The Mary Mine, taking over from the deceased Valentine. Yet from the correspondence of future years she knew this was not how it worked out, it was George who'd stayed in Manitoba until after his father died in 1928.

At the end of October, Mary again wrote to her brother saying how pleased she was with the arrangements for the voyage to Canada from Liverpool in November: *Few luxuries and probably a boat full of poor souls from the trenches, but with God's blessing it will get them there.* The implications were clear: a troopship carrying sick and injured to Canada. Which surely must have required some special influence on the part of Sir Edwin to get the two young men apparently unfit for active service booked onto for a private journey. She turned again to the photograph of Sir Edwin in the same album. He'd have been around fifty-five, and Lydia imagined him wheeled out of retirement to take command of a local reserve unit. Imagination was one thing but there'd be a record in the military archives, there'd be details to be discovered another day.

There were certainly records for transatlantic voyages, whole crew and passenger lists for thousands of sailings between the old countries of Europe and the brave new world of the Americas. In this case Lydia had one full name to go by, one first name, a port of departure and an approximate date. With a speed that would have astonished those who'd sailed on *SS Saxonia* from Liverpool to Halifax, Nova Scotia on 17th November 1917, Lydia had the details on her screen in two minutes. The ship arrived in Halifax on the last day of the month. And yes, the passengers included one George M

Stoppes. Among the nearly two thousand others onboard she found twenty-seven Williams.

"Lunch?" Georgina Stoppes asked from the doorway, breaking the reverie of research Lydia had sunk into, oblivious of time and space.

A little reluctantly Lydia followed Georgina into the kitchen where wine and cheese and fruit and bread were waiting.

"I know what it's like," said Georgina, "Chris would go all day sometimes, if I let him. It's better to stop, think about other things, then go back refreshed. Tell me, have you stopped looking at Chris and how he might have had a child I didn't know about?"

Caught off guard by the simple directness of the question, Lydia hesitated. "Not exactly. So far I've found nothing that might suggest it, nothing that I can follow up. I haven't spoken to his aunt yet, or anybody else so, something might come out of that or talking to his colleagues might throw up something. But there's so much information here and I can't do everything at once. I'm following my nose, following the unusual, seeing where the most likely possibilities might be. It's not quite as butterfly as it might look. I'm seeing Amanda at the flat tomorrow. It seems the third baronet, Sir George, purchased it in 1933."

They mulled over possibilities and the difficulty of putting yourself in another's shoes, the more so when those shoes walked a different road in a different age. They talked of change, the unexpected forced on a person by good, or ill, fortune and the change of attitudes as the generations came and went. Lydia could have cited herself for the good fortune of her sizable inheritance, or the good fortune of meeting Stephen, yet she wasn't at all sure what fundamental changes had resulted.

When lunch was done, at Lydia's suggestion, the two women walked to the churchyard. She wasn't expecting any new revelation, no additional Stoppes grave to be hidden in an overgrown corner, rather, it was a place of peace and shade, a place to share a bench or wander among past generations of the village. And it was a change of scene from the manor house.

After they'd sat a few minutes Lydia said, "What will you do, if there is a sixth baronet and he claims the benefit of the trust, I mean, if he comes to live at the manor?"

"I'm not expecting that," Georgina said, clearly having given the question some thought. "Do you think it's likely?"

"I've no idea, but my guess is it's most likely there isn't a sixth baronet waiting in the wings. But what if there is, what then for you?"

"Funnily enough, I think it'll be the same either way. If the girls have it all, there'll be huge death duties to pay and my guess is they'll want to sell up everything. So I'll look for somewhere smaller, a cottage somewhere. As I'm sure you can guess, I won't be exactly penniless. Chris left a sizable estate in his own right. And the girls have the trust fund he set up for them."

"Leaving here will be difficult after all these years."

"Maybe. We'll see."

In the library the papers lay where she'd left them, her notebook open to the page of careful notes she'd made through the morning. Where next, research what she had or finish the file? She was tempted to the former as being more interesting, possibly more revealing, but some sense of not being her own boss, of an expectation she should finish one thing before starting another, took her back to the correspondence.

The first letter from George, in his careful boyish hand, had been written on Monday 3rd December on headed notepaper from the King Edward Hotel, Halifax, Nova Scotia. It told his father that they were safely arrived but too late to attend to business the previous week. They'd encountered a further delay at the bank and were now expecting to stay in Halifax until Thursday when they'd booked railway accommodation on *The Ocean Limited* to Montreal.

The next document was not a letter at all, but a telegram, shocking in all its stark brevity:

Halifax, NS 10/12/17

William dead in catastrophe self injured now recovering letter follows

George

Catastrophe? What catastrophe? Lydia turned a few pages until she reached the letter mentioned, neatly written in a looping feminine hand:

Halifax 10th December

My dear Father and Mother

You will know by now of the disaster which befell this city last Thursday morning and which took William from us. He was not alone, many hundreds perhaps thousands are slaughtered, blown apart and hurled in pieces across the city. I escaped by chance and good fortune with small injuries. We were at the hotel preparing ourselves to leave for the station which was close by. A ship was burning but we had no clear view of it before it exploded and made a living hell of this place. We were caught as the ceiling came down upon us, William with a beam across his head. After a time we woke in the rubble. He did not speak but he was yet alive. It was quiet but very soon there arose the most terrible cries and screams. I was able to move and pull William free and thought to get help although from where in such destruction I did not know. In the black rain and smoke outside men women and children lay terribly injured and mutilated, some scarce recognizable as human, some no more than limbs. Words cannot begin to give a true picture of the horrors all around and I cannot single out one poor wretch without writing of all I saw that day. Suffice that they will stay with me for all my life however long that shall be. I left him in the care of a woman at the hotel who seemed no worse than stunned and deafened and sought help.

After a time of which I have no count I met a soldier pushing a hand cart with an injured woman stretched across it. He said he was going to an aid station at the barracks and I begged that he take William also and he agreed. Together we carried him to the cart and pushed it up the hill behind the hotel, although my leg was bleeding more and my arm of little use. We joined an awful procession of the dead and dying, most blinded and all bloody. When we were taken in the nurse shook her head and said that both our patients were dead. Neither the soldier nor I knew anything of the woman we tried to save, but I sadly furnished William's details. Then she took me to another place to have my lesser wounds dressed.

I lay there for a time, all the while surrounded by the most awful sights and sounds, the people there overwhelmed by more casualties than there were space for. When I could walk again I left that place and returned to the hotel through streets still littered with the dead and what buildings remained were burning with those still alive within them. The hotel was still standing but shattered while the railway station was all but demolished. I heard that as many as a hundred may have died there in an instant. It is hard to know what more to relate, so much still swirls in my head, the horrors vivid but the details half-remembered.

Since I cannot write for the present I have employed Miss Jepson to write this at my dictation. I have today gathered something of my wits and made plans for the next few days. Despite everything, including deep snow which has only added to the misery and dire conditions of the whole population, the railway is again operating and I will resume the journey tomorrow. Once in Montreal I will send word again.

George

His signature was a stuttering scrawl under Miss Jepson's clear loops, written left-handed Lydia guessed. It was a shocking account, not quite like anything Lydia had read before, more a dispatch from the trenches than anything else. Yet for all the carnage George described, for all he had lost his friend, that boarding-school stiff upper lip kept his emotions in check. For an instant Lydia wondered if it could be a fiction, for she'd never heard of such a calamity.

It didn't take long to discover: the world's largest man-made explosion until the dawn of the atomic age. A ship loaded down with explosives, a collision, a fire, catastrophe. Hundreds dead, many never found, many never identified, thousands more appallingly injured. She read the reports of the events, watched short jerky films and read other eye-witness accounts, all confirming and amplifying the dreadful picture painted by George. In any other time it would surely have been an event echoing down the years, yet compared to the unspeakable carnage of the war in Europe, it was hardly more than a couple of hours' worth of killing.

As terrible as the blast had been, as vivid and personal as George's account had made it, more than a century later the effect was quite simple: whoever William was, he'd have no further role to play in her investigations. She could tidy up the loose ends of his true identity in her own good time, for he was one of twenty-seven Williams on the *Saxonia* who might be cross-matched to the roll of casualties from the Halifax Explosion.

5

"I spoke to Gloria, my friend in Oxford," Lydia told Derek Ballard when she saw him at Town's End Cottage. "She's coming over to Wheadon St James on Friday. She can meet Georgina, Lady Stoppes, and I can show her what's to be done. If everyone's happy I'll pay her for Friday and she can come back next week. If she doesn't much like it then it'll just be a day out and we'll have lunch together."

"That sounds ideal," he nodded, "And the rest? You know I have to ask."

"At the moment nothing to ruffle any feathers. A couple of things that I'm curious about but that's all. But I'll say again, this is likely to be a long process. I'm thinking months rather than weeks."

"That's not a problem. We're doing this properly and really that's all that matters."

"I've asked Georgina if she'll do a DNA test and she's agreed. She thinks Amanda or Felicity will too."

"Lady Stoppes? I'm not sure how that could help. Surely she has no connection to the Stoppes genes? I assume that's what you're thinking of."

"You're right, but I have an idea, so here's the plan. There are many different family history sites offering DNA services but their purpose is to see if you match up with or are in some way connected to another member of that site. It's a way of connecting to distant cousins you might not otherwise find.

"It's a long shot, but I thought if Georgina and her daughters put their DNA on file then any matches that Georgina had, the girls would have too. Any that the girls had which Georgina didn't should be Stoppes connections. And they'd be worth investigating. I might ask Sir Christopher's aunt to do the same thing. What do you think?"

"I think I'm glad I asked you to look into all this, because I would never have thought of that."

"Even if there are no matches it won't be proof of anything one way or the other, but it will be another avenue we've tried."

Lydia showed him her notebook entries of her activities so far and the list of all the documents she'd examined, what files they were in and what potential for further research they might have.

"That's the kind of thing that'll be in the final report. Of course if there's a sixth baronet to be found it might have a different emphasis."

"That's exactly what I asked for, keep it like that," he said, "Now, come into the kitchen, I've something to show you."

Spread out on the table were pieces of a picture frame and the glass in three jagged pieces.

"Oh, that is such a shame," Lydia commiserated.

"My own fault, too heavy handed. But look at the back of the painting."

He held it and flipped it over, resting it face-down on a piece of cloth.

"That is very interesting," she said, studying the faint pencil writing so similar to the inscription on the back of her Prudence Mallingford portrait. *Mistress Sophia Cummins 1846 taken by Mr ----*. Again the artist's name could only be guessed at.

"Does that name, Cummins, mean anything in your family, Derek?"

"It didn't until an hour ago," he said proudly, "but there was also this in the frame."

He produced a handwritten note from his shirt pocket, with something of a conjurer's flourish:

> *A portrait of my mother's mother, who I did not know. This picture hung in my mother's house until her death when it passed to me. My mother told me that the artist's name was Aylton. It has no value for probate. RHB. June 1948.*

"RHB? Your uncle?"

"No, Robert Henry Ballard, his father, my grandfather."

"That's excellent, thank you. I don't know why exactly, but I'd always assumed that the inscription was written by the sitter or the sitter's family, but now I see your painting it makes no sense. I think the person who wrote that was connected to the painter, it looks like the same handwriting, the same wording, almost like a catalogue entry when you think about it. And the sitter's name is written clearly so it's easy to identify, it's the artist's name which is a squiggle, the name that was written on every piece of work and a name very familiar to the writer."

"I think it was worth the broken glass, don't you?"

"Thank you, can I get it re-framed for you? I'd like to do that, and maybe get mine done at the same time. I'll see if Mr Aylton is a better subject for searching than my Prudence Mallingford has been."

ooo

The novelty of being on a train in England – how many years had it been? – occupied Lydia completely, even though she'd brought a few of Robert Ballard's diaries to browse through. Mid-morning there weren't many passengers to people-watch, but it was smooth and just about comfortable enough to sit for an hour without the need to fidget. Unfamiliar countryside slid by, interrupted by old market towns, now dormitories for London workers. To travel like this every day would encourage the reading habit for sure, but for Lydia the novelty of the experience took all of her attention.

Arriving at Liverpool Street was almost a disappointment after the pleasure of travel through the landscape, enough that the idea of taking another railway journey, on a train she could sleep on, popped into her head. It was triggered, no doubt, by the letter from George Stoppes and his journey to Montreal from Halifax. Even so, it was an idea, one she might mention to Stephen when next they spoke.

The Central Line dispelled any romantic notions about trains. It is always a losing battle for underground railways: always too hot, too dirty, too noisy or too crowded for the slightest pleasure to be had in using them. But it was at least efficient, depositing her at Bond Street and out into the frantic busyness of the West End, all fumes and tourists, movement and noise, a confusing, constantly changing kaleidoscope. Lydia was so little used to the helter-skelter it almost took her breath away. She had a good idea of where she was headed but felt vague and undecided while all those around her had purpose and direction. More than once she was pushed and jostled by street-savvy speedsters and clutched her bag tightly for fear of it being snatched.

Once in James Street the melee thinned out a little. Café tables spilled out across the street but the lunch rush was still an hour away. By Mandeville Place she was in the heart of Marylebone, then, in the High Street, turning, then turning again at the library to find Whitecross Mansions. She hadn't expected to find anything modest, certainly not run-down or neglected. She was not disappointed: an immaculate red-brick edifice, the basement half sunk below street level with four or five storeys rising above it.

Amanda Stoppes answered at the first ring and buzzed Lydia in. Up one flight of carpeted stairs and the door was already open, Amanda smiling in the entrance.

"Welcome, come on in," she said.

Lydia stood for a moment, amazed by the size of the apartment. To call it a flat suggested something functional, something modest. Flats had a kitchen and bathroom, a living room and a bedroom, maybe two. This was something else.

"The family call it St James South, or, more often, just South." Amanda said.

"I can see why."

"I think all the apartments here used to be like this, with enough room for a live-in maid and cook as well as his and hers bedrooms for sir and madam. Most have been divided up but not this one. Disgusting isn't it?"

"I suppose you could share," Lydia suggested lamely.

"What I'd like to do is give beds to a couple of rough sleepers, but the sainted trust has absolutely forbidden it."

Lydia could see why that might be so, although she couldn't quite see Derek Ballard as a forbidding figure. He must have his reasons, Derek would be practical. Idealistic philanthropy probably wouldn't cut it.

"Employ them as your maid and cook?"

Amanda considered this for a moment then saw the snag. "My mother would object, I live here full time, but she uses the place quite often, so does Flicky sometimes. Besides, I don't think having a cook and a maid is really me, do you? Flicky would laugh for a month. I'd never hear the end of it."

"Did your parents ever have people in the manor, a cook or anything?"

"When we were young we had a housekeeper and a nanny. Not the same person all the time, the nannies came and went. I suppose they were *au pairs* mainly."

Amanda brought coffee while Lydia toured the apartment admiring beautiful Art Deco furniture and trailing her fingers across sumptuous pieces of glass cast in fabulous designs. Calling them ornaments, even in her head, did them no justice. Like the manor house itself, the contents of St James South were a collector's dream, probably worth as much as the apartment. By now she should have grown accustomed to the wealth and luxury that surrounded the Stoppes. Yet to their credit they made little show of it.

"A happy childhood would you say?" Lydia asked, resuming where their conversation had been interrupted.

"Happy enough," she said quickly, then, with the same keenness of mind and directness of her mother, "Lydia, I can't stop thinking that everything you ask is really asking whether my father had an illegitimate son somewhere. It makes talking difficult."

"Yes, I know, I'm sorry, I feel the same. Your mother is OK with it though. We came to an agreement. I'll tell her first if I find anything, or if I even suspect anything. I'll tell you second if you like."

"Deal."

They talked about Amanda's childhood at the manor, how it lacked for nothing, certainly not in material terms, and, so far as she was concerned, she lacked no warmth or comfort from her parents, even if her care was sometimes delegated to a visiting Czech or Polish student. And no, she did not think it likely that she had a half brother somewhere in Prague or Warsaw.

"What was it like living in the same house as your grandparents? I know it's big enough for everyone, but it's not the usual set-up, is it?"

"It was for us. We never thought twice about it. And really I don't remember us living that close. My memories are of people always being busy, not sitting around the house playing lord of the manor all the time."

"Did you get on well with your grandfather, your father's father?"

"He was all right, always sweet to me and Flicky, but I wouldn't say we were especially close. Flicky more than me probably, I've always been the prickly one, I expect my mother told you. Now if Granddad Charles had a love-child somewhere it was probably on the golf course. But Granny Kate was always there too, so that wouldn't have been easy. They were very conventional, stodgy even. My mother's parents, they were altogether different. Sparky, I'd say. But you're not interested in them."

"Actually, I am slightly," Lydia said, taking the opportunity to introduce the DNA test idea. "Do you know if any of your mother's family have ever researched your family history, or had any interest in it?"

"Not sure. I'd say probably not. Why?"

Lydia outlined her idea of comparing any resulting DNA matches with her mother's matches to try and find Stoppes connections. Then she invited Amanda to contribute her own sample to the scheme.

"The quick answer is no, I don't trust anybody with my DNA. Who knows what they'll do with it? And, if I understand correctly, it might help you find a long lost heir, right?"

"A long shot, but yes."

"And, as I've already told you, I'd really like to see the end of hereditary titles, so I'd rather you didn't find anyone."

"I understand, really I do. It's fine," Lydia reassured her.

"You'll ask Flicky? Yes of course you will. She'll say yes. She says yes to anything. Even so I think I'll keep my DNA to myself."

It wasn't as if they were close friends who'd had a disagreement, there was no ill-feeling between the two women, they simply had different views. And yet that small difference hung between them, a chill to an otherwise pleasant encounter, a chill that briefly inhibited further conversation.

Then Lydia remembered her prime reason for being in Marylebone. "Do you think there's anything here that I should look at? I don't want to go through all your things, but old photos or files, if there's anything like that I really should take a look at it."

"I don't think you'll find anything of the slightest interest in our stuff, but in the cupboard in the small bedroom there are a few boxes, I saw some old records and a collection of Christmas cards. I don't know how long since anybody was in there. You're welcome to go through it all. Other than that I don't think there's anything here at all."

The smallest bedroom was indeed small, filled by a single bed with a small bedside cabinet, a chair and a narrow chest of drawers with a mirror resting on it. Above the bedhead the window was covered by a blind. A built-in cupboard offered storage space. From it Lydia removed seven boxes and placed them on the bed to examine their contents.

First were the Christmas decorations, not the gaudy shimmering plastic of today but dozens of concertina paper-chains, their colours faded with age, some so brittle they crumbled under her touch. Jumbled coils of fairy lights and boxes of glass baubles for the tree, big fold-out paper bells and lanterns to fill the corners and hide the joins in the chains, all these and more had her imagining the apartment in festive clothes, welcoming the London friends for drinks. The decorations could have no significance in her quest, but she still lingered over them.

A box of cookery books circa 1960 were next. *Good Housekeeping* provided several well-used volumes, some still in their dust jackets, stained from a dozen spills and splashes. Lydia pulled one from the box, the cover picture familiar. Was it a real memory, or simply the style that struck a distant chord. Her mother's kitchen perhaps – or more likely her grandmother's.

It was far too easy to get sucked down rabbit holes.

Next, two heavy boxes of LPs. A glance at the spines revealed so many that should be pulled out and reminisced over: Helen Shapiro, Dusty Springfield, Del Shannon, Neil

Sedaka, The Stones. Lydia daren't look any further for fear of disappearing into memories of her parents' record collection, the one she'd always been a little scornful of.

A shoe box full of postcards offered the chance of something more relevant to her enquiries. But even as she started leafing through them, she wondered how she would spot a coded message or a subtle hint at an extra-marital affair in such a public space. She looked at a few and found little encouragement. Another tempting diversion.

The box of Christmas cards still in their envelopes offered little more, but it did set her thinking. She sifted through twenty or more to check the address. Each was addressed to Whitecross Mansions. Was there an equivalent box at St James Manor containing the cards from the Bedfordshire circle of friends and relatives? Were the lives that divided? All the cards she had in her hand were addressed to *Mr & Mrs Charles Stoppes* – the stodgy couple – and postmarked the 1950s and 1960s. So, the separate circles were just that, and these were from the London circle of the young couple of the swinging sixties, perhaps before stodginess set in. What more likely decade could there be for a stray son to have been conceived?

Which, Lydia reminded herself, was pure speculation. What she was supposed to be doing was pure investigation.

There wasn't likely to be a card from such a child's mother wishing Mr & Mrs Stoppes a Merry Christmas. Although the more she thought about the times they lived in, the more possible such a thing became. She would go through each card and tabulate the senders' names and dates and any noteworthy messages. Who knew when such a list of Stoppes friends might prove useful? And besides, it could be another job for Gloria.

Last of the seven was another shoe box. More envelopes, but this time containing letters, and from twenty years earlier than the Christmas card collection. The first she opened was addressed to Lady M. Stoppes and dated April 1934. It was in a clear and educated hand and concerned the appointment of a new cook at St James Manor, the previous one having left at short notice. It closed with an enquiry into the health of *your dear little Charles*, a reference no doubt to the baby boy born to Sir George and his wife Miriam the previous year. The letter was signed by Elizabeth Calbain.

The elusive woman's role was at least becoming clearer, probably as the housekeeper, given her interest and actions in appointing a replacement cook. And yet that question regarding the baby seemed almost personal. A familiarity through long acquaintance with the family, a familiarity that grew stronger over the years to end with her buried right next to the whole Stoppes dynasty?

"How are you getting on, ready for lunch yet?" Amanda interrupted Lydia's wondering. Some slant of Amanda's face, her words and the way she spoke could all so easily have been her mother.

"May I take these boxes of cards and letters? They need a longer look through. You can have them back or they can stay at the manor."

ooo

"Jesus Christ!" Gloria stood on the drive looking up at the ivy-clad walls of St James Manor then turned slowly to take in the broad expanse of perfect lawn. "Is this what Stephen's place is like?"

"No, it's smaller. I mean yes, like this but a lot less of it."

Lydia's friend stood silent, not quite able to take in the luxury of space that such a garden, a private garden, afforded the occupants of such a house.

When she'd stood for a few moments, Lydia said, "Let's get inside and meet Georgina Stoppes."

She took Gloria round by the old stables and in by the side entrance, into the kitchen to be less formal, to avoid Gloria's first impression being of a stately home. Georgina was at the counter eating toast.

"Hello, can I call you Gloria?" she said without waiting for introductions. "I'm Georgina."

"Yeah, of course," said a slightly startled Gloria, "Yeah, great."

"I'm sure Lydia has told you the ground rules here at the manor."

She had. They had coffee and more toast, before Georgina gave Gloria a shortened tour which included only the ground floor.

When Gloria and Lydia settled in the library, Gloria whispered, "You fell on your feet with this little number, didn't you?"

"Yes, I did," Lydia nodded. "Nice place, nice people, doing what I love. Welcome to paradise. Now let me show you what I've got for you, see what you think. This is just a trial, for you, not for me, I already know you can do it, it's whether you want to or not."

Lydia pulled out the earliest of the account books, *The Manor House 1878-1885*.

"I haven't studied this one before, so you and I are starting at the same point." Lydia slowly flipped through a few pages to familiarize herself with the way the entries had been listed and the kinds of information they contained.

"Take a little time to get to grips with this flowery handwriting, and get a feel for the kinds of things that are covered. Then we'll need a spreadsheet with some codes to help analyze the results. It's when, what, who from or who to and how much. Just the round pounds will be fine. You'll quickly see the same things come up month after month."

"And how many years are there to do?"

"Not many," Lydia said straight faced, "Less than a hundred and fifty."

"That'll be ... twenty thousand entries!" Gloria said in horror.

"Yes. But if there's anything to find my guess is it'll be a lot less than that."

"And I'm looking for what?"

"I really don't know. An anomaly, something that doesn't quite fit. A bill for something that doesn't belong, the start of a series of new bills, a regular receipt that stops. We'll do the first year or two together and see what kind of thing pops up. But the idea of doing everything is that it might make it easier to spot the misfit. What do you think?"

"OK, if that's what you want it's easy enough. I thought it might be more, you know, interesting." She sounded distinctly disappointed.

"Ah, but I haven't told you about the box of Christmas cards yet. Hundreds of them."

"Right, that's enough, don't tell me any more, I'll wait for that pleasure. Now, before I get started, where do I smoke? And don't tell me I can't, because I'll be off."

"All arranged. Anywhere you like outside, but collect the dog-ends please. Umbrella by the back door in the event of rain."

And so, without any further discussion it was understood that Gloria was on the team from that moment on, not that Lydia had doubted her. For someone of Gloria's experience and skills, tabulating and recording was easy work, and Lydia knew she had a keen eye for the mistake, the oddball, the cuckoo in the nest.

After they'd looked through the first three years' accounts together, she left Gloria to it. Then Lydia was torn between the box of letters from the flat and the *Correspondence 1909-1914* file. She chose the latter, hoping there might be more from the young George Stoppes at Snaresby. From what little she knew of him already he seemed to have had a more interesting life than most of his family.

She found the usual run of letters covering every aspect of Sir Edwin's life and responsibilities of the manor and the farm. Those addressed to Lady Henrietta were almost exclusively from her mother or her three sisters. They were full of chatter and gossip about cousins and mutual acquaintances. On a different day in a different search they might have been invaluable and certainly fascinating, but for once Lydia remained determinedly single-minded.

The first relevant piece of information came in another letter from Sir Edwin's sister Mary. As previously, it was mainly regarding her son Valentine who in June of 1909 was leaving for Canada where he intended to prospect for precious metals. An ill-fated trip, as it turned out. Lydia tried to read the letter as if she did not know Valentine's fate, did not know he was killed in a mine in Manitoba eight years later. Mary had written full of excitement at his adventure, but also with a mother's anxiety for a son's welfare.

In September, the ten-year-old George wrote to his parents from Snaresby College reassuring them that he was *well and settled happily into life at The College*. It was a short letter, a just-arrived letter devoid of fact or incident, copied no doubt from a standard template, its writing supervised by a prefect or house-master. It held no hint of affection or hankering for home life, it was the beginning of how that oppressive school system turned boys into men – men ready to serve in any part of the far-flung empire. Never mind the boys' misery nor the repressed and often sadistic men they became.

A few weeks later, George wrote again. Another short letter and predictably, everything was still going extremely well without being specific. But the phrase which caught Lydia's attention was near the end. *William has been most generous in helping me settle into the ways of College*. William, again. And perhaps most importantly, a William who needed no surname to be recognized by the reader. The same William pictured with George in 1917? The William he went to Canada with? The William killed in Halifax? Possibly, and if so, the root of their friendship lay in schooldays. Lydia reminded herself of the neglected task of finding William's surname by cross-matching *SS Saxonia* passengers with the death roll from the explosion.

By lunch, 1909 had turned into 1911 with more of the same: letters that followed familiar themes, minor incidents in local life, news of births and deaths from friends and more distant relatives. There was also more uninformative news from the stiff-upper-lip schoolboy George and one from his house-master saying there'd been an incident with a gas fire in the school sick-bay during his confinement with chickenpox.

Georgina Stoppes had put out the usual lunch along with a bottle of wine, although she'd left for a few days in town. While Lydia cut bread and opened the bottle, Gloria set out the cheese and cold meat and told Lydia of her morning's progress. She had a few uncertainties over some of the handwriting which she'd marked for further examination, but otherwise it was easy going.

"Before you ask, 1881, but I'm getting quicker."

"Anything interesting?"

"Big wedding last year. Paid for the church, the choir, the bells, the whole works I'd say. 'Course, it only cost a few quid really."

"How the other half lived. Actually, how they still do."

"I can't believe all this," Gloria said, pouring a second glass. "And you've got the run of the place with lunch laid on too."

"Not next week, we'll need to bring our own, I don't want to be raiding the fridge, although we can. It just feels like pushing it too far. Do you want to come and stay in Grantchester, maybe next weekend?"

Gloria stopped eating and looked at her friend closely.

"What, like grown-up people do? Being civilized and

refined and spending the weekend in the country?" she said in her best fake-posh. "Eddie too?"

"Of course Eddie too."

"Yeah, we'll do that. It's time we saw what Snooty Towers was like."

"Gloria, he's not ..."

"Yeah, yeah, I know, but let me have my fun."

While Gloria stayed in the garden, enjoying the dual benefits of a cigarette and the fresh air, Lydia went back to the correspondence. She hadn't been there more than a few minutes when she read another letter from Snaresby College, this one not from George but from the Warden:

> *Sir Edwin,*
>
> *I write with great sadness to inform you that an accident has befallen your son George Melville Stoppes, an accident from which he has mercifully escaped with his life although I fear his injury may be long-lasting. I am personally conducting a stringent enquiry into the exact circumstances under which he was injured. At the present time the known facts appear to be these: George was wounded in the shoulder from the accidental discharge of a training rifle in the range-hut during firing practice with The College's Army Volunteer Cadet Force. It appears that the bullet passed cleanly through George's shoulder which has resulted in great discomfort, although you will be pleased to know that he is bearing up well. Prompt attention to his wound staunched the flow of blood. He was promptly attended by Matron Queasly. Sir Emmanuel Rossiter, the highly respected surgeon was called from London and has been in attendance since yesterday. I should say at once that The College will meet all his expenses and will accept without question any alternative you may wish to involve in the matter.*

It is known that at least two other cadets, namely Cpl Creswell and Pte Tremain, were present at the time of the incident and these two are providing me with every assistance in establishing the sequence of events. I can confirm that no officer was present at the time of the accidental firing. As the senior cadet present Cadet Creswell has had his rank reduced to L/cpl.

I will personally keep you informed as to the outcome of my enquiry and the continued recovery of your son. If you wish to call upon me at any time I will be completely at your disposal.

A more interesting life! No doubt about that, how many thirteen-year-olds had been accidentally shot? Little wonder that the Snaresby College Warden was so willing to pay the costs of George's medical care, handled badly the accident could surely have ruined the college's reputation. On a whim, Lydia checked if the college still existed. It did, with a caring prospectus written in political-correct-speak all about equality and opportunity, but no mention of a volunteer cadet force. Clearly the grovelling had paid dividends.

Was this injury the one obliquely referred to in Mary's letter of 1917, *what one cannot do will be done by the other and vice versa*? So if George had a bullet wound in his shoulder, what disability did William have that balanced the pair? Lydia recalled the last photo in the 1917 album, where George and William were shown, one sitting, one standing with a walking stick. She found the album quickly enough and turned to the last page. With what she already knew she saw the two young men with fresh eyes. The one seated did look the younger of the two and his pose had something artificial about it. He appeared to have been arranged in the chair, as if the photographer had carefully posed a mannequin.

Lydia imagined herself injured, a bullet irreparably

damaging her shoulder, her arm able to be raised only by using her good arm to lift it into place. The chair she sat in was not unlike the one in the photograph, similar to the carver in a dining table set, but wider. She tried lifting her dead left arm and placing it on the chair's arm, mimicking the pose of the young man in uniform.

To sit like that felt awkward, unnatural, but the idea seemed to fit well. If the seated soldier was George, then the standing one was William and his balancing disability concerned a leg. She should find William's name. He may have been killed in Halifax but he certainly played a part in George's life.

Twenty-seven Williams on the *Saxonia*. Three were crew and immediately excluded, sixteen were Canadian soldiers returning injured to their homes, which left eight to cross-reference to the newspaper lists of dead in the explosion. Only one William appeared on both: William Tremain.

As Lydia made a note of her findings, careful to spell out William's name correctly, she knew it was familiar. Who was present at the shooting at Snaresby? She turned back to the Warden's letter. George Stoppes, Corporal Creswell and Private Tremain.

After a few moments to consider her discovery, Lydia typed the name again, this time into her genealogy search. Male, born England 1898 give or take five years, gave eighteen results, a very manageable number. She scanned the list of births from many parts of the country, but her eye rested on William Edwin Tremain, born 1897 in Lincolnshire. Wasn't the second baronet Edwin Tremain Stoppes? To Lydia's mind it could be no coincidence. She could order a birth certificate but there was more to find before she did so.

Knowing who she was looking for, it was a simple task to find William on the 1901 census. There he was, a four-year-old boy living in Lincolnshire with his grandparents William and Susanna Calbain, a couple who were already in Lydia's database as the parents of one of her people of potential interest. They were the parents of Elizabeth Calbain, the *truly loyal and loving mother* buried so close to the Stoppes in the churchyard just across the lane. Who but her son would have placed her there and provided such an epitaph? Yet that son was dead in Canada many years before Elizabeth's grave had been dug.

ooo

The beauty of the evening, all gentle breezes and slanting golden light, begged her to be outside. She sat in a deckchair by the summerhouse, her summerhouse, as she thought of it now: it had her things in it, the furniture was arranged as she wanted it, the fridge held her preferred wine. It was hers. The Stoppes and all their history swirled around her head, fact upon fact, letter upon letter, dates and events without number. If it weren't for her careful note taking it would be easy to lose track of where she'd looked and where she had not.

As she composed an update for Derek Ballard it was easy to think she was no closer to the solution, easy to forget that the only requirement was to look and report. There was absolutely no need to find anything at all. William Tremain was an interesting discovery, a possible alternative male line, but he had been snuffed out before that line could be extended. She could find no hint of an illegitimate son for any of the more recent baronets, although there remained more to be discovered for both the third and fourth. And Lydia remained hopeful that her DNA matching plan might yet throw up something to inspire fresh impetus to her work. As Amanda had correctly predicted, her sister Felicity had no qualms about supplying a sample.

As Lydia poured herself a second glass of Bousval, her phone buzzed with a call from Stephen. As his face appeared she couldn't help but notice a change in him, more gaunt, greyer. Too big a change in too short a time.

"Hello!" she said with genuine excitement, determined not to immediately ask about his health. "How's it going in the Caribbean? I bet it can't beat Cambridge on an evening like this."

She swept her phone in a gentle arc to show him the garden, his garden, bathed in the evening sun.

"That's cruel," he said, "I'd very much like to be there with you right now."

"Sorry, I don't mean to taunt you. Still doing full days of the bad stuff?"

They chatted amiably for a few minutes, without really saying anything but reminding themselves how they talked to each other. He sounded fine and Lydia hung on to that thought, pushing aside her real concerns.

"Did I tell you of my plan to use Lady Georgina's and her daughter Felicity's DNA to see what matches come up and where any differences might be? I'm still feeling quite clever about that."

"Have you done it yet?"

"Sent them off yesterday. Has your DNA analysis thrown up anything interesting?"

"No results in yet, and really, it'll only be background information, a context in which we might place some individuals or a group of individuals," he said, traces of the indulgent university professor leaking into his way of speaking as if he'd not quite switched off from work. Once, in what now seemed the very long ago, she'd found his academic manners, his formality, a little condescending. Compared to her own insecurities, he'd always seemed so secure in his knowledge, so precise in his statements, emotion rarely evident. Now she knew this to be a product of upbringing and education, a veneer on a truly caring man, as respectful of her skills and talents as she was of his.

"Why don't you do what I'm doing," Lydia said with a sudden inspiration, "Match them up to a commercial genealogy database? Not through their normal channels like me, but through the UN, I'm sure any one of them would love to help out and tell the world what great corporate citizens they are."

"I'd never considered such a thing. I don't think anybody has."

"And even if it only solved one family mystery about a lost great-grandfather," Lydia added, warming to her theme, "it might link some of your victims to a family tree. That would be real context. That would make them real people again."

"It's an excellent idea, thank you," he nodded, "I'll look into what would be involved. But I do wonder whether my lords and masters will want to turn these long-forgotten remains into real people with real relatives alive today."

"Don't tell them, make it just another part of your background context."

"That's subversive," he said, without actually disapproving.

"I'm feeling subversive."

"Good for you. Any particular reason?"

"Just a general dissatisfaction. Nothing that looks promising seems to lead anywhere."

Lydia told him about William Tremain, and about the second baronet most likely being his father, how he'd been involved with the young George in a shooting accident at school, but how he'd died young in the Great Halifax Explosion.

"I haven't heard about that."

"Nor had I," she said, then gave him a thumbnail sketch of the calamity, the deaths, the forever missing, the mangled unidentified corpses.

"Sounds appalling, chaotic. They wouldn't have had much to go on, and not much science back then."

"Yes, from what I've read, it was." As she said it, Lydia realized she hadn't even looked for official confirmation of William's death, instead she had relied entirely on a letter from George Stoppes and a newspaper report of the names of some of the dead. In his shocked and injured condition George could've been mistaken, it was possible that William had survived.

"What do you use for your DNA samples, Stephen? Bones?"

"Bones sometimes, teeth more often."

"What about hair, can you use that?"

"Sometimes. The trouble with extracting DNA from hair is that it's an expensive process. Sometimes we can't get anything. But we always pay close attention to clothes and the manner of death. You know all this, everything goes to making up the picture, getting close to the person and the life they led. And sadly, the manner of their death."

"Would I be right in guessing at gunshots?"

"Ah, that I cannot tell you," Stephen said, weariness creeping into his voice. "But of all those we've examined so far, none appear to have died of natural causes."

It closed the conversation, gently but firmly, as he intended it should. They looked at each other, uncertain as to how to continue, for of course they could neither of them think of anything but how the long-dead victims of Guanito met their ends. For an instant those thoughts included their own ends and Lydia had a momentary vision of a day in the future when she might lose Stephen for ever.

Then Gloria Fitzgerald came to her rescue.

"Gloria and Eddie are coming for the weekend!" she announced joyfully.

"That's wonderful," he said, knowing well that such an invitation signalled another small step towards Lydia treating The Old Rectory as her home. "Anything new on your Mistress Mallingford portrait?"

"Yes! It turns out that Derek Ballard has a family picture by the same artist whose name is Aylton. Same kind of inscription on the back too."

"That's exciting news, did you find Mr Aylton?"

"No. To be honest, I haven't even looked, my head's been full of Stoppes and all their doings."

ooo

Elizabeth Claire Wykham lived in a solid, late Victorian house in the unremarkable village of Fringly Green, north of Bedford and almost in Northants where brick and ironstone cottages alternate along the main street. According to her nephew's widow, Georgina, Elizabeth remained fiercely independent, even in her late eighties. She'd agreed easily enough to Lydia's request for an interview about her memories of family life and wasn't in the least disturbed when she heard the reason behind the request. "Nothing to tell," she'd said, "but you're welcome to it. Come after lunch, I'm not feeding you too."

She must have been formidable in her prime, Lydia thought as she was ushered through to a neat and uncluttered sitting room by a robust, white-haired woman, clearly still fit and in full command of her senses. Her solid features and enquiring eyes were softened a little by age, and she may have been a little shrunken from her former self, but she was alert and watchful as she studied her visitor. Lydia offered her the little gift, a tin of chocolate biscuits, which she'd brought by way of a peace offering in case one should be needed. For a moment Elizabeth Wykham looked surprised, genuinely taken aback by the gift.

"Did I scare you so much you had to bring your own biscuits?"

"No, no, I ..." Lydia stumbled.

"Oh, don't mind me, Miss Silverstream. Thank you, I like

chocolate biscuits. Now sit down and tell me what you want to know about the Baronets of St James."

"Please, call me Lydia. May I call you Elizabeth?"

"It's Lizzie to my friends. Will we be friends, Lydia?"

"I hope so," Lydia said, regaining something of her poise.

"Fire away. I've been wondering what you want to know from me that could possibly be of any interest or relevance to your enquiries."

"Funnily enough, the first thing I wanted to ask you wasn't about family matters at all, it was about you. I wondered if George and Miriam, your parents, had ever mentioned why they chose to name you Elizabeth. I ask because many names in the Stoppes family you can see straight away come from the mother or the father or the grandparents, which I suppose is also true of many other families. But I didn't see an Elizabeth there. Perhaps it was from your mother's side, someone I haven't come across yet."

"They never said, and I never asked. Claire is from my mother, and her mother before her. If I had to guess then ... but you don't want guesses, do you."

"Oh yes, I like guesses, they're much more interesting."

Elizabeth allowed herself a smile before saying, "My guess would be Nanny C, she was Elizabeth Calbain."

"I know she was close to the family. What do you remember of her?"

"She was our nanny. She looked after Charles and me, probably more than our parents did. They were always away somewhere. St James South, that's the flat in London, quite a lot, except during the war. I don't remember anything before the war, but afterwards they were always down there."

"What was she like?"

"Soft spoken, that's what I always remember when I think of her. She could be strict, but she wasn't one for shouting. She was more than a nanny too, I think she more or less ran the manor, even when my mother was at home. I think she'd been there in my grandfather's time, before my father came back. I think she came with the house. I have no idea really, it's just an impression."

Impression or not, it was exactly the kind of thing Lydia had wanted to hear, there was nothing so good as a first-hand account, even one that was seventy or eighty years old.

"Any other special memories?"

"When she died in 1952, she left me all her things, and a little money too. I think she knew she was dying. A few weeks before, she had a long talk with me, told me I should stand up for myself and how she was leaving me some money and her things and how I might need my own money one day."

"What kind of thing did she leave you?"

"All her personal things, everything from books to her hair brushes, her watch. Not a lot to show for a whole lifetime, but I don't suppose she needed much, living all those years at the manor."

"Is there anything left?" Lydia asked, with the faint hope that she might get a little closer to Nanny C by holding her watch or a favourite book.

"No, I don't think so. There was nothing of any real value. You can only hold on to things for so long."

Which Lydia knew was true, but which never made it any easier to part with keepsakes and mementos.

"What about the war years at the manor, do you remember anything from those days? I've seen a few pictures of a big marquee in front of the house and your mother in her WAAF uniform."

"I remember that big marquee, it was there for years. There was no lawn left when they took it down. It was always full of people doing things but I never knew what.

"We had RAF officers in the house, I mean staying there for a few weeks at a time. There were a lot of comings and goings. My mother did something with the officers in the house, I always thought she was a secretary of some kind, but I don't know really. Of course she never spoke about it, not then, not afterwards."

"Any particular events that come to mind now?"

"The local airfield got bombed now and again. One time we had dozens of the aircrew in tents for a few days after their huts were blown apart on the base. And that reminds me, the officers who stayed with us, some of them were Canadian, so were the aircrew in the tents." She paused for a moment, her face lighting up with the vivid flash of memory. "One of them, Ken somebody he was, gave me something, a badge or a patch or something like that. My brother got one too, but I lost mine soon afterwards."

"Did your brother keep his?"

"No idea, but probably. He collected all sorts of things. He'd ask all the officers and the aircrew for souvenirs. That's how I came to get a badge, Ken said I shouldn't be left out when he gave Charles something."

"I wonder where that little collection went."

"It's probably still at the manor. In the attic most likely."

"Your father had been in Canada hadn't he?"

"Yes. He came back when his father died. I don't really know anything about his time there and I don't remember him speaking about it. I don't remember anyone speaking about it. Something to do with mining, wasn't it?"

"Yes, The Mary Mine. It was in Manitoba. I've seen some of his letters to his father, perhaps you have too. Very uninformative."

"Sounds like my father. If he could say nothing he generally did so."

"But he was affectionate, a loving father?"

"Oh yes, certainly. Me more than Charles, but that's fathers for you. Fathers and daughters, mothers and sons. It was definitely like that in our family."

"Did he ever mention the Halifax Explosion? His friend

William was killed. It was just a day or so after they arrived from England."

"Halifax? In Canada? No, I don't think I ever heard that."

The story of the explosion and her father's and William's accidental parts in it were simple enough to relate. Elizabeth pressed for more details than Lydia had, but she recalled a few of the graphic phrases from the letter he'd sent a few days after the event.

"How awful, I knew nothing of it at all," said the old lady with regret.

"Did your father suffer any lasting disability from those injuries? I've no idea how serious they were."

"Not his arm, not that I knew of. His leg troubled him, he almost always walked with a stick, but I never knew that was from an explosion, somehow I had the impression that was from something else, something from childhood." Elizabeth closed her eyes, the better to remember what might or might not have been said so many years previously. "I thought I had a good memory for such things, but it seems you already know more than I do. What other little gems have you discovered?"

"I know a good deal about trusts that I didn't know before. Am I right in thinking that you still benefit from the St James Trust, as a child of the third baronet?"

"I do and I'm glad of it. I suppose my nephew's girls Amanda and Felicity will get my share when I pop off."

Lydia was about to explain that there may soon be no trust if she failed to find an heir, when it struck her that no one had mentioned what would happen to Elizabeth's benefits if the trust were wound up before her death. Perhaps it had never been considered, or perhaps Lydia had misread the provisions, perhaps she'd get her share. Either way, Lydia wasn't sure it was her place to raise that question.

"Did you know about the trust when it was being set up? I

mean, did you ever hear why it was set up, did your father ever speak about it?"

"He did, he had us all in the study on a bleak Saturday morning in February and told us what he'd done, put all the big property into a trust along with some capital to keep it going. I didn't think it really made much difference to anything, not that I really knew what it all meant. I'd only just turned eighteen that week and I was having a party that evening."

"He didn't say why he'd done it, did he?"

"Wasn't it to avoid death duties? I know he said it was something he should have done years previously, he said it put things right."

"Do you know what your brother thought about it?"

"He wasn't very pleased at first, but father explained it all and Charles just shrugged as if it didn't really matter. And I don't think it did. Of course it matters a bit more now, otherwise you wouldn't be here."

"Quite. And the real purpose is to see if there's any possibility of there being a male heir, a sixth baronet, who might not be aware of his position." Lydia tried to choose her next words carefully. "If there were such a person, somewhere in the world, who would you guess was the most likely to have produced an unrecorded, unacknowledged offspring?"

"Of my father, brother and nephew? Oh dear, what a choice. Of course you can never tell with men, can you? They're consummate liars, the lot of them, and I'd have been the last to know anyway. But if I had to choose one, it would be my father. He hated socializing, never had his picture taken, never went out unless he had to. He was such an introvert, you never knew what he was really thinking. But don't they say it's always the quiet ones? Although how he'd have found the opportunity I don't know. Maybe when he was in Canada, when he was young and fancy-free, maybe he was different then, maybe that's why he never talked about those days. There, that's my best guess for you."

"Yes, I think you're right, it would be a likely time. Unfortunately, even if such a child existed, finding any record would be extremely difficult. Most places in Canada have strict privacy laws about birth records. They're not regarded as public documents like they are here."

They chatted on for a while about men and somewhat inevitably, about their failings, which in turn led Lydia to mention her own circumstances, although she was quick to exclude Stephen from the general round of criticism. With regard to her own marriage, Elizabeth made no pretence of it being a great success.

"We lasted the course, that's all that can be said for it. Richard had a reputation, well-earned from what I've heard. Now, if you'd included him in the list of men most likely to have a bastard son somewhere, he'd have been an easy first choice. There may still be stray Wykhams waiting to come and claim an inheritance, although I think they'd probably have done so by now."

Elizabeth said these things about her late husband without malice or resentment, more to illustrate the point about male reliability, or the lack of it. Her husband's infidelities were gone with him to the grave, forgiven or forgotten it made no difference now.

"I have a favour to ask of you, Lizzie," Lydia said, the conversation reminding her of genetics. "Would you donate a DNA sample? You're the oldest relative close to the line of succession. If there should be someone making a claim, you would make an excellent reference point."

Elizabeth Wykham hesitated, circling the idea to test for traps and dangers.

"I brought a spare kit with me, just in case."

6

"Oh, no Eddie?"

With Gloria standing alone on the doorstep, Lydia was stating the obvious.

"No, sorry, some urgent repair to a roof on the estate," Gloria said, her face revealing her own disappointment.

"But you'll still stay for a couple of nights?"

"Unless you throw me out."

One guest was better than no guests. Lydia had found herself very much looking forward to having her friends to stay, far more than she might have imagined. It wasn't only the first time she'd hosted anyone at The Old Rectory, it was the first time in many years she'd hosted anyone anywhere. The house in West Street had never lent itself to visitors, not that Lydia really had any other friends to speak of. Her brother and his family had visited only once and the idea of one of her nieces staying with her had been quietly forgotten long ago. She hadn't renewed the invitation since moving in with Stephen.

Lydia played tour guide while Gloria silently whistled and shook her head in disbelief.

"You were right," she said as they finished in the conservatory, "it's like the manor, just smaller."

"Now the summerhouse, it's my little corner, my thinking space. And there's wine waiting."

"Christ, Lydia, I know I said it before, but you're a ..."

"Lucky cow. I know, I really do."

They settled themselves on the little verandah and toasted their good health and happiness. Gloria was still getting used to her surroundings, while Lydia was buzzing with the pleasure of having a companion as well as a thousand things to talk about. But as she ordered her thoughts she found nothing but the Stoppes project came to her mind, whether it was Stoppes in the manor house, Stoppes in Marylebone, Stoppes in Canada or a Calbain in the churchyard.

"How was it at the manor today?" she said, unable to hold back her most pressing question.

"Quiet. To tell you the truth, Lydia, when you're not there it's extremely quiet and boring. I know all the codes for the household expenses by heart now. No wonder you didn't want to do it yourself."

"Anything that stood out?"

"Something stopped appearing each month and a couple more have started. Boring things."

"Yes, but what? Do you remember?"

"Maybe, but only if you pour more wine and only if you don't ask me about the bloody account books all night."

Lydia poured, and then under encouragement from Gloria, poured a little more.

"That's better," she agreed, lighting a cigarette and drawing deeply on it. "You'll have to check the dates, but around 1895 they stopped paying someone called a land agent, whatever that is. I'm all the way to 1905 and it hasn't re-started. There are plenty of what seem like one-offs, funerals, parties and so on, but there's a new regular receipt which started in 1898, or maybe 1899. It's rent for somewhere, Priory Villas I think."

"Now that might be really interesting. Number 1 or number 2?"

"Are you serious? If that's what you call interesting then you should get out more. As I've always said."

"And look where it got me!" Lydia spread her arms wide to include the garden and The Old Rectory itself.

"OK, point taken, but a rent payment is not that exciting.

Anyway, it's all on my laptop, we can have a look later. But not now. Please."

After dinner at The Green Man in Trumpington, they walked leisurely back to Grantchester in the last of the evening light, swapping memories of their previous time working together, each with very different views of those days. For most of them Lydia had been the odd one out, the non-drinking, non-partying, boring stay-at-home. Gloria had been the party-girl and, above all, the man-hunter. In what seemed like such a short time, their two worlds had grown closer together, each settled into monogamy, both surprised in their different ways that such a thing would happen to them.

"When will you see Stephen again?" Gloria said as they passed the church.

"A few weeks, actually a couple of months, unless I go to see him first. He's only been back a short time but I should, I think he needs the break. But there's the project and I know it shouldn't come first, it doesn't come first. I don't know. Maybe if I think I've reached some kind of milestone or made some discovery, then I'll take a week off and go to Cancun."

"You're sure about the whole deal with Stephen now? Not that long ago it was definitely only a trial."

"Oh yes, pretty sure, even though I can't tell you exactly what changed," Lydia answered without hesitation.

"I know, you don't even know what day it changes, do you? It's just like, oh yeah, when did that happen?"

"Same for you and Eddie?"

"Yeah, like pigs in shit, the both of us. Having your place makes all the difference."

"A place you can share and be comfortable in does wonders. I didn't think I'd ever be like that in Grantchester, but I am."

"Stephen's got a daughter hasn't he? How's that going?"

"It's had its moments, mostly my imagination, I think. Anyway, she's away, California I think."

Saturday dawned cool and grey and remained that way. By midday a steady drizzle had set in, enough to deter them from walking into Cambridge. While Lydia might have been content to read or investigate the Mallingford portrait, Gloria was less easily amused, so they drove to Trumpington and took the bus into the city.

The attractions of Cambridge were muted in the dull damp day, the tourist crowds huddled in plastic macs and crowded into bars and restaurants. A few hardy souls persevered under picnic table umbrellas outside pubs, but for the two visitors from Oxford there was little novelty in anything the city had to offer. At length they squeezed themselves into a corner of The Bath House and laughed at their foolishness as they ate macaroni cheese and dawdled over two glasses of lager.

"How long do you think this business at the manor house will go on?" Gloria asked.

"A very long time, months maybe, unless we find something, I mean find a sixth baronet."

"Do you reckon there'll be something for me to do for that long?"

"Probably. But only if you want to and it could be very boring. Like the rent from Priory Villas."

"What's so special about that?"

"If it's from number 1 then it might be just a tenant paying rent. If it's from number 2 then the person paying is someone of great interest. But here's the thing, if the person in number 2 is not paying rent while their neighbour is, then that person becomes even more interesting, because you would really like to know why not."

"OK, but if they're already a person of interest, you've probably got a good idea why they're not paying rent."

"I have. My guess is that person, her name was Elizabeth Calbain, had a baby fathered by the second baronet, and the family, or Sir Edwin himself, maintained Elizabeth and possibly, to some extent, her son William too."

"So he'd be the missing baronet?"

"No, too long ago, and besides, he died very young, killed in an explosion."

"So what's the big deal?"

"We have to explore every possibility, so where there's one there might be another. Elizabeth ended up living at the manor house as a nanny and housekeeper for sure, and as who knows what else."

"Sounds like *Downton Abbey*. Come on, finish that, I need a smoke."

The bus back to Trumpington took them out of the city past the Botanic Gardens, reminding Lydia once more of Laurence Durham and the search for his father, which in turn reminded her of what that whole saga had involved: wills. Elizabeth Calbain's will might make interesting reading, even though Lydia already knew what happened to her personal things. And had Elizabeth used a solicitor to draw it up? If she had, then who other than Ballard, Edwards & Joyce, the family's loyal advisors?

ooo

A stone relief set in the brick above the two front doors declared the building's origin: *Priory Villas 1895*. The rounded archways of the entrances were reflected in the window openings, giving the whole building an elegance that recent owners had done nothing to enhance.

New Street in St Neots was not what it once was, neither were Priory Villas, despite their obvious former status. Number 1 had become an alternative health clinic hosting a chiropractor, an aromatherapist and a reiki practitioner. Number 2 was apparently unoccupied. As Lydia approached, a sagging For Sale sign was being reinforced by a suited man wielding a hammer to little effect.

The temptation was too great.

"Hello," she said, "are you the agent?"

"Yes," he said, slightly startled by the enquiry.

"I wonder," she said, adopting her most timid and tentative voice, "I mean I haven't got an appointment or anything, I can call if it's easier, but as I'm here, if you have time, I wonder could I have a look inside? I mean just to get an idea if it's the kind of place I'm looking for."

He looked uncertain, this was not at all how business was meant to be done, although he was young and had only slight acquaintance with selling property. But a prospect was a prospect, even early on a dull Monday morning.

"Yes, I can give you a look round, if you'd fill in a few details for me. We can do it inside, it'll be easier, Mrs ...?"

"Oh thank you," Lydia said warmly, while weighing the idea of giving a false name and address. Instead she listed herself as being a resident of Osney, which was technically true and matched her driving licence which she was surprised to find she needed to show him.

The house was white, everywhere, even the floors had been painted. Or rather, it was dirty white. Every surface needed cleaning, or better, the whole house needed redecorating. There was no character, no trace of the history of a century and more, no sense of its place in the town or even in the street. It still stood, it looked solid, no water apparent where water shouldn't be, but it offered nothing when the high ceilings, the period door frames and those arched windows should all have offered so much. Even the back garden, like the neighbour's, had been paved over to provide car parking. At best it would become another set of offices like so many other once-fine town houses.

Curiosity satisfied, Lydia made her excuses – "sorry to have troubled you, so disappointing, not at all suitable" – and continued her journey to St James Manor. She had a full day planned, working through more correspondence, searching for wills and documents about the baronetcy itself, checking for the existence of a family safety deposit box, and on a whim, looking for badges in the attic.

The first thing she did, before even getting out of the car, was to send Derek Ballard a message about the Elizabeth Calbain will. With no Gloria until Wednesday, she wished she could delegate more of the mountain of work in front of her. No rush, Derek had said, but even so, Lydia really wanted to make some progress. It seemed that at every turn a fresh line of enquiry opened up and so far, all led down blind alleys.

"Safety deposit box?" Georgina queried. "No, I don't think so. And yet, now that you've asked, I have a very vague memory of something, somewhere. Why would that be if we don't have one?"

"Some banks stopped having them. But others are starting them up again."

"I'll call them. No, better than that, you can never get through, I'll go into the branch later when I'm in town."

"Do you have a bank in London as well as one locally?" Lydia wondered on a sudden inspiration.

"Yes, we do, but a different bank. Very old-school. Hoares. A great name for a bank, don't you think? Chris could never resist a schoolboy joke about that. Actually I think the trust uses them too."

"Could you call them and see if you have a box?"

"Looking for anything in particular?" Georgina said warily.

"Not yet, but it would be good to know what there is, if anything. I'm particularly interested in seeing the original documents about the baronetcy. From when it was granted back in 1874."

"They're not here?"

"Not that I've found. You think they might be here?"

Georgina Stoppes shrugged.

"I'm on a bit of a mission today. Do you mind if I go up to the attic to look in those old trunks? Sir Christopher's Aunt Elizabeth mentioned something, a collection of war mementos that her brother, Sir Charles, had as a boy. She thought they might be there or in the nursery."

"Of course." If Georgina wondered why such a collection could be of any relevance to Lydia's enquiries, she didn't ask.

Up under the roof in the old servants' quarters, Lydia found the trunks she'd remembered from her first-day tour of the manor. Three of them, all of a similar design, brass-bound and black with curved lids like treasure chests. She guessed them to be late Victorian. The first she tackled was locked, or jammed shut, either way she couldn't open it. When she pushed against it the weight told her it wasn't empty.

The second opened easily enough to reveal a space crammed full of magazines: *National Geographic, Punch, The Illustrated London News* and others she'd never heard of. Lydia took out a stack from one corner, enough to tell if there was anything other than magazines hidden beneath them but there wasn't; hundreds if not a thousand or more, and all in apparently good condition with no sign of mould or mouse attack. On another day she could have sat leafing through such a fabulous collection for hours, drawn into the stories and photos of a century of big events and everyday lives.

The third was closer to what she was seeking: antique toys of all kinds, carefully layered with a thin woollen blanket between each layer. She cautiously removed each layer, marvelling at the condition of each item. It was as if they had been played with for no more than a week before being discarded. They would most certainly be valuable. More hidden treasures, she thought, in this house of treasures. Were they part of the trust, like the furniture, or part of Sir Christopher's personal effects handed down from each of his predecessors?

It was easy enough to explore old trunks in the attic, but the nursery felt more like an inhabited space. Rummaging there felt more intrusive, more like an invasion of privacy, not that the rooms were currently in use. But it reminded her that Elizabeth Calbain probably slept there during her nannying years. Here too was where, in later years, a succession of Eastern European *au pairs* would've rested their heads. The nursery consisted of a bedroom with a single bed and a small bathroom off it, plus a large room furnished with another bed and a baby's cot, chests of drawers, a dressing table, a rocking horse and a pair of easy chairs. Even with all that there was plenty of room for infants to crawl and toddlers to toddle.

Behind the rocking horse was a floor-to-ceiling built-in cupboard. Lydia tentatively swung the doors open, fearing that some precious antique might fall out as she did so. Instead, she saw a dozen shelves, mainly empty but with several biscuit tins resting on them. She took down the nearest and was surprised by the weight. Easing it open she found dozens, perhaps hundreds of brass shells, all bullet casings of various calibres. Hardly a significant find, but to Lydia it was a sure sign that the young Charles Stoppes' collection of patches and badges couldn't be far away.

She was right. The next tin she chose held exactly what she was looking for. She took it to a chair and ran her fingers through the contents. The tin held badges of all kinds, some felt, some cloth, some embroidered, some printed, but all with a military connection. The greatest number by far were the little country-title shoulder patches denoting an airman's nationality. There were examples from practically every country and colony of the British Empire together with the European countries fighting with them. And there, jumping out at her, were two from Canada. Were these the two from Ken, the flyer in a temporary tent while the airfield huts were rebuilt?

How many Kens had served at RAF Little Wheadon, Lydia wondered, as if such a search would take her closer to anything of importance in her real objective. How many of those young men who'd given Charles their flashes and badges had lived to tell the tales of their wars? The badges and insignia in the tin on her lap might well be all that remained of them.

Pulling herself from her reverie, Lydia looked about her. She should at least see what else was in the nursery, not to examine everything right away, but to know roughly what was here. It wouldn't take long, and it might pay dividends in the long run.

To her surprise the chests of drawers still held small children's clothes. Pulling a few out she reckoned they were modern, most likely belonging to the most recent children in the house, Felicity and Amanda, putting them at around thirty-five years old. A few seemed even more recent: Felicity's children, Matthew and Catherine? It seemed strange to Lydia, but then she'd never had children, nor a house so large that three generations could easily share it.

She turned her attention to the dressing table, an ornate white piece at odds with the heavy polished chests and bed ends. Beneath the central mirror a series of small drawers were arranged in two rows. The first few she tried were empty but the widest, the middle drawer, rattled as she pulled it out. It held a selection of small cases, mainly round, but one oval and two rectangular. In all, there were nine little boxes, each small enough to sit in the palm of her hand. Some were decorated with beautiful enamel, one of the rectangular boxes appeared to be silver, while the oval was golden, decorated with a ruby-coloured stone in the centre.

For a moment Lydia thought they might be a collection of ladies' powder compacts, but as she gently twisted the little clasp of the oval box she saw it was something else entirely. Inside the lid was a head and shoulders photograph of a young girl. The photo was bright and clear despite its age. In the tray was a lock of hair and two baby teeth, under which was a piece of paper with *Mary Eloise 1866* written upon it.

Lydia hardly dared breathe on it for fear of disturbing the hair. She set it gently down on the dressing table. Next she opened the silver rectangle. Another child, *George Melville 1906*, and just as the first box, with two teeth, a lock of hair and a photo as fresh as the day it was placed in the lid.

When she'd opened them all she had a collection which included each of the four baronets from second to fifth plus their siblings, Elizabeth Wykham's daughter Ann, and Albert, the cousin who died at Ypres. As she sat staring at the incredible collection, wondering just what value might be put on the boxes alone, it slowly dawned on her that there, right in front of her, might be the perfect DNA data bank by which any claimant to the baronetcy could easily be proved or denied.

Georgina Stoppes was nearly as amazed as Lydia.

"I think I knew about them," she said, "but it was a long time ago. I think Chris said something when Flicky lost her first tooth but we never did anything about it. I don't know why but I've always thought there was something slightly peculiar about saving hair and teeth. Maybe it was a thing when children often died young, maybe it was something to remember them by, maybe all there was to remember them by. But not these days."

"How would you feel if I took one tooth and some hair from each box to see if I can find a way to collect the DNA?"

"You can take it all as far as I'm concerned, but leave me the boxes please," Georgina said, then as an afterthought, "And maybe the photos too."

ooo

There he was, William Tremain, duly recorded in the newspaper cutting from the immediate aftermath of the explosion in 1917. It was a long list of fatalities, as were the lists published every day for weeks. Alongside those lists were the desperate notices of those seeking news of the missing, those seeking relatives of unclaimed and unrecognizable remains, those seeking the parents of maimed and shocked babies and small children. Many of the lost were never found, vaporized in the first instant of the explosion or shattered into so many pieces as to be unrecognizable as people at all.

Not only was William reported in the newspaper casualty list, he was also shown on the official roll of the dead. But, try as she might, Lydia could not find his death certificate for December 1917 in the archives. And yet, when she took a random sample of the names from the official roll she found each of their death certificates, each with the same cause of death: *shock due to injuries in explosion.*

From all she read, it seemed that in the chaos and confusion of those hours after the explosion, it was possible William and his identifying details had been separated, in which case he'd have been buried amongst the unknown dead and her search was futile. But she also read how some badly injured people had been left for dead in waiting rooms, makeshift wards and even in morgues, until by accident or good fortune their silent suffering had been recognized and they'd finally been attended to. But even if he'd survived those first hours, or even days, he might still have succumbed to his injuries in the bitter winter days that followed.

Or, despite being injured, unconscious and declared dead, he might still have survived. If Lydia could find no trace of him, then it was a good bet that he was buried with the unclaimed and unknown. Unless he had moved on to another province or another country. Another country might even include England, in which case she'd be right back where she started, chasing ifs and maybes. No death record in Nova Scotia really meant nothing at all.

She found twenty-six deaths of Tremains and Tremaines on

the record up until 1970, the last year available to researchers, with not a single William amongst them. But there were six marriages, and in pride of place there in 1921 was William Edwin Tremain, aged twenty-four, a railway clerk born in England, married in Halifax County. Lydia could scarcely believe her luck after so many dead ends. It didn't prove it was her William Edwin, it didn't prove anything, but it was a start. The bride was Mildred Luckhurst aged twenty-one years and born in Boston. Her occupation was nurse, which seemed to Lydia to be significant. Don't patients always fall for their nurses? Now what of births? Did that happy couple have children? If they did, the archives were not about to give up their secrets: the hundred-year moratorium on birth details blocked all enquiries.

A call from Derek Ballard prevented further frustration.

"Sorry to disturb you, but I missed your call earlier. Can you talk now?" he said.

"Yes, of course. I'd just hit another obstacle in my searches, so you've saved me from dwelling on that. And besides it might be quite irrelevant. As you know, sometimes I follow a lead for no good reason."

"Was there anything in particular you called about?"

"Yes and no. A general update on progress or lack of it, plus there may be a new expense coming up with some DNA analysis. Not the commercial ones I've already sent off, but something that might be more difficult, extracting it from teeth and hair. I haven't done anything about it yet, but I wanted to let you know it might happen, and check that the trust will be OK with that."

"Yes, I said before, it's for you to decide. The trust will pay if you think it necessary."

"Talking of the trust paying, who does the trust bank with?"

"The same as it always has, Hoares in London. Not convenient in some ways, but everything is electronic nowadays, it's not as if I have to go into the branch for anything."

"And that's because the third baronet, Sir George Stoppes, set it up that way? Because they were the family bankers?"

"Probably. Any particular reason to ask?"

"Curiosity. Lady Stoppes is checking to see if the family has a safety deposit box with them. I still haven't found any of the wills, apart from Sir Christopher's."

"But there's a registry isn't there, even if they were lost, you could get copies?"

"Yes, I can get them online too, but it can take a couple of weeks and I keep putting it off thinking I'll find the originals."

There was little of real progress or discovery to report, but Lydia let him know how many letters she'd looked through, how many account books Gloria had transcribed, how much information she'd gathered, how many old toys she'd played with, how many magazines she hadn't read, and how she was no nearer to finding a sixth baronet.

"What I keep forgetting is that not finding is as important as finding, that every dead end is one step closer to the trust being completely satisfied. But I'm loving it really. It would be so easy to disappear down rabbit holes. When it's all finished I may go back to some of them."

"How about your little portrait? Have you got anywhere with that?"

"Er, no, I've done nothing. Maybe this week."

"It doesn't matter, I'm just curious about my Sophia Cummins painting, that's all."

Wasn't she meant to be getting that portrait re-framed for him? Something else she'd done nothing about. For a moment she was tempted to lie and tell him it would be ready soon, let him continue to think she was reliable and conscientious, despite what she knew to be otherwise. What on earth was she doing accepting fat fees to bumble around in the Stoppes family saga with no qualifications or even a serious plan?

She hurried her goodbye then poured herself another glass of wine. Sitting there in Stephen's chair behind his desk, in his study, in his house – in his world – she felt the ground shift from under her feet. The momentary high of *loving it* was left far behind as a curious oddity, a diminishing point of light in her plunge towards the black sea of unworthiness. It would be best to accept it, to let gravity and the currents of uncertainty take her where they would. She would finish her drink, and perhaps another, then get her coat and drive away. From the front door her ghost would see the car turn out of the drive, the lights disappearing into the evening gloom, gone for ever, gone back to Oxford, to the little house in Osney where she could close and bolt the door behind her.

If Gloria and Eddie weren't living there.

Her refuge out of reach, her escape blocked, Lydia steadied herself. Closing her eyes, she concentrated on the last good image she had, the trunk full of magazines and their potential for hours of pleasurable reading, a single-minded rabbit hole down which she could dive at her leisure. She embraced the thought of the Cummins portrait and her Mallingford one too, allowed the wave of guilt to run over her and waited for it to recede.

Little by little she recovered from the abrupt descent, all the worse for being so sudden, so unexpected. In recent times she'd been able to see these episodes approach, to recognize the symptoms, but this had ambushed her.

She was still taking stock when her phone buzzed again. Stephen on a video call. Just as she'd considered lying to Derek, Lydia thought for a moment of rejecting the call, blaming a poor connection. But while she might not deserve Stephen, he did not deserve deception from her. She waited for the fifth buzz before accepting the call. Five buzzes to find a smile for him.

"Hello," she said with an attempt at cheeriness that came out strangled.

"Hello, are you OK?"

"Yes," she gulped, "wine went down the wrong way." White lies didn't count.

He looked as weary and undernourished as she'd last seen him, but he didn't look any worse, so she drew a little comfort from that. They spoke of the small things in life, how the visit from Gloria had gone, their visit to rainy Cambridge, his day off sitting by the ocean with a colleague, reading and recovering.

"Any progress you can tell me about?" Lydia asked.

"More of the same. At all levels. It's getting to the point where to find something different would be a real surprise. We're not expecting that."

"When you send samples away for testing, is it just DNA or other things too?"

"We do everything here, apart from DNA. We've got a lot of equipment, a first-class lab and some very good people."

"And the DNA?"

"Goes to Paris. They're regarded as a clean pair of hands, beyond reproach."

"Ah, right." Lydia's disappointment showed.

"Not what you hoped?"

"No, I was hoping for Cambridge. I have some samples of my own I might like to get analyzed."

"Cambridge was ruled out because of me. Paris has no conceivable conflict with the work here on the ground. I thought you were using the commercial family history sites, sending samples off to them."

"Yes, I am, but now I have teeth and hair from four deceased baronets and their siblings." She said, as if these samples were great trophies from her battles, rather than accidental finds in a disused drawer. "They were all in the most beautiful little gold and enamel boxes tucked away in the nursery."

"There is a lab at college, a very good one. Shall I talk to them? I can email tonight."

"Would you? That would be wonderful."

More small talk and then he was gone. Unsaid things threatened to break through the false normality of their separate lives: how Lydia wanted more than anything to get the next plane to Havana or Cancun, somewhere close to him just to spend a few hours together; how he doubted she was anywhere near as buoyant as she made herself out to be; how he could come home for a long weekend if it would help. But these things, and more, remained unspoken.

ooo

"It turns out that we do have a box at the bank," Georgina said, "but I can't access it because it's in Chris's name. I've asked Derek Ballard to send them whatever paperwork they need. You've made me very curious as to what it might contain. I thought we might go up to town together one day and find out."

"I'd like that very much," Lydia said. "I'm about to have a look at Elizabeth Calbain's will, it arrived this morning but I didn't have time to look before leaving. Want to look at it with me? Sir Christopher's Aunt Elizabeth told me what was in it, but I wanted to see for myself."

Together they hunched over the screen as Lydia opened the document. The usual preamble was followed by:

> *To Charles Melville Stoppes I leave my constant love and affection in the full knowledge that he will be well provided for throughout his life and will be in no need of my small property. To Elizabeth Claire Stoppes in addition to my love and affection I leave all my personal effects for her to enjoy for herself only. I also leave to Elizabeth Claire Stoppes all monies,*

investments and accounts as I have, for her use entirely.

Aside from the executor, Sir George Stoppes, and the witnesses, that was it. It was dated September 1952, those few weeks before her death, almost certainly around the time she had that conversation with Elizabeth about standing up for herself.

It seemed to Lydia that more than being a nanny, more than being a housekeeper, Elizabeth Calbain had also stood in as a grandmother to the young fourth baronet and his sister. And with Sir George as the executor, didn't that also say something about their relationship?

"That was sweet of her," Georgina said, "but is it significant in any way?"

"Probably not, but it confirms the picture we're building of that lady, confirms how close she was to the family."

"Who else do you have?"

Lydia clicked on the link for the will of George Melville Stoppes, Elizabeth Calbain's executor and the third baronet. Given the extent of his estate it was remarkably brief. Bequests of £100 to each of five individuals who Lydia guessed worked at the manor and all of whom lived in the village, another £100 to the parish church, and £50 to an animal charity, the PDSA, were the only bequests outside the family. £10,000 each to his children Charles and Elizabeth *who are otherwise well provided for through the trust previously established*, and after them the residue went to his wife Miriam. The will was dated five years before Sir George's death in 1972.

Nothing at all to suggest a secret love child.

"Another blank," Lydia reflected.

By the time Gloria arrived, late and flustered, falling through the door in a rush of apologies, Lydia was leafing through more correspondence files, each as unremarkable as Sir George's will.

"Gloria, thank goodness you're here, I need some distraction from these deadly letters. Coffee?"

"Oh, I'm so sorry I'm late," she pleaded, "Bloody traffic, bloody roadworks, nothing went my way today. And I got up late. And I really need a ciggy, but I can't do that straight away."

"Yes, you can. I'll go with you, we'll have coffee on the terrace. This isn't how it was, this is a different life now. Now we're valued for our skills, even if they don't seem much to us." Telling Gloria helped Lydia believe it, if only for the moment.

She took one of the files of tedious letters, while Gloria salved her conscience by taking her laptop. They looked at neither but Lydia was prompted to stand back from all that she'd examined, all that still remained, to see the project as a whole. It was too easy, it was always too easy, to get sucked into detail and lose sight of the bigger picture, the true sweep of a family's history. The Stoppes, much as she had anticipated, were turning out to be solid and reliable pillars of the community, as upper middle class as the baronetcy would suggest, stuck firmly between the aristocracy and the commoners. They might yet have secrets to be discovered, but the longer she looked, the more Lydia thought they would be small secrets, lesser secrets, as would become the lesser position of a baronet. Big secrets, important secrets were reserved for the rarefied levels of barons and earls.

In the library, Lydia weighed the choices of either continuing with correspondence through the start of the Second World War or filling the gap between 1890 and 1909. She chose the latter, partly to be working closer to the time frame Gloria was immersed in.

The details of the letters were unique, but the letter writers were largely the same, or at least held similar positions in the Stoppes circle: Lady Evelyn's daughters and female cousins wrote to Lady Evelyn, wife of Sir Clarence, the first baronet;

their son Edwin wrote to them both; local worthies wrote to Sir Clarence requesting his presence or his support or money, sometimes all three. Even the most personal communication was stilted and formal, despite the odd domestic crisis or a sad passing of a friend or relative. All in all it amounted to very little in the grand scheme of things.

Then, in June 1897, a letter that seemed completely out of place, almost as if it had been misfiled:

My dear Edwin

Thank you for confiding your news to me, it was and is a difficult matter to speak of. I am gratified that you were able to broach the subject with me and I hope nothing in my reaction led you to regret doing so. As I told you, it is nothing of which you should be proud but the laws of nature are ever strong. I must repeat my assertion that the child is not to blame for his condition even though there are some who will consider the situation differently.

I urge you to give him every support and advantage. And even though you and his mother may never come to agreement or a proper union, you should not abandon her, nor let her want for sustenance.

It is right that at this time you should be acquainted with something of your own history since it may be a lesson to you. My own origins are not widely known but may be shown in parallel to those of your child. My own dear mother, who you did not know, found herself situated similarly to your child's mother. Her and my paths in life would surely have been very different had it not been for the guiding influence of my father the Viscount Tremain. His position prevented him from making any public show, but he ensured that both my mother and I were without difficulty in life. I met him privately many times and he was always most affectionate during those encounters. It was he who suggested my entry into government service which in due course led to the unique honour which our family now enjoys and will benefit all who follow us. I have often felt that his influence aided my advancement although he claimed otherwise. This is not to say that you should follow any of his examples, but I urge you to have them foremost in your mind in matters concerning your son and the life he has before him.

There are many things yet to be considered, many things to be taken account of. We are our own masters and yet are never free to do purely as we wish so long as we maintain our Christian values.

I remain your affectionate father
Clarence

Lydia sat back, a little shocked by the contents. There was no mention of William by name, but surely it was a letter all about that baby boy, a letter which promoted her suspicions to fact. And also a letter which flew in the face of the stereotypical idea of Victorian hypocrisy, a letter from a caring father open about his own background. As the first baronet, Lydia had seen no need to investigate his origins, they could provide no insight to future generations. And yet Sir Clarence's own birth and upbringing had clearly affected his son's actions and possibly his illegitimate grandson's life and even his death.

Lydia made a note to look further into Sir Clarence's life, which until that moment, and with no evidence whatsoever, she'd assumed consisted of a genteel middle-class family who'd made good through diligence and loyalty in government service.

Between Sir Clarence and his son Edwin, Lydia weighed who was the more likely to have placed the letter in the family archive. Perhaps neither, perhaps it was done by a secretary or some later sorting and filing of uncategorized documents. However it came to be in her hand after more than a century, she was grateful. It was a letter shedding light on the people, their attitudes and their times, the very details so often missing from a family's history.

She read on through the file, hoping for another mention of the child or a new revelation, but found nothing. Then in 1898 with the death of Sir Clarence and the twenty or so letters of condolences, the possibility of any further intimacy between father and son was extinguished.

"Here's something," Gloria said.

"What've you got?"

"Sounds a little odd, but I think it reads *Snaresby College Fees – WT*. A school maybe?"

"Certainly a school. The Stoppes went to Snaresby, father and son since the 1870s. The late Sir Christoper, whose passing is the reason we're here, was the latest, back in the 1970s. Maybe his daughters too, I haven't asked. A hundred years of one family at one school makes you think. I bet it wasn't like that for you."

"You bet right."

"What date for WT?"

"January 1908."

"Anything else?"

"Several doctor's bills. All from Sir Bernard Rothwell with an address in London, again with *WT* as the reference. Any idea on that?"

"William Tremain. He was the second baronet's illegitimate son. It was an educated guess until this morning. Now in the space of a few minutes three confirmations. He might still be our best hope of a sixth baronet."

"You say that as if you'd like to find someone."

"I know. I can't get excited about *not* finding someone."

ooo

The results for 'Aylton artist Victorian' were discouraging. Running her eye down the links over several pages, there was still no mention of an artist or portrait painter named Aylton. There were hundreds of links Lydia might follow and which could conceivably identify her quarry but she was looking for a short cut rather than the long haul. The Aylton portraits, hers and Derek Ballard's, were an interesting side-show, only given a higher priority by her offer to find out more and to have his painting re-framed, but the puzzle intrigued her.

Previous searches for an 1841 or 1851 Mallingford had proved fruitless. The portrait was dated 1844, so was Prudence perhaps only a visitor for a few months? For Derek's Sophia Cummins she found a handful of entries, each far from Bedfordshire with the best geographical candidate a decade too young. Did the painter specialize in hard-to-find subjects?

If the subjects didn't want to be found on the census, what about the artist, now that she had a name? Aylton revealed only two for the 1841 census, the same two for 1851. In the earlier, her choice was between Cedric in Hastings, calling himself a painter, and Nathaniel in Catsfield, also Sussex, who was the predictable *Ag Lab*. In 1851 Cedric was still a painter, but by now was living in Bloomsbury, London. Nathaniel's wife, Louisa, was by then a widow.

1861 showed a change for Cedric, for he was now recorded as a photographer, but still in fashionable Bloomsbury. Apart from a new profession, Cedric had also acquired a wife, three small children and a housemaid. His new career clearly paid enough to support a comfortable lifestyle.

Now, with this additional information included in her searches, the world of Cedric Aylton, photographer, opened up. Dozens of entries, hundreds of images, references to museums, too much to take in. From the small evidence Lydia had, Cedric Aylton may not have been in the first, or even second, rank of portrait painters, but he'd quickly grasped the importance of the new art of photography and mastered its techniques. That Bloomsbury house had become his studio as well as his home, until by 1871 he'd moved his family to a new address a little distance away. It was an address Lydia found familiar. Marylebone Street. Surely she knew someone who lived there. Didn't Amanda Stoppes live in Marylebone Street, in Whitecross Mansions? She checked Cedric's address on the census once again: *No. 13 Marylebone St.* If there was a symmetry in life then it would have been Whitecross Mansions, but it was not. And really, same street, same district, same city all meant nothing, it was coincidence. We are amazed when we meet someone who was in Piccadilly Circus on the same day that we were, but in reality thousands shared that space on that day. That later we meet one of those thousands is meaningless, but we cannot help ourselves in searching for patterns. It's like seeing faces in clouds.

Which was all a diversion from the real purpose of her search. Lydia snapped herself away from philosophizing and musing on the chance of random events. Aside from prints in museum collections, personal details of Cedric Aylton were in short supply. Her simple census results gave her more than the Royal Academy or the Victoria and Albert collections combined. She might have to follow her more accustomed methods and find Cedric's descendants by family history sleuthing, just as she'd done previously for photo albums and medals, bibles and diaries.

Then, just as she'd decided that Google's fifth page of results was as far as she'd go, an entry caught her eye: *Arseneau Aylton & Berber images from the past*. It contained a huge collection of photographs from the three Victorian photographers. She scrolled through a hundred or so, nearly all of single buildings or cityscapes, but including a few of the busy Thames sailing barges. The history of the three men included how they'd all worked individually but come together for collaborative projects and special occasions. The site included a brief personal history of each: Arseneau originally from Normandy, Berber from Cornwall and, to Lydia's satisfaction, Cedric Aylton from the Sussex coast.

Cedric had indeed started out as a portrait painter, "*but had soon abandoned this for the new art of photography*". Hidden away on the contact pages was the name of the curator of the collection, Nigel Aylton. To Lydia's mind he must surely be a descendant of Cedric, a great-great-great-grandson perhaps. In one simple step she had moved from Mallingford and Cummins giving her nothing, to a living descendant of the artist.

Turning again to the catalogue she tried the Cedric Aylton subsection. More than a hundred images, the earliest of which was a painting, clearly in the same style as her Mallingford portrait, this one of a Mistress Crawford from 1848, who meant nothing to Lydia. Looking through the list for places of interest she was delighted to find *The Manor House at Wheadon St James, Beds, 1878*. It was unmistakable: a beautiful panoramic view of the house, taken from the gate, the same prospect that had greeted her at every visit she'd made. Had she seen that photo before? Wasn't it in that envelope of photos she'd lingered over with Georgina in the library that first day at work on not finding a Stoppes heir? Easy enough to check.

She wrote a long message to Nigel, asking about Cedric's earlier work and mentioning the portraits. As she was about to end, it occurred to her that there might be other, unpublished, photos of the house, perhaps even of its occupants. She added that enquiry and sat back satisfied, but wondering why it had taken her so long to find answers that were all there simply for the asking.

7

"I'm tempted to sleep in the summerhouse tonight, Stephen."

"It's that hot?"

"No, it's cooled off a bit now, it's lovely this evening, but the house is stifling, locked up all day in this heat. I forgot to close the shutters this morning."

Showery June had turned into blistering July. The soft greens of summer were already starting to fray and scorch at the edges as the heat rose inexorably day after day.

"Maybe we should get some cooling installed, it's only going to get worse," he suggested.

Maybe we should, Lydia thought. Stephen was always so careful to be inclusive when it came to anything which involved them both. He'd moved seamlessly from The Old Rectory being his house to it being their house. When Lydia spoke of such things she expressed no ownership at all, still nervous of treating anything as partly hers. It wasn't altogether rational, born in part from her inferiority complex, and part guilt at having brought nothing equivalent to their relationship.

"Did you get any reaction to the idea of using DNA to find living relatives of your victims?"

"Yes," he said, "they had a long think about it, then turned it down. I can't say I'm too surprised."

"Oh, what did they say?"

"They said that the commercial sites were 'not rigorous enough' in their science, and they feared false matches might lead to all manner of problems, including lawsuits."

"That's pretty damning. I don't suppose they wanted the

publicity that would go with it either. Which reminds me, is what you're doing in Cuba actually public knowledge? I assumed it must be."

"It's not a secret, but I think it's been pretty well buried in committee-speak. And besides, the media have a very short attention span and this will go on for a long time yet. There'll probably be no juicy headlines at the end of it all, either."

"Do you know it's nearly six weeks since you went back? Six weeks this weekend."

"Forty days. I know, I've been counting them. More than half way through this stint."

Forty. Something about the number made them pause and reflect. So often used over the centuries to mean simply 'a long time,' it carried that same weight for them now.

"If anything, I find it a little easier than I did a week ago," she said.

"I'm glad you said that, me too. And four weeks doesn't seem too much to do."

Again they paused in their exchange, comfortable to see without speaking, much as they would be if sitting in the same room.

"Have you heard from college yet, about getting DNA from the Stoppes teeth?"

"No, nothing yet, but I do have one result from the swabs I sent off, Felicity's, Lady Stoppes' daughter. On its own it doesn't mean much but it flagged up a potential cousin, or half cousin, but I can't get at the who or the where until I get the researcher's permission to look."

"And the work at the manor house, how's that going?"

"Well enough, but it's become a little repetitive lately. Gloria's ploughing through her accounts, and I'm into the 1940s with the personal correspondence. Lots of small things that fill out the picture of the family but not the slightest hint of a secret child. I think the third baronet was an extremely stingy man. I know times were difficult but he cut down on everything."

"How do you feel about the time? Another month or another six?"

"Somewhere between the two."

"That's what I'm thinking here. I know there'll be a lot of work still to do even when the site is all closed up and we're gone. There's talk of a memorial of some kind, but that'll be up to the Cubans to decide about that."

"I'm seeing Derek Ballard on Saturday, he's taking me to lunch for getting his picture re-framed."

"Did you hear back from the photographer's website?"

"No, I think it must be one of those sites that gets set up and then forgotten."

ooo

When Lydia arrived at the manor house on Friday, she was a little surprised to see Gloria's car parked outside the stables, the heat haze already rising from its roof. They had no timetable, no clocking on or off, they came and went as they pleased, but she couldn't remember her friend ever arriving before her. As she pushed through the door into the kitchen, Gloria was drinking coffee with Georgina Stoppes. Gloria raised her eyebrows, looked at her imaginary watch, and tutted loudly.

"And good morning to you, too," Lydia said, returning the sarcasm.

The greetings and coffee pouring were hardly complete before Georgina announced, "Lydia, I've got the all-clear to open our security box at the bank."

"Excellent, when do you want to go and look? It might be a real anticlimax."

"Yes, but it's bound to be interesting to me, even if it's not important to you. How about Monday?"

They agreed to go by train, Lydia would collect Georgina

from the manor, then drive to Bedford for the train to London.

Lydia paused a little before sharing her own news, uncertain herself as to the true importance of it, yet knowing she'd be asked by them both.

"I've had some results from the DNA samples, yours and Felicity's. And it's only from one service, so it might not be a hundred percent accurate."

Georgina's expression turned to stone, the colour draining from her face. "Is this your way of telling me something about Chris, something you agreed I'd be the first to know?"

"Oh no, no, certainly not." Lydia's words tumbled out, urgently seeking to repair the unintended suggestion. "There's room for interpretation, but I'm sure it has nothing to do with Sir Christopher. I'm so sorry, I didn't think of that, I should have said."

"No, it's me, I don't know why but I've been worrying about these results since you sent them off."

"Well I'll tell you straight away that the little plan I had about comparing your matches with Felicity's appears to have had a small success. Your results show a possible link to a very distant cousin, someone with whom you might share an ancestor maybe six or seven generations ago. And of course that distant cousin won't be a Stoppes connection. It's such a distant relation that it doesn't even show on Felicity's results. But Felicity has a much closer cousin, second or third most likely, someone who's not on your matches at all. Whoever they are must be a Stoppes connection, and more importantly, that connection doesn't go very far back, probably three or four generations."

"Which means what exactly?"

"It could mean there is another Stoppes line other than through the third and fourth baronets to Sir Christopher."

Georgina sat a little stunned, unsure of her ground, unsure if her world had shifted slightly on its axis. "Isn't that what you've been looking for?" she said tentatively after a few moments.

"Yes, and I have a good idea who it will be from, but it's a long way from finding a sixth baronet. And it could mean something else, it could mean that a female Stoppes had a baby who wasn't acknowledged. There aren't many candidates to choose from so it's not quite a needle in a haystack. I must still look at everything else, but I'm going to concentrate my efforts on this new information. I have no name for them, they are simply shown as initials, AM, but I've sent a message, although I've not heard back, so I have no more information than that."

"Any idea where this cousin is? Somewhere local?"

"No indication at all, could be here in Wheadon St James or in Timbuktu, they really could be anywhere."

"And the trust, did you tell Derek Ballard yet?"

"Tomorrow, he's taking me to lunch."

Once they were alone in the library, ready to resume their painstaking examination of the archives, Lydia had a pleasant surprise for Gloria.

"No more accounts!" she announced.

"Really?" said Gloria, delighted at the prospect of a change.

"No, not really, we'll go back to them, but I thought we'd give it a rest for a while. It's given us confirmation of all kinds of things, but nothing we hadn't already worked out for ourselves."

"No, things you'd worked out, not me. The house in St Neots, the Snaresby school fees, everything about Elizabeth Calbain, all your ideas."

"Team effort. So today I want to look at the letters and Christmas cards from the London flat."

Lydia explained how she wanted an index of all the letters, a short summary of each, together with the date, the sender and the sender's address and apparent relationship to the

Stoppes. It might reveal nothing of importance, but there was a chance that it would. After they'd read through a dozen letters together and Gloria had created suitable entries, Lydia added an extra detail: a note of any third party mentioned in the letters. That way she hoped could build up a comprehensive picture of the London social world of Sir George and Lady Miriam Stoppes, the seemingly tightfisted third baronet and his wife.

"And if you find anything sensational then just say so, I'm going to continue through the house correspondence, I'm at 1942."

It was all too easy to skim through the letters, anticipating their dull contents simply by identifying the sender. One or two, usually from female relatives, were more revealing of the family, and the events related to life in wartime Britain had a certain historical interest, but for the most part the letters were mundane. Lydia supposed that such tedium was something archaeologists encountered when excavating a potentially important site with nothing to go on but a hunch. It was like digging in a field to prove there was no Roman villa lurking beneath the topsoil. Lydia didn't even have the benefit of ground radar or crop marks to assist her.

The letter from Kenneth Tremain caught her eye before she reached it. The paper was different, the colour was different, even when it was still mostly hidden behind three other sheets, it stood out. She dutifully read those three in order before turning the last page in delight to see a letter on cheap paper with immature, perhaps uneducated, handwriting covering a single side. Lydia knew straight away that this was a new correspondent, which fact alone was enough to pique her interest. It was also a rarity in being addressed to the manor's housekeeper:

Dear Mrs Calbain

I hope you can help my mother with something

about my father who died a few years back. I got your name from the village post office.

My name is Kenneth Tremain. I am over here with the RCAF not far away but can't say where. Mom asked me to write you to know anyone at the House might know my father who was William. My mother is Mildred Tremain and she nursed him after an accident before they were married. He didn't know his life before but he was English. He thought he might know Wheadon St James and the Manor House and the name Stops. He had other ideas my mother wrote down but she could never know a true connection.

If you could help her then write me at the service post office or my mom at 20 Brookside Rd Dartmouth Nova Scotia. She would be most pleased to have any news from you.

Sincerely

Kenneth J Tremain RCAF R95067

Lydia sat back and let out a deep sigh. William didn't just survive his injuries in 1917, didn't only marry his nurse, but he had at least one son, Kenneth. A son who wound up back in Bedfordshire, most likely just down the road at RAF Little Wheadon. Or maybe he'd been even closer than that. Wasn't that flyer, the one who camped in the grounds and gave out patches to the children, wasn't he called Ken? She checked back in her notes from the interview with Aunt Elizabeth. Yes, Ken, a Canadian flyer. It wasn't proof of anything, none of it was, but the odds were that she was right. Lydia liked working with the odds.

"See this," she said to Gloria, who looked up from her letters and Christmas cards.

"I heard you sighing, something new?" she said, taking the letter.

"It's something that tells me there really is another line of

Stoppes, but probably not one that counts in the baronet stakes. We'll see."

ooo

"Coming here today reminds me that I should get out more," Derek Ballard said once they'd settled to their table at The Plough. "It's so easy to get stuck in a selfish routine, one which alternates between the office, the house and the club. It's not good for me. Our times together at the cottage or having lunch always remind me of that."

"But you've been here before?" Lydia said.

"A couple of times, just with clients. I tend to get invited when a junior partner feels the need for a senior presence at the table. Age has few advantages but I'm occasionally useful."

"This is still work though? Even if I'm not a client." Lydia sensed their lunch together might stray from the true purpose of their meeting unless she corrected the course from the outset.

"Yes, yes, certainly," he said quickly, "but it's also very pleasurable. And it's a long way from the usual office business, far more interesting."

"Aren't other people's jobs or their pastimes always more interesting than our own? Aren't we always a little jealous of a skill or talent we don't have ourselves? I know I am."

"You're right. And I suppose it's obvious, but I'd love to be doing what you do."

Lydia's instinct was to tell him she did nothing, and knew even less, that she simply followed her nose and blundered about in other people's families, but she thought better of it. She had grudgingly come to accept that she did have a value, even if it were not so high as that which Derek had put upon her.

Once they'd ordered their lunch and the wine had arrived,

Lydia took a parcel from her bag. "Your Cummins portrait," she said, passing it across to him.

The picture-framer had done a beautiful job, making a matte and frame that perfectly complimented the little watercolour.

"Oh that is so good," Derek said, holding the picture at arm's length to better appreciate it. "Did you get it done in Cambridge?"

"No, a little place near Halton. Old-fashioned craftsmen. I had mine done the same. I think the frames may be better than the artwork, but they do have meaning more than their merit."

She went on to tell Derek about the artist, Cedric Aylton, how she'd found the website and the connection to the Stoppes and St James Manor and how she'd received no reply to her enquiry.

"I did something else, too," Lydia said. She slipped an envelope across the table to Derek.

He opened it carefully and examined the sheet within.

"Oh, thank you!" he exclaimed. "That is so good. My own family tree, that's wonderful. Did it take you very long? It's so kind of you."

"It didn't take long and it's not diligently researched, one day I'll do a better job for you. The Ballards seem to have been prompt and dutiful in recording their births, marriages and deaths, both in church and on the registers. And I only followed the Ballard line, apart, of course, from a few Cummins. And you'll see that I'm pretty sure Sophia was your great-great-great-grandmother, I think your grandfather had it wrong, she was not his mother's mother but his mother's grandmother. I can look a bit harder when the Stoppes saga has been unravelled. As I've said before, a family tree is never anything but a work in progress."

"But thank you anyway, that's excellent. What is the latest in the Stoppes saga?"

"DNA and a 1943 letter from a Canadian airman. Do you remember it seemed there was another son of the second baronet, a child born before Sir Edwin married, a child he apparently supported. I don't know if he was publicly acknowledged as a son, but he was certainly not hidden away. Well, he and the third baronet went to Canada in 1917, where the older boy, the illegitimate son, was supposedly killed. It now seems possible that he wasn't, that he went on to have a family, that the Canadian airman might have been his son. I don't think it changes anything, unless it turns out that he wasn't illegitimate.

"The extra twist is that from what I can find and the hints from another earlier letter, the first baronet himself was illegitimate and his father, apparently Viscount Tremain, also looked out for him without publicly embracing him as his son."

"So at the moment there's no sixth baronet waiting in the wings?"

"Not yet."

"Not yet." Derek Ballard pressed his palms together in his customary prayerful pose, his index fingers just touching his lips and considered Lydia's news for a few moments before asking, "And the DNA?"

"It seems likely that there is another Stoppes line, which may be the Canadian airman's line or may be another line. From the samples I sent off, it's possible Sir Christopher's daughters have an as yet unknown cousin, second or third I think, somewhere in the world. It might not stand up to examination but it needs to be followed up."

"So nothing to point at Sir Christopher misbehaving himself?"

"Nothing at all, although I must always add, 'so far'."

"I'm glad of that, I liked the man, what little I knew of him, and Lady Stoppes seems pretty straight."

"Yes, I like her. We're going to London together on

Monday, hopefully to open her bank safety deposit box and discover any secrets it might hold. Did you check if the trust has one?"

"Oh, no. I'm so sorry, it completely slipped my mind."

Their lunches arrived to cut short his apologies. By the time they had toasted their health and taken a few mouthfuls, it was forgotten.

"I can see a difficulty ahead," Lydia said cautiously.

"Which is?"

"If there is a Canadian connection then we will be entirely reliant on what any possible cousins might tell us. There is no online access to most of the records I'd normally look to, especially the births. Not for the last hundred years. They're locked up behind their privacy laws."

"You wouldn't be telling me this if you hadn't already considered a solution."

"There are archives, newspapers, church records, burial grounds, registers, all the things you might expect, many available for personal inspection. It would be like going back to how it used to be here before everything went digital. Traipsing round county record offices and overgrown churchyards. I've done it before but didn't think I'd have to do it again."

"You'd hire a researcher in Canada?" he said, slightly surprised that Lydia would delegate work so critical to the project. Then he saw her expression. "Ah, no. You'd go to Canada yourself."

"Only if justified. And only if I could arrange it around ... other commitments."

"Stephen's still away? Yes, yes of course. Other commitments," he nodded, momentarily drifting away at the thought.

"And it might not be Canada, it might be Hong Kong or Australia or even Wheadon St James."

They finished their Cornish plaice fillets without further

discussion of the Stoppes, each content to enjoy the food and wine. Lydia also remembered to count her blessings: how better to enjoy her passion for family history than to be paid handsomely to do so and be wined and dined by her employer. But she wondered if that was perhaps too formal a term, he must by now be a friend as much as an employer.

Their dessert passed equally quietly and it was not until their coffee had been served that Derek Ballard returned to the Stoppes baronetcy. "What of the teeth and hair? You warned me a while ago of some additional costs. Have you started that process?"

"No, not quite. Actually not at all, I'm waiting for a reply. And you'll still have to give the final OK on the costs. I don't think I can push it at the moment."

ooo

The taxi brought them to 37 Fleet Street with ten minutes to spare before their appointment with the Stoppes' safety deposit box. Another baking day was in prospect and as they stepped from the cab, the acrid smell of the city assailed their senses, despite the regular wash and brushup given to the streets.

The cool quiet banking hall, no doubt as secure as any high-street bank, retained an old-world charm and the hushed tones of a library. After a brief delay they were ushered down a polished corridor to a private room, tastefully but sparsely furnished with two chairs at a large table and windows that gave out onto an enclosed private garden, so luxuriant that it cast a green hue on the pale walls of the room. From the longest wall the figure of one of the founder's family gazed benevolently down on them from a large canvas. A second door to the right of the painting led, presumably, to the vault and the boxes.

As they sat anticipating the pleasure, or anticlimax, of discovery, Georgina Stoppes suddenly clutched at Lydia's arm. “I don’t have a key,” she whispered anxiously. “Surely I’ll need a key to match the bank’s?”

Lydia supposed that she would, hadn’t everyone watched such scenes unfold in countless films? The process always required two keys.

“You can ask about that before we go down to the vault,” she said calmly, although the idea that they might have made the journey for nothing made her smile. From the painting above her she fancied that Henry Hoare might have been doing the same.

The second door opened and a white-haired man looked into the room and enquired, “Lady Stoppes?” Behind him came another man pulling a trolley upon which was placed a small trunk. It was domed, in the style of an old steamer trunk, although this was smaller, perhaps a couple of feet wide and tall, a little less from back to front. The body was black, trimmed with brown leather and leather straps. At the front it was secured with a brass lock in the style of an antique briefcase. Lydia thought it was a wonderful object on its own, never mind what it might contain.

The trolley-puller brought it close to them, then lifted it onto the baize-covered table.

“Is this it?” Georgina Stoppes said. “I mean, are they all like this? All the boxes?”

“No, madam, they are not. I think yours is unique, and, if I may say so, quite marvellous,” said the first man.

“I thought it would be a square metal thing in a wall of metal things tucked away in a vault. This is … different.”

“And this is your box, by that I mean it is physically yours. We store clients’ boxes securely, safely, but they are our clients’ own possessions.” He made to leave before pointing to the phone on the wall and adding, “If you need anything or when you have finished your business please lift the receiver and wait for an answer.”

The little trunk had three labels on it. One, a parcel tag tied on with brown string simply said *C. Hoare & Co for Stoppes 1375*. The second looked like a modern luggage label, attached by a plastic strap but where there might have been a name and address there was only a QR code. The third, stuck to the body of the trunk, read *London, Midland and Scottish Railway Delivered Luggage* and was franked 29th June 1933 over a one shilling railway stamp.

Georgina said, "Moment of truth," and tried the lock.

It slid easily to one side but the latch hesitated briefly before it flipped up. Gingerly she lifted the lid to reveal bundles of documents, all on parchment or vellum and tied with ribbon, apparently filling the trunk. Who knew how long they had lain folded in that place, but they were stiff and awkward to open. Besides which, both Georgina and Lydia were tentative in their purpose, unfamiliar with handling such things and wary of damaging them.

"I think they may be property deeds or conveyances. Perhaps no longer legally needed but certainly of interest," Lydia said after a few minutes studying the folds which could be most easily accessed.

As the documents were removed it became clear that they'd been resting on an internal tray which separated the space into two compartments. Georgina lifted the tray carefully from the trunk, revealing a pale blue box with the remains of a red wax seal on the lid. A faded script announced the contents: *The Patent of Baronet of Sir Clarence Charles Tremain Stoppes*. Apart from the box there were two black jewel cases of a size that might contain necklaces, two smaller cases and three envelopes.

The two women looked at each other, wide-eyed with expectation. It struck Lydia that while she might have been excited to find valuable treasure if it were her box, there would be no such anticipation from Georgina, who already had millions to her name. For them both it was purely the excitement of discovery.

"Box first?" Georgina said.

She lifted it out and placed it gingerly on the table. As she removed the lid a few crumbs of wax from the seal spilled on the floor. Inside was more vellum. It resisted their unfolding just as the conveyances had done but between them they smoothed the large sheet flat enough to read, if not to understand, the hand-written Gothic text. The headline, however, was unmistakable, taking up as it did the top six inches of the document: *Victoria by the Grace of God*. Here and there a few words were written larger and darker for emphasis or separation, *Whereas, And Moreover, And Have, Lastly* and *In Witness Whereof* all leapt from the page in their clarity while the words around them remained obscured by their ornate form. The sheet also had a huge seal attached. It would take some work to decipher but here at last was the Grant of Baronetcy that was at the root of Lydia's searches.

"I always feel I'm touching history itself when I'm close to old documents, whatever they might be, but especially parish registers or legal documents of any kind," Lydia whispered.

"This is certainly history," Georgina agreed. "Will you be able to read it? Does it really matter what it says, I mean what the details are?"

"No, I'm sure they're all the same, but it'll be interesting to find out," Lydia said.

"What now? Let's save the little boxes till last, so it's the envelopes next. They look like wills to me."

And so they were. Brown pocket envelopes, each inscribed with the testator's name: Sir Clarence C T Stoppes, Sir Edwin Tremain Stoppes and Sir George Melville Stoppes. One for each of the first three Baronets of St James. The handwriting on each was different and the earliest one, that of Sir Clarence, had once been sealed with wax.

"More history to touch," Georgina said.

"And history that could be informative, history that might have a bearing on our research. I've seen Sir George's before but the other two might reveal something useful. But it'll wait, I'm dying to look in the cases."

Georgina took both small cases from the bottom of the trunk. Each contained a gold coin, sullenly beautiful, as immaculate as the day they'd been minted.

"They're wonderful!" Georgina exclaimed. "I'm scared to touch them they're so perfect. Do you know anything about coins?"

"Not a thing. But they're old and gold so they'll be worth something. I wonder why they're here? I never asked, but do you have a safe at the manor house?"

"No. Unless it's hidden away behind a panel, but I've never seen it if we have."

"Which leaves ..."

"The jewellery."

But when they opened the cases they were empty. Whatever treasures they had once held were gone.

"That's peculiar don't you think?" Georgina said. "I mean, it suggests that someone came and took the contents but left the cases. Why would you do that?"

"In a hurry to raise some funds, but leave the cases so the casual observer would think they still held the jewels?"

"Hmm, not many casual observers likely to peer into this box."

"True. But it does make me wonder about taking things away. Do you want to leave everything here?" Lydia asked.

"Could we photograph everything then put it back and decide later? Or is there anything you really want to take?"

"Let's try some photographs, I think the wills could be the most important."

They photographed everything, checking each shot to be sure that the result would provide something readable. The vellum conveyances and Grant of Baronetcy proved most difficult, but Lydia thought she had enough to be able to stitch shots together into a readable mosaic.

"If we need to come back, we'll do so," Georgina announced firmly when they were done and had repacked the little trunk. Before it was placed on the trolley for its journey back to the vault, she was required to sign a client's inspection form, confirming that the contents were in order, which gave Lydia an idea.

"Do you keep a record of who accessed the Stoppes box and when?" she asked, "Could we see it?"

The white-haired man said that they did. A few minutes later he returned with an old ledger, bookmarked to a page headed *Stoppes 1375*. It contained a list of dates and signatures, the earliest from 1874, the latest from 1989.

"Nobody's opened our box in thirty-odd years?"

The official looked at the page and confirmed Lydia's observation. "Except," he added, "yourselves today. The register was computerised ten years ago, the ledgers are only kept for reference. I checked for digital entries and there are none."

Lydia took a photograph of the page before the ledger was closed and returned to its archive.

"What do you think Lydia? A worthwhile visit?" Georgina said as they stepped back into the noise and heat of Fleet Street.

"Yes, worthwhile. We don't have to wonder what might be there and we have those wills I'm keen to read, and when I've nothing better to do I'll decipher the grant, the Letters Patent of the Baronetcy of St James."

ooo

The journey from Grantchester to Wheadon St James was easy enough, but Lydia was growing weary of it, especially the return, which so often involved lines of queuing traffic, regardless of how she timed her travel. After the day in London – they'd dawdled over lunch with Amanda before Georgina needed 'just a few minutes' in Selfridges – Lydia had been looking forward to a day at The Old Rectory, a day in which she could enjoy her summerhouse, enjoy working alone with her thoughts and ideas. And besides, she needed to catch up on her journal of activity, exactly what had been searched and investigated and with what results. It was all too easy to fall behind with that and concentrate only on the research itself. As it was, her notes had become more brief and scribbled as the project had progressed.

Which was a fine intention, but what immediately took her attention was the first DNA analysis for Elizabeth Wykham, the fourth baronet's sister. Like her great niece Felicity, she too was shown as being related to an unspecified person identified only as AM. With so many overlaps in the ranges of matching DNA, the estimated relationships could never be relied on. To suggest simply that a person might have a second or third cousin was as near as could be reasonably forecast without mapping the actual relationship, which could only be done with certainty once the unspecified person was properly identified and the shared family history was examined.

For Elizabeth's match to include the same anonymous AM lent weight to both results. To Lydia's mind, them both being flagged up as a second or third cousin to AM suggested that AM might be of the same generation as Felicity's father, the fifth baronet. That way they could each have a similar relationship, perhaps a second cousin once removed, to the mystery person.

Doubtful that a second message would fare any better than her first, Lydia sent AM another plea for information. And she recorded her actions carefully in her log, before turning back through all her notes to begin the process of recording all those actions too.

To her shame, interpreting those notes proved far more difficult than it should have, but, spurred by the fact she was being paid to perform these tasks, she'd caught up enough to satisfy herself, or any other scrutiny, by mid-morning. Yet something told her it was later than mid-morning, surely nearer lunch time, nearer how-about-a-glass-of-wine time. Without really noticing it, she'd slipped into wine every day at the manor house, it was always available and Georgina was a generous host. Generous enough that every few days Lydia felt the need to take a bottle of her own to share. Which usually resulted in them simply drinking more.

There might come a day when she should consider reducing her intake, but, with a bottle of Bousval calling her name from the little fridge, she decided that today was not that day. To fool herself into thinking she'd made an effort, she waited until she'd printed copies of the wills from the safety deposit box before opening the bottle.

Sir Clarence Charles Tremain Stoppes, First Baronet of St James, had made his will in 1896, a little over two years before his death. It was a fairly short and straightforward document, witnessed by two names not known to Lydia, one of whom was the executor described as *my good friend and advisor Matthew Russett.* Lydia noted the name in her index of the Stoppes' circle. The substantial bequests to Clarence's wife Evelyn and their daughters Mary and Sarah, *for their own use entirely,* were naturally the largest, then there were smaller amounts for the local church and tokens of gratitude for his *loyal servants* at the manor house. After that the entire residue of the estate was left to his only son Edwin *on condition that he maintain and support his mother my beloved wife Lady Evelyn Stoppes at the Manor House at Wheadon St James for so long as she lives or so desires.*

One other item attracted a special condition: *it is well known that among my personal possessions will be found two gold coins bearing my birth date which were given to me by my father on condition that their value might only be realised when all other resources and possibilities had been exhausted and these I leave to my son Edwin with the same condition attached even though my father's original letter has been lost.*

Not only was that a charming curiosity, but it explained the two gold sovereigns that she and Georgina Stoppes had discovered at the bank. Lydia checked the photos she'd taken in the viewing room: George III sovereigns dated 1819. Then she checked the family tree: Clarence Stoppes born 1819, baptised November 19th at St John's, Bedford. It also suggested a caring father, as was reflected all those years later by the letter Clarence had written to his own son Edwin when he appeared to have fathered a son outside of marriage.

Lydia scrolled through her file of significant documents to turn up her copy of the letter. It was just as she remembered: Sir Clarence had written to Edwin that his father had *ensured that both my mother and I were without difficulty in life.*

Apart from the record of baptism Lydia had found no other confirmation of Clarence's parentage. Given what she now knew, that was perhaps not surprising, indeed what was most surprising was that she should have any supporting evidence at all. Viscount Tremain took little finding. Successive Viscount Tremains had been the sons of successive Marquesses of Rugby, a title dating back several centuries. A great deal of information was available about the family and its property, wealth and power, but with very little about individuals from the 19th century.

And really, what did it matter? Lydia's quest started with Sir Clarence, not his father, yet the urge to know more, to understand the people and how they lived was part of how she worked, part of her passion, as Stephen might say.

It was only five days since they'd spoken, but thinking of him as she sat in the summerhouse, enjoying his garden, enjoying everything about her life at The Old Rectory, made the urge to call him irresistible. The time in Cuba would be what? Quickly she checked: breakfast time. Yes, why not, what was the worst that could happen?

But her call remained unanswered. His voicemail clicked in and she manage to stutter, "Only me, nothing important, just thinking of you. Everything's fine here."

Perhaps this was the worst that could happen, for now she could only wonder at the reason, speculate on ifs and maybes, worry that something malign had occurred. How had he looked on Thursday? Worse than before? Or better? She couldn't remember the fine differences of his appearance from one call to another, most of which was probably due to the light and where he spoke from. If she tried hard she could rationalize all her concerns away. There were a hundred good reasons that he might not have answered and very few bad ones. But the bad ones obstinately stuck in her head.

To push these anxieties away and replace them with more agreeable thoughts, Lydia took her glass and her sunhat on a tour of the garden. All was in its place, all neatly tended, all freshly watered by the rarely-glimpsed gardener, Roger. His quiet care meant a burgeoning vegetable crop, the promise of apples and pears in the autumn and a walk sweetly scented by roses. At the furthest extreme, by the paddock fencing, Lydia paused while a glossy chestnut horse approached. Its interest was brief and after a few moments it turned away, tail swishing, back to the shade of the trees on the far side. Absentmindedly, Lydia wondered when the Stoppes had ceased keeping horses at the manor house.

The second baronet's will was as businesslike as the first's. Dated three years before his death in 1928, it contained the usual bequests to local charities and staff at the manor house, followed by the essence of the thing: *to my dear companion Elizabeth Calbain the sum of one thousand pounds for her use entirely* and for his son George *the remainder of my entire estate providing that he maintains and supports the aforesaid Elizabeth Calbain at the Manor House at Wheadon St James for so long as she lives or so desires.* There followed the same condition regarding the two sovereigns as his father had laid down, that they were only to be used as a last resort.

What could be clearer than Sir Edwin putting Elizabeth Calbain on exactly the same footing as his father had placed his wife Evelyn? Elizabeth was surely the mother of his son William and certainly his close friend during their time together at the manor after Edwin's wife Henrietta died in 1922.

Lydia had to remind herself that William had been reported dead in 1917 and was clearly still regarded as dead in 1925, for if not, then surely he would have been included in his father's will. Quite why she felt the need to pursue this line of her enquiry, she wasn't sure. As an illegitimate son William would never have inherited the title, and yet it was certainly possible for a descendant to appear at some future point and make an awkward claim. Wasn't anticipating such an event also part of her remit?

The special conditions of inheriting the two sovereigns also fascinated her. She could remember no such condition in the third baronet's will, but she checked again. There was none. She had the impression of Sir George as a man with no room for sentiment. In any event, it left the family free to keep them or sell them. To satisfy her curiosity she checked their possible value. Estimates of anything up to half a million took her breath away. Not that such a sum would make much difference to the Stoppes way of life.

Derek Ballard had told her more than once that time did not matter, she should take as long as was needed, but six weeks after starting she could still rule nothing in nor rule anything out. Even the unblemished character of the fifth baronet, Sir Christopher, came with no guarantee. More than anything Lydia wanted to kick the whole Stoppes tree and see what fell out of its branches. Despite her best endeavours her work so far felt more like a prod than a hefty kick.

8

"No Georgina?"

"Back mid-morning. She left a note. Coffee?" Lydia said.

"Yeah, great. What've we got today, more cards and letters or back to the dreaded account books?" Not that Gloria really cared which. The cards and letters had come as a welcome change, but were uninteresting enough that the accounts might now be a relief.

"Where are you up to? Or more importantly, is there anything remotely interesting from all that paperwork?"

"To be honest, I don't think so. You should have a look yourself but really there's very little beyond *Merry Christmas, hope to see you in the New Year*, or *at Wimbledon* or *missed you in Cannes again this year, it was wonderful by the way, you missed a super season.*"

"And the people, how big was the circle?"

"Getting smaller as the years went by. I think the London circle was entirely friends, there's hardly anything from relatives, so far as I'm aware."

"How far have you got?"

"Maybe three-quarters done?"

"Cards *and* letters?"

"Yeah."

Lydia stirred her coffee and wondered about the best use of Gloria's talents. She was worth a great deal more than a glorified card-indexer, but at least she'd produce trustworthy results. If the truth be told, Lydia had almost given up hope of there being anything of significance in the cards or the letters. If there were, she'd be proud of her diligence for checking, but like almost every other line of enquiry, it was beginning to look like a fool's errand.

"Better finish the job rather than leave it. Do you remember if there are any letters from here, from the manor house, to Sir George or Lady Miriam while they were at the Marylebone flat? I think there was one I saw when I was thumbing through them. Something about a new cook."

"Hmm, you'll have to look, I'm not sure off-hand. No, wait, yes there are. Two, perhaps three?"

"I'm going to get started in the library, I'll have a look at those letters now. See you in a minute, I'm sure you'll want to start with a ciggy," Lydia said.

"Yeah, maybe. Um, OK if I don't come over tomorrow? I've got something on, then Friday I'm temping at County Hall. I'll probably get the cards and letters done today, in fact, I'll stay till I do," Gloria said.

"Yes, of course, that's what we agreed, come when you can."

It wasn't like Gloria to be evasive, to not say what it was she had on, but Lydia didn't press her. They were good friends, better than they might ever have been, but there was plenty they didn't share. More accurately, there was plenty Lydia didn't share with Gloria unless asked directly, rather less that Gloria didn't share with Lydia.

In the library Lydia flipped open her laptop and found the spreadsheet Gloria had been working on. Three tabs: xmas, pcards, letters. She clicked on letters, sorted them by origin, then by sender. Three entries from St James Manor, all sent by Elizabeth Calbain. 1934, 1936 and 1937 – hardly a regular correspondent. From the spreadsheet entries she found the letters easily enough in the shoe box.

The first was as she remembered it, a business-like communication concerning a new cook, yet with that personal intimacy of *your dear Charles* included in it. But no *love* or *affection* in the closing, just her name, *Elizabeth*

Calbain. The second was similar, another domestic matter needing Lady Miriam's approval, or rather, informing her of a change already made to the housekeeping staff. Elizabeth clearly had full authority to act in such matters. And again she wrote an effusive and fond reference to the boy Charles and the new baby Elizabeth, the same Elizabeth who'd become Sir Christopher's aunt and whose saliva sample Lydia had recently had DNA tested.

The envelope of the third letter was addressed to Sir George Stoppes, although curiously the letter itself had no salutation, no *Dear Sir George*, no opening of any kind. It concerned another domestic matter, but this time relating to the garden and the use of the old stables. In the main text Elizabeth used the phrase *in your dear father's time*, and later *I feel sure your dear father would have approved of this.* Again in closing she made an affectionate reference to the two children before signing herself simply *Elizabeth C.*

Elizabeth Calbain may have been in charge of the manor but her intimacy with the family was confirmed time and again. It made Lydia wonder if her being William's mother was known and accepted within the family, even if it wasn't publicly recognized. Her place at the manor house was written into Sir Edwin's will, she was supported and apparently valued, and certainly trusted – enough to become the children's nanny. And one of those children might well have been named after her.

Lydia was staring at the ceiling contemplating Elizabeth's place in the family, not just in the family but her place right there in the library, possibly in the same chair as Lydia was using, when her email pinged. A sender she didn't recognize, but the telltale *.cam.ac.uk* at the end of the address told her it was from Cambridge.

It was the long-awaited response to Stephen's request for assistance with analyzing the Stoppes baby teeth and hair. The message, from the facility manager, Dr Charmaine

Thibaud, was little more than a note asking for a discussion about details, giving a suggested time that afternoon for a video call. In Lydia's imagination the terse nature of the email suggested Dr Thibaud was not enthusiastic about the project.

Gloria joined her and Lydia noticed that for once her friend was not wrapped in a cloak of smoke and nicotine. A thought sprang to her mind but she bit her tongue before it found voice. The logical detective in her guessed the reason for tomorrow's absence: a hypnotherapy session to help Gloria stop smoking – it was something she'd tried once before without success. But if Gloria wasn't going to mention it, Lydia certainly wouldn't.

It was nearly two before Georgina Stoppes returned to the manor, subdued and far from her normal self.

"Are you OK?" Lydia asked tentatively, a little unsure whether or not they were sufficiently close for personal enquiry.

"Yes, I am, but thank you for asking. Someone in the village, she's had cancer, was doing well it seemed, but now it's back with a poor prognosis. I went to see her and ended up staying longer than I thought. It reminds me, as if I needed reminding, that we're all mortal, it's just a question of when, never of if."

"I know, and we were all immortal once. Just like all those that've gone before us. They're easy to see in a place like this, where you know who's lived here before. I was thinking about Elizabeth Calbain, thinking about her being in the library, sitting in the chair I was sitting in. She was young and immortal once, maybe before she had William, who knows when, but there would have been a time in her life. Now she and her world have all but disappeared."

Georgina paused to digest this idea before asking, "Too late for a glass of wine?"

"Or too early. I have a call to make soon, but don't mind me. Before I do, can I just ask again if you'll allow me to take the baby teeth and locks of hair. I know you said it would be OK, but I want to confirm that."

"Yes, certainly. After all, what are they anyway? Better they have a use, I don't want them and I can't imagine anybody else wanting them. But you'll leave the lockets and the photos?"

If Lydia had imagined anything of Dr Charmaine Thibaud it was not the smiling woman who greeted her on the video call. She also appeared to be far too young to be a manager of any facility, or any kind of doctor come to that.

"It sounds fascinating," she said when Lydia had explained the background, "and yes, I think we can help. But we'll have to move quickly, we have our first academic project coming up in about four weeks."

"Your first?"

"First with the new set-up, the new equipment. We've all been training on it for the last few weeks. No academic pressure in the summer. We'll slot your project into the training. How quickly can you deliver your samples?"

"How about Friday morning? In labelled plastic bags, would that be all right?"

"Perfect. We'll discuss details then."

It was all over in less than ten minutes. Charmaine Thibaud was not at all terse, she was direct and business-like, wasting no time or words on inessentials, but still personable and engaging.

"Freezer bags," Lydia said to Georgina, "Do you have nine I can use? And can you please double check I label each of them correctly."

ooo

The bus from Trumpington deposited Lydia outside the Fitzwilliam, that astonishingly grand edifice full of such treasures as wealthier foundations can only dream about. It is one of the gems of Cambridge, of which there are many.

She'd only visited once but had always promised herself a return. Perhaps today might be that day but she'd wait and see how her meeting with Dr Thibaud went. Despite their agreeable conversation, despite Stephen commending the project on her behalf, Lydia was still wary of being seen as an amateur, her samples inadequate, the project laughable, the academics of Cambridge sniggering behind their hands as she closed the door behind her. It was, she realised, her first venture into the university without Stephen's presence to reassure her.

But there was still time to compose herself, time to collect her thoughts and regain her balance before she met Charmaine Thibaud. She crossed the road and turned into Fitzwilliam Street, all fresh paint and neatness despite the bicycles chained to railings outside many of the houses. To judge by the uniform white windows and blue front doors, it was all owned by one of the colleges. On a quiet summer's day, before the heat or the tourists had got up, Fitzwilliam Street struck her as a tranquil place to live, a street of untold histories and academic excellence. What was it? Victorian? Georgian? Either way, it appeared little changed in the nearly two centuries of its existence. Its occupants had been looking out on the life of Cambridge before the Stoppes and their baronetcy had even been thought of, yet here she was, carrying their baby teeth in her briefcase to an appointment with a very special dentist.

At Tennis Court Road she swung left towards the city centre until she reached the entrance to the Downing Site. She was a minute or two early, but Dr Thibaud was waiting at the entrance.

"Registration first, then it's not far. Easier for me to meet you than for you to find your way."

The formalities concluded, they followed a zigzag route to a side entrance into a grand building and from there down stairs and along corridors to a suite of rooms that struck

Lydia as something between a clinic and a laboratory. Two young men, hunched over machines, looked up from their work as the women entered, gave brief acknowledgement and returned to their duties. It was a place in which Lydia felt the need to speak in hushed tones.

"I really appreciate this, Dr Thibaud," she said softly. "I hope it's not going to be a complete waste of your time."

"It won't be. If we get good results or we get nothing, it'll still be practice. And we don't use titles here, it's Charmaine please. And no need to whisper. Now, let's see what you have."

Lydia retrieved the nine plastic bags from her case and spread them on the table.

"I don't know who might've touched them in the past, but since they were found recently nobody's touched them at all. We used tweezers and plastic gloves to put them in the bags. And I know who each one is supposed to be from, but they're just dates and initials on the bags. I'd really like to see what familial connections come up from the DNA."

"The hair will be difficult," Charmaine Thibaud said, placing a bag on a light box. "Very little of it and no roots. Not impossible, but unlikely to find anything usable, maybe some mitochondrial traces. We'll see."

"And the teeth? The youngest is around 1960 and the oldest 1866."

"In theory they would be good samples, but you can't tell just by looking. The problem is that they might only yield a small amount of DNA. And to work on a sample it's basically a matter of the more you have the better. That's where we start amplifying a sample."

"Amplifying? As in reproducing it in some way?"

"Exactly so. It's a process using some special biological agents, enzymes mainly. It's been around for a good few years."

"So your new equipment does what?"

"Nothing original, but it brings all the latest techniques together and gives us extremely precise control. It also takes away some of the try-it-and-see process that's needed to get the best results from amplification. It uses AI to more accurately predict the best temperatures and concentration of the agent. We've been practising on pig bones."

"Any idea on timing? And, I should have asked before, what about cost?"

"Cost? I was told it was not commercial, something we could train on, something Professor Kellaway had suggested. I assumed you knew him."

"Ah, yes, I do know him, I know him very well, he's my, um, partner. I'm never sure what word to use. Partner makes it sound like a legal firm but it's not. We, um, he's away at the moment, but ..." Lydia realized she was speaking without needing to and trailed off, embarrassed at her awkwardness, heat flooding her cheeks.

"Partners. Yes, I know what you mean. You want to say something without the baggage that wife or husband carry with them. He's with the UN at the moment isn't he?" She paused briefly as if an unspoken thought had interrupted her flow. "Anyway, cost. No cost as far as I know, but I'll check."

"And timing? There's no pressure at all."

"But sooner rather than later, I'm guessing. Three weeks maximum, simply because if we're not done by then we'll be starting up the new academic project. And after that it could be a year before we could look again. I'd be surprised if we didn't have something for you in three weeks, perhaps even two."

"That's wonderful, thank you."

"Are there two teeth for each sample?"

"Yes. Three for one of them."

"Then I'm going to split each sample in two. One to work on, one for emergencies or in case something odd shows up.

We'll have something to try again. Help me separate them will you, then you can be sure we've got it right."

She pulled latex gloves from a box and handed a pair to Lydia. From a cabinet she took small plastic boxes, each little bigger than a matchbox. Then she began entering information on a keyboard. Behind her, Lydia saw her name being typed together with a summary of the project. Next, Charmaine took the first bag and copied the information Lydia had written. Two bar-coded labels emerged from a little printer. One tooth and a few strands of hair were placed carefully in each box before they were snapped shut and the labels attached. Lydia examined them both and agreed they were correct.

Eight bags later and the job was done, all sentimentality having been completely removed in the journey from beautifully jewelled cases in an antique nursery dresser to cool forensic catalogue. That baseline DNA Lydia had considered when she'd first found the teeth would soon be a reality, she was sure of it. And what surprises might that lead to? The prospect was tantalizing, yet some small part of her regretted the role of science over sleuthing.

As Lydia handed back her badge and thanked Charmaine Thibaud again, she was left feeling that she knew nothing of the person she'd spent nearly an hour with. Business-like, thorough, confident was all she could think of, was all she'd been presented with. Ah, and comfortable in her own skin, yes, she was certainly that and Lydia was a little jealous of that assurance.

ooo

By the time Lydia returned to The Old Rectory the day was half done. The Fitzwilliam had lured her in, just as she thought it might, and then pleasantly delayed her. Like her walks by the Thames, and more recently the Cam, the museum and its art slowed her, gave her space and solitude enough to restore her perspective on life.

Now The Old Rectory welcomed her back. Little by little it became more her home each time she returned to it. Odd, she thought, that the act of returning rather than the days spent being there, should engender that feeling. But home was a very comfortable feeling, nowhere more so than in the summerhouse. She'd picked up some sushi in the city, and the bottle of Prosecco waiting in her fridge was its obvious companion.

Most likely Stephen would call, Fridays had become one of their regular times and it seemed that his end of week work was less pressured, less dealing with disinterred bodies, more completing paperwork and calling bureaucrats in Paris or New York. Until he did, Lydia decided she would enjoy her lunch and the small pleasures of the garden.

But the Stoppes could not be kept at bay for very long. Enjoying the garden led to thoughts of the garden at St James Manor, reflecting on her solitary drinking brought her to Lady Georgina and her endless supply of wine, Stephen's work took her to the university and that led right back to Charmaine Thibaud.

In theory the results from the baby teeth shouldn't tell her anything she didn't already know, the true value lay in matching those results to any possible claimant to the title, or finding a distant relative. The elusive AM was one such, almost certainly a Stoppes relative, yet knowing that, but without the details to confirm it, was immensely frustrating.

Her phone buzzed just as she finished eating.

"You caught me with wine in my hand again," she said, raising her glass.

"Cheers!" he said, lifting his breakfast orange juice.

"I was at the university today, one of your regular haunts, The Downing Site. The DNA testing finally got sorted out and I was there delivering samples this morning."

"Excellent! Who did you see?"

"Dr Charmaine Thibaud."

"I know her slightly. She has a good reputation. Very competent, apparently."

"Competent describes her precisely."

Then the rush of speaking about something shared, something easy to talk about was gone and they looked at each other silently, as long-distance partners are often wont to do.

"I called you my partner today," she said, "I hate the word but don't know a better one, then I got in a tangle trying to explain it. What do you call me?"

For a moment he hesitated, trying to recall what he might say. "I think I just say Lydia, anyone I mention you to would know who you were. But I don't like partner very much either."

As soon as she'd asked, she knew he wouldn't know. Why would he ever refer to her when speaking to someone who didn't know who she was? Men generally don't talk about their wives or girlfriends, or their partners, and certainly not when they're with strangers or casual acquaintances.

"You know it's only twenty-two days?" she said.

"I do," he said, lifting his diary to the camera. Each day was numbered, counting down to the next flight home. "Unless you'd like to come and visit."

"Oh, yes, very much, but three weeks isn't too long, let's save it for another time."

They chatted for another few minutes, he in his guarded way about progress with the exhumations and what they might do when he was home, she about all things Stoppes, the frustrations and the minor successes, until they were interrupted by an unseen assistant begging his urgent presence for something unspecified. Lydia didn't speculate on what new horror that my be.

When he'd gone with hurried goodbyes she was suddenly

empty, emptier than before he'd called. For a few moments she felt bereft, utterly abandoned, even as she recognized such extreme was completely unwarranted. A sign of how deeply she felt about him, or a sign of her inner instability? Something of both, she reasoned, as the day came slowly back into focus.

The Grant of Baronetcy, the Letters Patent from the safety deposit box, remained a little mystery. Not that it was likely to have any real bearing on her project, but curiosity demanded that the document be deciphered. After all, it was the very thing that the whole project depended on. If there were no baronetcy there'd be no investigation, there'd be no well-paid days simply doing what she enjoyed most.

The photos took more stitching together than she'd bargained on. Dimly, she recalled some software that might help her do that, but she was halfway through the job before she thought of it. And despite her best efforts, and despite checking each shot as she'd taken it, it was not going to be an easy task to transcribe the wording. It opened up easily enough with *Victoria by the Grace of God* in large bold letters, but it quickly became unreadable. After only a few words, *We of our ... Grace ... knowledge mere...* Lydia was stumped. Not only was the language antique, the obscure formal language of the court, but the script was an unhappy cross between old English and medieval German. Some words she could guess at from the context, but whole strings of words were beyond definition. Perhaps with a few hours spent on each line of the document she might get a reasonable result, but what she really needed was some expert help. Surely someone must have been down the same road previously? And surely the results would be online somewhere?

They had and they were.

After an hour or so of searching – and following some fascinating red-herrings – Lydia came to *A History Of The*

Baronetage by Francis W Pixley, first published in 1900. With one search of the document for 'Victoria' she had the template for the Letters Patent of the Baronetcy of St James. No need to work through every word, the whole thing, apart from the first baronet's name, was right there. With the transcript as a guide Lydia could easily follow the first few lines. Even so, it was a difficult document, entirely devoid of punctuation and with apparently random use of capital letters. Drawn up by lawyers, to be read by lawyers.

She printed a copy of the page for Georgina Stoppes, it could go in the box with the original vellum and save some future researcher the trouble of deciphering it. And she should tell Derek Ballard about it, too. She hadn't been in touch with him since their lunch at The Plough. Plenty had happened but she wasn't sure that any of it constituted progress. But there were a finite number of things to be done and she'd done more of them – which was, in itself, progress of a kind.

Her inbox pinged just as she was about to pour another glass. A name new to her, Nigel Aylton. Aylton! The photographer's website, at last.

He was full of apologies, delighted to have someone interested in his website, and extremely excited to think that he might be able to add two of his three-times great-grandfather's paintings to the catalogue. He had the great man's journals and was aware of the earlier work, the likenesses taken for a few shillings each before he abandoned painting for photography. All in all, Lydia had the impression of a puppy dashing from excitement to excitement and not knowing where to stop and take breath.

Could she send him copies of the portraits as soon as possible? As for more photos of the manor house at Wheadon St James, he would search through the collection and if he found anything of interest, contact her immediately. He explained that he didn't have prints of all the photographs and hundreds of the glass slides remained unindexed.

Lydia had copies of the two portraits on her phone. No sooner had she sent them than another effusive email thanked her and promised to search every part of the collection for anything, anything at all, that might be connected to her work.

What a lucky man to have inherited such an archive, lucky to have it and luckier still that successive generations had understood its value. Of the millions of those early photographs what percentage had survived, she wondered. And of the billions since then, how many would be around for research or amusement in a hundred or two hundred years?

ooo

The summer sun, slanting through the windows, woke her early. The room was familiar and yet somehow unexpected until she remembered she was in Jacqueline's room, the room she'd used when she'd first stayed at The Old Rectory. It was cooler than Stephen's bedroom, their bedroom as it had become, but she'd forgotten that Jacqueline's room caught the early light. On that July morning, it was a very early light.

For a while she lay still, letting herself catch up with all that had brought her there. As the curtains rippled gently in the lazy air she remembered how they'd billowed out on that first morning, how she'd been excited by the prospect of the day, curious about the paths it might take her down. Now here she was, mistress of this grand house, a woman of independent means, a woman who shared her life with a good man who, against all reason, willingly shared his with her.

Despite her blessings, she had a sudden desire to be back in her house in Osney, back by her Thames. On such a day, on this day, she would rise early and walk the empty towpath into her Oxford, and treat herself to breakfast at Brown's in the Covered Market. And when she was full of bacon and egg and sausage, she'd walk back again, more slowly, breathing in all the river could give her. She knew each step, could anticipate every scene, yet still the river and all its business drew her.

Why not walk to Cambridge and get an early breakfast in that fair city? She saw the path by the sleepy Cam, the early dog-walker, the lone fisherman hunched on the bank, a jogger pounding up unexpectedly from behind her. It was all about the path, nothing about the river. And breakfast? There'd be some somewhere, certainly, but where? Stephen would know where, but she didn't, and Stephen was in Cuba.

That final down note could have sunk her, but some change in light, some angle of the sun, called her from bed. She'd take coffee to the early morning cool of the garden, then make her own bacon and eggs and be at her desk in the summerhouse before the rest of Grantchester was even awake.

Which she did, letting herself enjoy the novelty of cooking a breakfast, the pleasure of being where she was, and remembering she enjoyed privileges far beyond the reach of most. These were good days in her life, better than many that had gone before. Not that her hard days had been so unbearable, no, the hard days had been unfulfilled, disappointing, a succession of failures of which she had been the greatest, but they had not been hard on the body, she had not wanted for creature comforts.

At length, she opened her laptop and stepped back into the Stoppes world, a world in which any kind of hardship appeared to be absent. Although, who knew the truth behind that comfortable facade, weren't Sir Christopher and Georgina a couple who'd lost a four-day old baby boy? It wasn't something Lydia had ever had to deal with, so who was she to think they'd not known hardship?

Her email had three more results from each of the Stoppes DNA samples she'd sent off, all from family history sites with a lesser reach than the first. Two had no matches within their databases, but the third linked both Felicity and her great Aunt Elizabeth with a Megan Parslow. The name was slightly familiar. Lydia turned to her Stoppes family tree and found her easily enough. She was Elizabeth Wykham's granddaughter, and Felicity's second cousin. It didn't shed any new light on the enquiry, but it would be another reference point if one should be needed. And it might yet be useful to have found another family historian with Stoppes heritage.

A look at Megan Parslow's tree showed the Stoppes branches to be the same as those Lydia had created, apart from two small differences: Sir Christopher and Georgina's baby boy did not feature and neither did William Tremain. The child wasn't a secret, he wasn't forgotten, but most likely Megan Parslow had never known she'd once, briefly, had another cousin and she'd never thought to ask. Why would she? And as for William, the connection would be impossible to make from the records alone.

The morning which had started so early and with such purpose slipped away as the heat rose. Birdsong shrivelled to nothing, the carefully tended plants drew into themselves, hunkering down to survive another day, while Lydia sought refuge in the house, the shutters blinding every window. Stephen was right, they should consider air conditioning.

The heat brought lethargy, along with a desire for cool wine which she took in Stephen's study while aimlessly browsing unconnected topics, disappearing down one rabbit hole after another. But once she'd been led to Google Earth by a reference to boating in Cambridge, it was only a single spin of the globe to look at Cuba, or more particularly, that portion of the island a little to the east of the American base at Guantanamo. It was that little patch of land where she knew bodies were being dug up, where tents and trailers were ranged in rows and generators hummed all day and night, where a village of temporary buildings covered Google's apparently empty landscape. It was where Stephen was.

Three weeks and he'd be back.

A little after two an unfamiliar sender pinged her inbox: AnneMarie51. The elusive AM at last?

> *Re access to my family tree: What is your interest? I see no links to Silverstream. What name are you interested in? The suggested DNA links are to Elizabeth Wykham and Felicity Maynes.*
>
> *Thanks Anne-Marie Tremain*

Not a promising start, but AM was a Tremain.

Hoping that the sender might still be online Lydia quickly replied, saying she was being employed as a researcher by a family trust, without giving details of the greater purpose. She honestly stated that her interest was in William Tremain, whose birth date she included without suggesting anything of his life in Nova Scotia. Finally she attached the letter from Derek Ballard asking that she be offered help from anyone who might have information.

It brought a rapid response. *Let me look at your tree so I can check. Sorry but too many scammers around.* Lydia clicked the link and waited hopefully. The Stoppes family tree she had constructed online was truthful in every aspect, but light on detail. It did not mention the baronetcy at all, although she knew that a determined researcher could easily find the link between the Stoppes name and the title.

While she waited she realised that she didn't have a plan for how she would proceed. She'd waited for this response and now it was here she didn't know what she'd do with it. Perhaps once she'd seen AM's information the next step would become clear.

The wait turned out to be a lot longer than she'd hoped. And waiting meant constantly checking her mail and being quite unable to settle to anything else, which in turn meant a nearly wasted day. As she was opening a second bottle and beginning to think about food, her email pinged again.

> *Thanks. Interesting possibility. I have never found anything about my grandfather William Tremain apart from his father possibly being Edwin Tremain and his mother being Elizabeth. Here's the link to my tree. See what you think.*

Lydia poured a fresh glass and clicked. Anne-Marie Tremain had done a lot of work, but the greater part of it was her mother's family: Careys, Macdonalds, MacLeans and Murphys. Her father's side was limited to his two marriages, his parents William Tremain and Mildred Luckhurst, and the questionable – so far as Anne-Marie was concerned – link from William to Edwin and Elizabeth. For Lydia, that marriage between William and Mildred Luckhurst was the key entry. Her William and Anne-Marie's William were the same person, the DNA connection virtually proved that, and proved he hadn't died in the Halifax Explosion. Anne-Marie was Elizabeth Wykham's half first cousin once removed and Felicity's half second cousin once removed. Both were in the range of relationships predicted by the DNA results. The chance that they could be related in the same way by any other connection was too remote to calculate. Even as she worked out the probabilities, the idea of there being another half brother to another of the baronets crept into a corner of her thoughts. Maybe she'd missed something, maybe she'd taken the wrong approach. As ever, the seed of doubt came from within.

From Anne-Marie's information she saw William and Mildred had three children: Kenneth, Ameline and Elizabeth. Kenneth? Surely the Kenneth Tremain who'd written to Elizabeth Calbain at the manor house in 1943 asking for information to help his mother. Yes! there in the details Anne-Marie had noted that he served in the RCAF in

England. Kenneth had a son, Gilbert, by his first wife Maureen, but he had apparently died childless in 2016, aged 73.

Elizabeth Tremain had died unmarried in 2016 aged 90. Her sister Ameline was also unmarried but shown as still going strong at 94.

From Kenneth's second marriage to Margaret Carey, two more children: Anne-Marie herself and Robert Charles, deceased in 2013. Either Anne-Marie had no children or she'd decided not to record them, but Robert Charles, like his father, was also married twice. From his first Lydia saw a fresh family tragedy: the death of a son aged six years. Anxious as she was to quickly absorb every detail, finding another event that must have brought such sorrow made her pause. There were no details of the boy's life, simply the fact that Gavin Henry Tremain had existed from 1981 to 1987. Better than just four days, Lydia wondered, or far worse for having seen your child grow for six years?

Robert's second marriage, to Rachel Streetly in 1989, produced two more sons: Andrew and Peter. Andrew died aged twenty from meningitis. Why were the deaths of the young so much more distressing than those of older people? Unfulfilled lives? The misery of what might have been? Yet the same regrets can be found at any age. For Peter, Anne-Marie had included only his birth date: 1993.

When Lydia had made notes of all the vital details of the significant members of the family she sat back and considered the implications. Most likely it changed nothing, for although William was the oldest son of Sir Edwin Stoppes, it was his bad luck to be illegitimate, and so blight all his heirs' and successors' chances of inheritance. But what it most certainly did demonstrate was a route by which a claim on the title might be made, even if it was unlikely to succeed. But who knew what interpretation a twenty-first century court might put on a nineteenth century grant? And wasn't that just what

Derek Ballard wanted to know about? He wanted no surprises in a year's time when the trust had been wound up, he wanted no would-be sixth baronet knocking on his door without warning.

Lydia saw one problem right away. What she'd discovered was only what Anne-Marie had recorded in the family tree, she had none of her own researches to rely on since the Nova Scotia records were closed. Some of that could certainly be remedied by having sight of whatever certificates Anne-Marie already had, so long as she was willing to share them. In terms of finding a sixth baronet, the living were of far greater importance than the dead, but would Anne-Marie share details of the living, or more especially those of Peter Alan Tremain?

ooo

"Lydia, you left a message. I'm sorry, I didn't get it until this morning. Sounded important, what can I do for you?" Derek Ballard, as affable as ever.

"It could have waited, but something came up yesterday. I was in touch with someone who I think is William Tremain's granddaughter. William was the second baronet's first son, an apparently illegitimate son. I've mentioned him before."

"You have. What did the granddaughter have to say."

"Quite a lot. After a few emails we eventually spoke. There's a lot to tell, but the key point is that she has a nephew, Peter Tremain, who as William Tremain's great-grandson, is a direct descendent of the first and second baronets."

"Ah. The possible sixth baronet."

"Emphasis on the possible, not probable."

"What are you doing right now?" he asked after a pause. "I mean, are you free?"

Lydia looked around her. Neither the dishes from her breakfast nor any of Saturday's meals had yet made it to the dishwasher. She was still in her dressing gown and hadn't had any intention of hurrying her morning. Then it occurred to her that Derek Ballard might be on the verge of suggesting he come to Grantchester. Meeting him for lunch was one thing, having him come to The Old Rectory was quite another. How, or why, it would be different, she wasn't sure.

"I could be," she said lamely.

"Shall I come over? I could bring something."

"No, no, of course not. What about The Plough, halfway between us?" It wasn't halfway, it wasn't what she wanted to do, but it was all she could think of and far better than having him come to the house.

As might be expected in the height of summer, The Plough was crowded. The predictable Sunday lunchtime busyness was compounded by a wedding party in one of the function rooms.

Derek Ballard was waiting when she arrived a little late, and flustered by being so.

"Sit," he said, "and relax. I should never have accepted your suggestion, I should have come closer to you, or even to Cambridge. I've ordered lunch and wine, the same as last week, hope that's OK." He lifted the bottle from the cooler and turned the label towards her.

"Thank you, that's perfect."

"Now, tell me about Anne-Marie Tremain and her family."

Which Lydia did, with the help of a family diagram she'd remembered to print before leaving home. With it she showed Derek how Elizabeth Wykham's and Felicity Maynes' DNA matches linked them to Anne-Marie.

"So there's no doubt about the relationship, the Tremains have Stoppes blood in their veins?"

"It would be astonishing if their connection to Anne-Marie came about in any other way."

"But Peter Tremain might be something different?"

"No, he's probably the real deal, but at the moment I have,

we have, no birth certificates, no marriage certificates to support this. I'm sure Anne-Marie has recorded her family history honestly and to the best of her knowledge but without seeing the official record or any certificates. It's all what she already knew or what she's been told. She and her brother were estranged for many years before he died. Her nephew Peter's DNA could short-cut all that and give a definitive answer."

"But?"

"Peter Tremain's whereabouts are unknown."

Derek raised his eyebrows and adopted his familiar contemplative pose.

"Another mystery. Are there any suggestions as to where he might be?"

"He may be running a bar in South East Asia, perhaps Thailand or Cambodia, a tourist spot she thought. Peter's mother is alive and well the last that Anne-Marie knew, but it seems she may not know either. Another fuzzy unknown."

"What else is there?"

"One of William's children, Ameline, is still alive, in her nineties. She lives in a care home. I think she'd be an interesting person to speak to, but probably not essential in the final analysis, although her DNA would be useful. What might be more interesting are Ameline's mother's papers, especially her journal. She wrote a lot about her time in Halifax in 1917 and her life in the years afterwards. Ameline gave it all to the archives on the centenary of the explosion in 2017."

"Which archives? Where do these Tremains live?"

"In Nova Scotia, in Canada."

Again the thoughtful pose, this time interrupted by their lunch arriving. It signalled a change from business to pleasure as they chatted about their lives without either of them really giving away much more than they already knew. They were almost finished their plaice fillets before Derek returned to the subject of the St James Trust.

"What will you do next, Lydia?"

"Continue with the papers at the manor house, I suppose. They haven't given up much but they have certainly confirmed some things and helped paint the whole Stoppes picture. And wait for the new DNA results. Oh, I'm sorry, I didn't tell you. The teeth and hair samples, they're in a lab in Cambridge being analyzed. Full results expected in about three weeks."

"Likely cost?"

"Zero, I think. I had help from Stephen, he, um, knows people at the college."

Why couldn't she say how and why he would know such people? In case Derek Ballard would be amazed that she, Lydia Silverstream, could even know a professor, let alone one who'd been knighted years previously for services to forensics? More likely because she was still amazed herself.

If Derek Ballard would have been surprised, or even interested, he said nothing of it.

"And the Nova Scotia connection? What next there? Will you go to meet Anne-Marie, talk with Ameline, find Peter's mother?"

"Go there? To Canada?" They'd spoken of such a thing previously, but now that it might be a real thing, an imminent thing, it suddenly became a huge and impossible thing. And besides, in three weeks to the day she'd be pacing around The Old Rectory, unable to settle, full of anticipation at the prospect of Stephen's homecoming. A trip to Canada would take time to organize, time to plan, time to be there.

"Yes, go to Canada," he said. "Supposing the Tremains were in Dublin or Berlin, you'd think nothing of jumping on a plane and going to meet them. In fact you'd have probably called me to tell me you were already booked. Nova Scotia is just a little longer in the air. Or is there another reason? Do you have other doubts?"

"No," she said, but thought otherwise. She always had doubts.

"Then I think you should go, not that I want to direct your work in any way. Go for a week or two and if you need to go back then go again. I've a good mind to come with you."

The suggestion was so unexpected, Lydia felt sure that her expression must have revealed her dismay. Derek Ballard was a nice man, she enjoyed his company and he clearly enjoyed hers, but the idea of travelling together, staying together in a distant city, was as unsettling as him coming to The Old Rectory.

"No, but seriously," he continued, apparently unaware of her discomfort, "this is exactly what the trust needs."

"Yes, I know."

"Now," he said in softer tones, stabbing the family tree diagram with his index finger, "what chance that this William Tremain, this illegitimate first son of Sir Edwin, was not illegitimate at all? What if he and the mother were secretly married and the third baronet was actually the son of a bigamous marriage? Wouldn't that be a thing?"

"Oh, I don't think that's true," Lydia said quickly. "If it were, then why ..."

"No, I don't think it's true either, because if it were then I think you'd have found it. But it makes you think, doesn't it? It certainly makes me think."

"It does. And another thing, have you ever read the actual Grant of the Baronetcy of St James? I have a copy of the standard version, the template. I know these things are supposed to be set in stone, but I wondered what a modern court would decide if any of the terms were challenged. Illegitimacy, for example."

"I'll get counsel's opinion on that. Let me know about your travel. Now, dessert?"

9

It was two hours into the flight before Lydia's anxiety began to ebb away, both the lulling drone of the engines and a second glass of wine each contributing to the improvement. She had never made such a trip at short notice. It was one thing to decide on a day in Cambridge a couple of days in advance, but to arrange a week in Canada on the same basis was completely foreign to her. Yet Derek Ballard was right, had it been only a few hours by train or a hop across the Irish Sea, she wouldn't have thought twice.

Stephen was quite calm about it, no more than another trip to him, one to wish her well on, one that would somehow hasten their next reunion, which, when she thought about it seemed true for her too. But no one had been more taken aback than Gloria. "Just when I think I know you," she'd said, "you do something completely unexpected." But the way she'd said it lacked her usual spark, lacked the outraged indignation she might have usually expressed. Afterwards, Lydia wondered vaguely if Gloria might be unwell, but she hadn't asked.

Anne-Marie sounded equally surprised when Lydia announced her visit, not that she needed to do much in preparation apart from contact her Aunt Ameline and Peter Tremain's mother, Rachel. Anne-Marie gave no promises about either being co-operative. The result was that Lydia had seven days in which to find the truth about the Tremain family, examine the papers in the archives to see if they shed any fresh light on the events of 1917, and hear from Ameline anything that she might remember of her father. And, if Ameline was amenable, take a mouth swab sample to later test her DNA. Lydia had no expectation of significant revelations from Rachel Tremain, but it might be helpful to at least meet Peter Tremain's mother.

What she would have really liked was a solid plan rather than woolly intentions.

Sleep came stealthily upon her. Nonsensical dreams of driving a ridiculously overcrowded car down an ever-narrowing lane, of stopping by a windmill whose sails were a blur of motion on a still day, were thankfully swept away by the announcement of their imminent arrival in Halifax. Below, the blue-green Atlantic had given way to a billion trees and a thousand sparkling lakes. It was an astonishing and sparsely populated landscape with clusters of dwellings joined by slender threads stretched through infinite forests.

Halifax's little airport, puffing out its chest to be *international*, was like a Lego toy after the maelstrom of Heathrow. But none the worse for that, she thought, as the formalities were concluded with smiles and welcomes not often found at Europe's busiest. It picked up her spirits, gave her hope for the week to come: perhaps Ameline and Rachel would be equally welcoming.

With so little time for research or careful selection, her chosen hotel was a massive brick block by the railway station, close to the cruise liner terminal. Proximity to the waterfront had sold it to her and the view from her room did not disappoint: to the left were The Narrows and the site of the great explosion, and beyond that the broad expanse of Bedford Basin; straight ahead, following the course of the fussing ferries past Georges Island, lay Dartmouth and its industry; right, down the shipping lane and beyond McNabs Island, stretched the broad Atlantic. The archives and a couple of museums were out of sight, yet all were within walking distance, as was the city centre should she seek any other amusement. Being car-free for a week was a bonus, even if it did mean she was reliant on Anne-Marie's generosity. And if that was found lacking she'd hire one easily enough.

Watching the water from a distance was never Lydia's preference. To be beside it, to smell it and listen to its busyness, that was always her choice. On a magnificent July day, with a gentle warmth without the stifling heat she'd left in England, and a soft breeze driving puffy white clouds, the urge to walk was irresistible.

In a couple of minutes she was down to the boardwalk by the old customs house and breathing the ocean. There, she joined a dawdling stream of people doing what she was also intent on doing: taking the air and seeing what was to be seen. All along the route, benches, chairs and even hammocks invited the walker to pause awhile but each twist and turn in the path as it snaked round every dock and quay, invited her on.

At the pilot station she found the little flotilla of yellow boats lashed together, bobbing and jostling in the wash of a ferry. To her eye they had a restlessness about them, like working dogs keen to be busy. By the Maritime Museum lay a corvette from the 1940s, the *Sackville*, looking as ready for service as ever she did during the desperate days of the Battle of the Atlantic. It made her think of her uncle Bill's neatly sloping writing in his wartime journals. Maybe he'd even set eyes on K181 as it escorted his wallowing tanker home to England.

And right by *Sackville*, the *Acadia* looking all of her hundred and something years old, with such elegant lines she might have stepped straight from an Edwardian film-set. When Lydia paused to read information about the ship, she read how *Acadia* was believed to be the only surviving vessel to have been afloat in Halifax harbour in December 1917 at the time of the explosion. There was no escape from her purpose in being there, even when she took an hour off to see the sights.

ooo

Anne-Marie Tremain immediately reminded Lydia of someone, but she couldn't think who. In modern times when seventy is no age at all, Anne-Marie carried her years badly. She made a dumpy figure coming into the grand foyer of the Nova Scotian and walked with the gait of someone who finds no pleasure in it. She wasn't carrying a placard with Lydia's name on it as limousine drivers do at airports, but she might as well have been. Lydia had no doubt who she was and crossed over to rescue her visitor from confusedly scanning the area for some recognizable landmark. "Anne-Marie?" she said in her friendliest voice.

"Oh, yes, are you Lydia?"

"I am. Thank you so much for coming today, and at such short notice."

"I can't believe what's happened. Last week I didn't know you and here's you flying in a few days later. Must be important, I reckon, more important than what you said, too."

"Let's go somewhere for a coffee, we can have a chat about the whole business of the trust and what I'm doing for them. I saw a place along the boardwalk yesterday, just a coffee shop with a few tables and chairs, we could go there."

"Is it far?" Anne-Marie said doubtfully.

"Five minutes."

It was more than five, as Lydia should have realized, and further than Anne-Marie would have chosen, but the tourist day had hardly started on the boardwalk and they strolled at leisure to the coffee stand. The urgency of Cambridge, the near-daily drive to the manor house and back, the need to make progress, identifiable progress, with the Stoppes enquiry, all these things had been left far behind. The St James Trust, the manor house, Fleet Street bankers and DNA labs suddenly seemed light-years away. As they receded from view, their importance diminished with them. The serious business was the business at hand, the waterfront, the promise of new discoveries, adventures in a foreign land.

They settled with their coffees and doughnuts close to the water's edge while walkers drifted in little eddies around them. For a few minutes they made the small talk of strangers forced into closer company than would have been natural to either of them. No, Anne-Marie hardly ever came to the waterfront, certainly not for pleasure; no, she had no family, had never married; no, she no longer worked, having retired from years as an administrator with local government. It was something they had in common, one thing Lydia could have picked up on, but she was in no mood to revisit her former life.

"So," Anne-Marie said after a long pause, "you're looking for who exactly? I thought I understood but tell me again."

"The short version is I'm looking to see if there is anyone who might benefit from the family trust. If there's no one, it'll be wound up, which is why the trustees want to know if there's likely to be anyone. They have to be as sure as possible that nobody will turn up unexpectedly and claim they were a beneficiary." Still she kept back the title and how a claimant might benefit from the inheritance. For what reason she wasn't entirely sure, apart from a vague idea that she might be more likely to hear the truth if the tellers were not dazzled by great estates and millions in assets. And if Anne-Marie had not discovered the baronetcy for herself after learning of the Stoppes name then that would tell Lydia something of how resourceful she'd been in researching her own family history.

"And Peter might be such a person?"

"He might, although most likely he wouldn't qualify because your grandfather, William, appears to have been illegitimate. I need to find out anything and everything I can about your grandfather and his descendants. There's almost nothing available online, so you're the best source I have at the moment."

"Tell me about my grandfather, I found his likely birth record, Edwin Tremain and Elizabeth, but I could never find mention of his father anywhere else."

Lydia did so, telling Anne-Marie what she knew of William, from his birth through his school days to his arrival in Halifax, and she told what clues and documents had led her to reach the conclusions she had. She told how he was part of the family although never quite a complete part, how his grandfather Clarence had also been illegitimate and how his attitude to William had probably benefited his position and progress immensely.

"At one time," Lydia said by way of concluding, "It looked as if your grandfather died in the Halifax Explosion. His name was published in the list of casualties. Did you know that?"

"My William Tremain? No, I didn't know that. Are you sure?"

"Pretty sure. But why would you? Why would you look for a death record of someone you knew well enough had not died?"

"He could have died, he was injured, that's how my grandmother met him, she was a nurse come up from Boston."

"Exactly. Have you seen the exhibit at the Maritime Museum?" Lydia said, waving vaguely along the boardwalk in the direction of the *Acadia* and the *Sackville*. "I'd love to go there and see what they have, just to have the feel of the explosion, to know what we're talking about. I've seen a couple of videos and some very blurry old film, but they need a lot of imagination as well."

The museum was almost deserted and so quiet Lydia and Anne-Marie were inclined to whisper as they toured the exhibits. The sinking of the Titanic occupied the largest space, no doubt that infamous event held more interest than anything else on offer, but the Halifax Explosion was their main objective.

Amongst the carefully prepared information boards, the accounts of heroism and the photographs of destruction were some of the pathetic personal items which such a catastrophe throws up: shattered eyeglasses, a battered pair of shoes, a single white glove blackened by oily residue, a blue and white polka-dot handkerchief. It seemed that such small things were all that might identify a victim, so unrecognizable were the remains themselves.

The narrative display spoke of the never-found bodies, those totally consumed in the fireball, of the unclaimed, unidentified corpses given mass burials, of the lost and the brutally injured. It also spoke of the misidentified and the dead found to be living and the living found, after all, to be dead.

Towards the end of the exhibit were reproduced pages from a newspaper listing the dead and injured. Lydia and Anne-Marie were drawn to it, their eyes going immediately towards the end of the alphabet to see if William Tremain might be there. He was. *Tremain, William, King Edward Hotel, English.*

"Oh, that's a shock to see that," Anne-Marie said softly.

"Yes, even though you know it wasn't true."

"If it had been true, we wouldn't be stood here now."

"Maybe Mildred would have fallen for another of her patients. You'd be a different you."

"It doesn't do to think about that kind of thing too much."

There was plenty more to be seen, but nothing that could come close to what they had already found.

"Where now? Or is that enough for you today?" Anne-Marie asked as they emerged into the sunshine.

"I wondered about going to Dartmouth, to see the house

your grandparents had, the one in Brookside Road. Would it take long?"

"How did you know about that? I haven't been near it for ages, not since before Granny died. That must be forty years now."

"Did you know your father wrote to Elizabeth Calbain during the war when he was stationed near the Stoppes house?" Anne-Marie shook her head. "When he wrote, he gave your grandmother's address in Dartmouth if Elizabeth could help with answers to any of your grandfather's missing memories. I've no idea if Elizabeth did write back. My guess is that she didn't. She thought her son was dead, so maybe she didn't trust a letter from an unknown airman suggesting that he might not be. But even so, the more I've thought about it the more I wonder why that never came to anything. You'd think she'd be at least curious."

"Maybe she never saw the letter," Anne-Marie suggested. "Or maybe she did write back and the letter was lost. I think there was a lot of mail went missing in the war. I don't think my dad ever said about it. I know whenever Granny would mention about Granddad's story and his not knowing where he came from, we'd roll our eyes a bit, like, you know, here goes Granny again. When I started looking at family history I could see how it could become a fixation, wanting to find out. But I don't think she ever did, not that I heard of."

"And did all those papers go to the archive? Are there any left?"

"No, they all went."

The drive to Dartmouth took only a few minutes, across the Macdonald Bridge, swinging left past the tollbooths and a few turns later they were there. Brookside Road was a quiet street with narrow detached houses on narrow plots. A between-the-wars development, Lydia guessed. Number twenty looked much like all the others, a few steps up to a verandah across the front with a window each side of a central front door, clapboard walls in the same light grey paint popular among its neighbours, although it could have benefited from a fresh coat. They parked a few doors away then walked up the street and back down again to pass it twice.

"What do you think? Just the same or ...?" Lydia asked.

"Smarter. I remember it always seemed run-down when I was a kid. Maybe it was. It'll be inside that's different."

"Does it stir any special memories?"

Anne-Marie stopped and looked again at the house, then shook her head. "No, nothing really, it's just another house now, could be anywhere. It doesn't mean a thing. It doesn't even feel like a house I was ever in. Sorry."

ooo

Anne-Marie's car turned into the hotel entrance at exactly the arranged time, early enough to not waste the day, late enough that Lydia had no need to hurry her breakfast. It was the day to visit Ameline Tremain in her retirement home an hour or so away on what Anne-Marie referred to as the South Shore.

As they drove out of the city it struck Lydia how lived-in Halifax was. She'd half-noticed it yesterday on their journey to Dartmouth, but now as they passed low-rise apartment buildings and streets of much older housing close to the city centre, it became more obvious. Most modern cities have all but lost their old, residential communities, pushed further and further out by commerce and property values. Not so Halifax, it seemed. She was about to comment on this to Anne-Marie when she realised she had no idea where Anne-Marie herself lived.

"In Halifax," she said, "off North Street. About ten minutes from your hotel. Ten minutes' driving, not walking."

In her mind's eye Lydia saw a house like her own in Osney, saw a life like her own had been, if a little further advanced.

But while she was active and engaged with life, she had yet to discover how Anne-Marie normally spent her days.

In a few minutes they joined the highway, then quickly the suburbs were gone and they travelled on a wide road with little traffic through a wooded landscape dotted with lakes and ponds. Periodically the ocean glittered in the distance, never far away, reappearing unexpectedly just as it seemed the highway had forgotten about it, preoccupied with more trees and lakes. Further south a massive road scheme was leaving its indelible scar on the land as a second carriageway was being blasted out of the rock, even though to Lydia's mind there was scarcely enough traffic for one.

"How long since you've seen your Aunt Ameline?" Lydia asked, as they took the exit to Chester.

"A few months. I came down in the spring. We went to lunch. And I phoned a couple of times."

Harbourview House had exactly that. Down a little side street, away from the town centre and set back from the water, the old house had a modern extension to it. It was a pattern Lydia remembered from the place her own grandmother had come to rest in. It was no doubt a pattern often repeated by those setting up such homes, although few would have had such a pleasant outlook across a little harbour to moored dinghies and yachts.

"I hope she's on a good day," Anne-Marie said as they approached the entrance. "She can be a bit off sometimes, like she's angry about something and not sure what."

"I think I might be angry about a few things if I get to her age. Ninety-four isn't she? There must be plenty to be cross about at that age."

Ameline Tremain was waiting for them in the lounge. Whether it was a good day or a poor one was not immediately apparent. From her previous dealings with residents of such homes Lydia knew it could easily be both.

"Is it true what Anne-Marie says, you've come from

England to talk to me?" Ameline said after they were introduced. She was a small woman, shrunk into herself in her ninety-fifth year, and clearly frail but her intellect appeared to be still sharp. Lydia was aware of being closely studied by dark eyes behind rimless glasses.

"Yes, it's true, all the way from England. But not just you, I've come to talk to Anne-Marie and your nephew Robert's widow, Rachel. And I'm really keen to go to the archives and look at the papers you donated."

"Why have you come? What's it all about?" the old lady said sharply.

Lydia explained again about the trust and how it would be wound up if no beneficiaries could be found, concluding with, "But the snag is your father, William, was probably illegitimate which might prevent any successful claim by any of his descendants."

"If you know all that then why bother?"

"My job is to report to the trust, tell them who's who so far as I can find. Then they can decide about beneficiaries. Or maybe a court can."

"Well, what is it then, what do you think I can tell you?" Having been a little excited by the prospect of their meeting, Ameline was deflated. Lydia wondered if she might even be disappointed and considered casually mentioning the baronetcy or hinting at the wealth involved in the trust. But she stopped short, that would be ammunition for later should she need it.

"I'd love to hear about your father, about life at home. Can you tell me what you remember of Dartmouth, about the house in Brookside Road."

"You know about that?" Ameline said, surprised.

"We went and looked at it yesterday," Anne-Marie said.

"What for? What's to see there?"

"So that when you tell me about your life there I'll know just what it looks like, just where you're talking about. Tell me, where did you sleep, at the back of the house or the front?" Lydia said, soothing away the old lady's doubts and scorn.

After a few moments gathering her thoughts, Ameline began her stories. "I shared a room with my sister, Beth. We were at the back of the house. I remember when we moved there it seemed like such a big room – and separate beds we had! I was seven or eight, Beth was two years older than me. And dear Kenny, he was older again. Six years older than me, four more than Beth. He slept at the front on his own. My mother and father were downstairs."

"I can see the house, Ameline. Were they left or right of the front door as you looked at it?"

"Right," Anne-Marie chipped in as her aunt hesitated. "Granny always slept there. She always called it 'our room' even though Granddad died before the war."

With the reminiscences beginning to flow, Lydia took out her notebook and let the two Tremains carry the conversation as they bounced off each other, sparking new memories as they did so. Sadly, Ameline's memories of her father were limited, she being barely eleven when he'd died in an accident at the railway yards.

"But I remember the day they came to the house, I was out front and two men came up from the yards and looked at me and Beth funny, then said where was our mother, where was Kenny. Mother was out somewhere but Kenny was at work in the yards. We wondered why they didn't look for him there."

"What happened?"

"They waited till mother came up the street, then they went in the parlour. In a while they came out and mother came and told us there'd been an accident and our father was dead. Kenny came home then and put his arms around us all. I don't remember there being a lot of tears. Maybe we were too shocked, but I think back then there was more of an acceptance that these things happened. I always thought it was funny he worked in a railway yard but got killed by a truck."

"What was he like, your father?"

"I don't remember really. He wasn't much with hugs and that, least, not that I remember. He could be a bit moody, sometimes bite your head off for nothing. We'd leave him alone when mother made a sign, when he was mad about something. I know mother said later it was on account of him being frustrated he couldn't remember things from before. There must have been some good times. I remember it was quite hard times, we had enough, we ate all right, but there weren't luxuries. I don't remember too many treats. Nothing like today. After he'd gone mother said a bit of him was always somewhere else. She said it was on account of him not knowing where he came from."

"Did you ever talk about that with him?"

"I don't think so. I know one day he said something had come to him, I'll always remember it, it seemed like such a funny name, Mary Valentine. We were at tea and Mother said how she'd write it down and she left the table and went and got her notebook right then."

It took Lydia a moment to realize exactly how that name might mean anything in William Tremain's life. In 1917 in Halifax he was en route to The Mary Mine in Manitoba when the explosion changed everything. And the person he and George were travelling to replace was their cousin Valentine Valence who'd died in an accident at the mine.

"Do you know why your father was in Halifax in the first place?"

"We've no idea. Mother said he had his papers and some money and nothing else. He'd never have known his name without them."

"Well," said Lydia slowly, and trying not to appear as the clever outsider come to tell the two women what they could never discover for themselves, “I think he was on his way to Manitoba, to a place called The Mary Mine. A cousin of his had been killed there and he and George Stoppes were going there to take over the running of it. George was only slightly hurt in the Halifax Explosion and carried on to Manitoba. He ran the mine for more than ten years. The cousin who was killed was Valentine Valence. Maybe in your mother’s papers there could have been another reference to the mine, something never known for what it was. Like Mary Valentine could have been.”

Anne-Marie and Ameline looked at each other, the old lady shaking her head in astonishment. “You might look at those journals of my mother’s and know what all kinds of things meant, things that were just little fragments to him.” Then a sudden thought came to her and she added, “Was there a shooting? She thought it was the war, thought maybe he’d been in the war. Anyway, he said there were soldiers. He said something else but I don’t recall what just now.”

“Are you tired, Aunt Ameline?” Anne-Marie had spotted the signs that Lydia had missed.

“I’m all right,” Ameline said indignantly. “Don’t cut me off now.”

“Shall we go out for lunch?” Lydia asked her. It had been their plan all along, depending on how they found Ameline.

They chose a pub the other side of the harbour, right down by the waterside, where Lydia did most of the talking by way of giving Ameline a rest. She told them about Stephen and The Old Rectory, about how she’d met Derek Ballard and how it was he who was now employing her. She said a little of St James Manor without describing its full magnificence but she told them nothing of the baronetcy or the trust’s millions.

Ameline brought the conversation back to her family. “My mother came to Halifax just after the explosion, did you know that? She came from Boston on a relief train. She was a nurse, it's how she met father, in hospital."

"And she stayed." Lydia said, happy to hear her own deductions were correct.

"Yes, she did. She said how the rest all went back to Boston after a few months. She said she went and waved them goodbye. She said she knew she'd marry our father, even then. I think it was a few years before she did. He was partially paralyzed for a long time. Even when I was young he'd sometimes use a stick."

"Did she ever go back and see her family in Boston?"

"I don't think so. And I don't think they came here, but I don't know. I never met them and of course they're all gone now."

"How long did she keep her journal going?"

"She wrote that all her life. After father died she wrote less, I think the real purpose of it faded away. At the end she didn't write much at all, she was too ill."

When they took Ameline back to Harbourview House Lydia thought it safe to broach the subject of a DNA sample. "Did Anne-Marie tell you how we came to be in touch?"

"Through the internet wasn't it?"

"Yes, but did she tell you it was because her DNA matched DNA from the Stoppes family?"

"No," Ameline said, shaking her head, "you never mentioned that did you, Anne-Marie?"

"Would you let me have a DNA sample from you, Ameline?"

"What do you think, Anne-Marie?"

"Oh, your choice, but I think it would be fine. I did it. It's nothing really."

"All right then. I thought I'd seen everything but here's something new. What do I do?"

Lydia gave Anne-Marie the phial and the mouth swab, asking her to take the sample from her aunt.

"That's it?" Ameline asked, "Not much was it, I thought it would be more interesting."

They were making ready to leave when Lydia remembered the letter from Kenneth Tremain which had contained the family's Dartmouth address.

"Ameline, I wonder if you remember your mother ever getting a letter from a woman called Elizabeth Calbain or possibly from your brother, maybe in 1943? It would have been a letter regarding anything Elizabeth knew about your father's parents in England."

"Kenny wrote all the time, he was in the air force. He never said much, but you could read between the lines. He was different when he came back, lost his smile. And moody like father had been. You didn't go near him when he was like that. But the other name, no, maybe she wrote but it doesn't mean anything to me. If it was important mother would have had it with all her papers. There were a lot of them. I never looked at them all, not even all the journals."

ooo

"How's it going, Lydia?" Stephen, smiling, subtly healthier, on the video call.

"Oh, very well. Everything's fine here." It was. She was eating breakfast in her room before heading out to the archives where she'd be meeting Anne-Marie again.

"Me too," he said.

She was about to say that she could see that, but held back. She'd avoided voicing her concerns so she thought it better not to mention her relief.

"Anything new, anything you can talk about?"

"Nothing good. And the bad will wait for another time."

She could imagine the nature of the bad, if not the specifics. It would be the discovery of a child or evidence of abuse or torture, it would be something far, far removed from their normal lives, something foul that couldn't be denied or brushed away.

She waited a moment or two before saying, "In two weeks you'll be packing to come home," then, as the remembered the uncertainty factor, added, "I hope. Do you think you will?"

"Right now I can't see anything stopping me, and I'm hoping for three weeks, but only banking on two. I don't know if we'll get away anywhere."

No, she thought, they probably wouldn't. Getting away would be something when they wanted to be away from the house, away from Grantchester, not when it was their refuge.

"I met Ameline Tremain yesterday, one of William Tremain's children. He was the ..."

"I remember, the one who was supposed to have been killed in Halifax."

"You're good at that, knowing who's who in my world. Anyway, Ameline was really interesting, not just about her father, but generally. She was a teacher all her working life but with none of that bossiness you can sometimes find with a spinster schoolmistress."

They chatted on for a few minutes about nothing of consequence, each happy to simply have the contact of the other, in video if not in body. Then their days called them and they spoke of longing and of the time between that moment and the moment when they'd be together again as being nothing at all in the bigger picture.

Lydia turned to her window and the view across Halifax harbour. A new cruise ship had docked overnight and a steady stream of tourists were spilling into the city. The boardwalk would be busy today. A good day to be in the archives.

And a good day to walk there in the sunshine up South Street, a sharp climb, then the long gentle slope down to Robie Street before the turn and in another two minutes she was there. A formidable brick building appearing as safe and secure as you'd want an archive to be, a building that gave nothing of itself away.

Lydia was still registering for a reader's card when Anne-Marie joined her.

"Are you a regular here?" Lydia asked as the lift whisked them upwards.

"Not really, and hardly at all now."

"But at least you know your way around."

On the third floor the soft silence of the research area embraced them. It sets libraries and archives apart as oases of reading and learning. Just being there gave Lydia the secret pleasure of anticipation.

"It will take a few minutes," the research assistant told them when they handed her the request form.

While they waited, Anne-Marie introduced Lydia to the rows of index files. To test the system Lydia looked for newspaper reports of the Halifax Explosion. In particular anything connected with the name Tremain, and as an afterthought, also for Luckhurst, Mildred's maiden name. Then she reversed the search, looking for Tremain or Luckhurst and seeing what they might be connected with. A couple of trails emerged as possibilities and Lydia suggested that perhaps Anne-Marie could concentrate on them while Lydia read Mildred's journals.

They were delivered in two cardboard boxes, labelled with references and a summary of the contents. Within the boxes, bundles of papers were contained in separate files, also labelled and summarized. Ameline had said there were a lot of papers – she was right. To go through them all would be impossible in a day, it might take two or three and then not be as thorough as she wanted.

But there were two prime targets for her enquiry. First and foremost, the journals Mildred had kept, especially when she arrived in Halifax immediately after the explosion, but also to tease out the references to fragments of William's memory. Secondly, it would be good to look through any correspondence to see if there'd been contact between Mildred and the manor house.

As she lifted the bundles from their boxes it was a relief to find the contents had been dated. She turned immediately to a notebook marked *To Halifax 1917* in a precise female hand.

> *December 8th 1917 Embarked today on the third relief train towards Halifax of which we hear the most terrible reports. I am one of only a handful of juniors permitted to join the relief with no expectation of nursing only of assisting those who are qualified.*

The entry was long, describing Mildred's fellow passengers and the journey in some detail. Most of Sunday's entry was similar but shorter, until the final line: *We are almost arrived and have been warned of dreadful sights that we will encounter.*

Her records of the following days were compelling and terrible, and yet somehow innocent in their brutal frankness. Mildred didn't hesitate to describe some of the appalling injuries she encountered, noting *splintered bones protruding from arms and legs* and her own small contribution to easing the end for a woman *too burned to survive*. These and many other sights she recorded, quite matter-of-factly, as another day of *my new duties*.

She wrote of her own situation with similar directness and modesty. On December 11th she noted that the previous day she worked *too long to sleep or write and had only water and a plate of beans but it was enough*. On the 12th Mildred was promoted to assist a surgeon removing eyes shredded by flying glass: *I have new responsibilities and will discharge them, but would do without them. Little food or rest again today.*

For Lydia the journal was engrossing, as only first-hand accounts of drama can be and surely the basis for a story in its own right, but if she read every entry in full she would hardly scratch the surface of the papers in front of her. She must try and scan each day's entry rather than read it as a diligent researcher should. Scan for her first encounter with William Tremain.

She didn't have long to wait. On December 15th, nearly a week after she'd arrived in Halifax, Mildred was again re-assigned, this time to care for eight casualties with broken limbs and head injuries. She wrote specifically of William, the first of her patients she named in her journal. *New charges today, all immobile some scarcely alive one unconscious. According to his record W Tremain was dead and yet he lives although he may have little time*. But a day later came a turning point: *a sound from WT he took a little water*.

In this way WT progressed over the next week or so until he asked where he was and who he was. When he was told he made no sign of recognizing his name nor of understanding how he came to be in Halifax. Lydia skimmed each entry but while mentions of WT became fewer they were always attentive. And besides, Lydia knew exactly how the story ended, there was no suspense in following his progress. What she wanted now was to find where Mildred had written her notes of his fragments, his snatches of memory that had led to his son Kenneth writing for information from Elizabeth Calbain at the manor house.

Anne-Marie interrupted Lydia's searches with an excited whisper. "I've found that newspaper entry we saw at the museum. I haven't seen anything for Mildred, not even in the honour roll of Boston volunteers."

"She may have been considered too junior to be worth mentioning. She was certainly very young. Maybe they honoured those who returned and she was overlooked. Have you read your grandmother's journals?"

Lydia had never thought to ask before, she'd simply assumed Anne-Marie had done so.

"No, Aunt Ameline had given them to the archives before I'd got going with the family's history and they never seemed very important. I'll have a look now though."

Lydia handed over the first notebook. While Anne-Marie settled down to read about her grandparents' first meeting, Lydia leafed through the folders looking for a different journal. *William's Memory Book* appeared to be exactly the thing.

> *In this book are all the sayings and thoughts of William Tremain regarding his life before The Great Explosion in Halifax in which he was sorely injured. The first entries here are faithfully copied from my notebooks made while he was being cared for and slowly gained a better health.*
>
> *Mildred Tremain*

How wonderful, thought Lydia. Mildred had been a well organized diarist and clearly had an eye to future generations reading her journals. No wonder such a diligent girl had been selected as one of the handful of juniors to come on a relief train from Massachusetts with the surgeons and the qualified nurses. This reminded her that Mildred was still a month short of her eighteenth birthday when she'd arrived in Halifax. Like the young men in the trenches, much had been expected of teenagers in 1917.

The first entry was copied from the notebook she'd just read, how he'd been told his name and age and where he'd been born but recognized none of it. Lydia imagined him repeating this new information and rolling it around his mouth to see how it felt, to find some familiarity with the sound and shape of *William Tremain*.

A few days later he asked again, having forgotten what he'd been told. Mildred noted WT *thought it might be another name, something other than William but he did not know what.* After a few more reminders William came to know his name, which the doctors took as being a sign of improvement.

On a particularly bad day when his head ached terribly, William said *I've been hit on the head before. A cricket ball. Did I play cricket?* This entry was followed by several that hinted at games or sport. Then weeks passed with nothing until he remembered standing by a horse looking up at a woman who was looking down at him. Apart from him thinking that she was smiling at him, no details of the woman were recorded.

For Mildred to still be in regular contact with William, Lydia assumed that he was still under some kind of medical care. Perhaps his head injury had disabled him in other ways. Mildred's daily journal might reveal more, but that would be for another day.

In the middle of January a new topic appeared: *WT remembers army uniforms and rifles and shooting. He cannot say how many soldiers but he can see two faces although he recognizes neither. They are both young but he thinks they are older than him. They are inside a building on a wooden floor by a window. He cannot say what is beyond the window other than grass.*

In February Mildred recorded a rush of new images. He is a boy standing by a grave in a churchyard, a heavy hand resting on his shoulder, the sound of earth rattling on the coffin lid. Mildred wrote *WT said Do you think that was my father's hand?* Next, clearly still a child, William recalled playing in a hayloft, relived the sweet smell of the hay, saw how, when it was thrown, the dry fibres hung a little in the air. He was with someone but he had no knowledge of who. Hard on the heels of that memory came feeding pigs and picking strawberries. Again, William was sure that these were scenes from his childhood.

Less pleasant moments from that childhood also emerged. Being caned while knowing it was for something he hadn't done; hiding in a cupboard fearful of discovery and shaking so much he thought he'd give himself away; being made to eat burnt toast as a punishment for complaining about breakfast. All nightmares from a harsh upbringing. Lydia wondered if they might also be nightmares from life at a boarding school in 1910, a boarding school like Snaresby College. And the earlier memory of uniforms and shooting, might that not be an echo of the incident in which George Stoppes was shot?

Lydia looked across to see Anne-Marie engrossed in the journals. "Aren't they wonderful?" she whispered.

"They are. I can't believe I've never read them. I might never have done so without you coming over."

"You should take some photos, or see about getting them copied."

After a brief lunch they returned to their tasks, both enthusiastic to discover more, each for their different reasons. First-hand accounts of historic events, be they personal or public, have a compulsion all of their own.

Lydia noted each of the memories Mildred had so faithfully recorded in her neat pencil script. It had clearly become a preoccupation of hers, or perhaps more likely, a labour of love. It was certainly one way a girl of eighteen could show her English patient that she was interested in more than his headaches.

At the end of 1918, just as the war in Europe was ending, so Mildred's notes ceased to be transcriptions from her journals. William was still in some kind of medical care, possibly in convalescence along with thousands of others shipped home broken from the Western Front. Whether Mildred was still nursing him was unclear from the memory book, but she must have seen him regularly as no doubt her journals would show. A year on from the explosion Mildred noted *William knows the name Stops which came to him during a conversation about trains and a journey he took or a journey he didn't take*. Lydia smiled at the small change from *WT* to *William*.

As the afternoon wore on, so Lydia collected the puzzle pieces from William's lost life. Now that she could see them, see how small they were in the overall picture, it was no wonder that he could never recover his memory from them. Nothing fitted together to make even the smallest corner of the whole picture. Only his parents might have been able to arrange those pieces in their rightful places or, quite remarkably, Lydia herself more than a century later.

ooo

"How long will the drive take?" Lydia asked as she and Anne-Marie headed north through Rockingham along the western shore of the Bedford Basin.

"Something over an hour. This is the scenic route for now."

"I love being so close to the water."

But it didn't last long. In a few minutes they left the basin behind and joined a highway that might take them to such familiar sounding places as Windsor and Avonport, Berwick and Yarmouth. Their destination, however, was the less recognizable New Minas, which so far as Lydia could discover was a small town with a big shopping centre. It was also the home of Rachel, mother of Peter Tremain, Anne-Marie's nephew. He was the man who might, if Lydia's research was accurate and if his ancestry had been wholly legitimate, have been the sixth Baronet of St James. He was also the man who Derek Ballard wished to be forewarned about, the man whose existence had brought Lydia to Nova Scotia.

"Have you thought about getting copies of your grandmother Mildred's papers?"

"Yes, I have. I asked at the archive yesterday and

apparently I need permission from the donor, from Aunt Ameline. I'm going to ask her next week."

"They're a wonderful collection, a unique first-hand account. There's a really good book in there, for someone who's got the time. It might be something Ameline would enjoy getting involved in, too. That moment she mentioned about her mother getting up from tea to write in the memory book, I saw that entry yesterday. It was May 1938. It was funny seeing that, knowing Mildred had been having tea with her family just before she wrote that."

"What will you do on Monday? It's your last day isn't it?"

"I'm not sure, maybe the archive again just because I love those journals, or maybe another visit to Ameline. I don't know what more there is to find, but let's see how today goes."

The two women chatted through the rest of the journey, each a little more at ease in the other's company. So much so that Lydia began to feel guilty for not telling the whole truth about the trust, the baronetcy and the wealth associated with both. Even so, she'd keep her silence until she'd met Peter's mother.

At the first exit to the town they dropped down off the highway and were immediately into the world of big-box stores and acres of parking. For all Nova Scotia's lakes and forests, its picturesque harbours and tumbling rivers, it was inevitable there would also be the brash and ugly somewhere. Just off the main street, Anne-Marie took them into a maze of short roads and cul-de-sacs, stopping in front of a nondescript single storey home similar to all the others in the row.

As they stopped, Anne-Marie looked at Lydia, paused a moment and said awkwardly, "Rachel's had a, um, difficult life. In some ways."

It seemed like a warning, but of what? To be

understanding, patient? Before she could ask, Anne-Marie was out of the car.

Lydia saw a figure watching them as they approached the house. The shadow passed behind the frosted glass entry before opening the door. They were greeted by a dark-suited woman of late middle age, her steel grey hair perfectly groomed, her make-up discretely applied. Lydia thought she might be about to host a board meeting or impress a corporate client. It seemed too unlikely that Rachel Tremain had dressed herself like this simply to meet Lydia. For the briefest moment Lydia wondered if something bad had happened to Rachel and the lady who'd opened the door might be a doctor or worse still, an undertaker. Her face, stone cold and utterly neutral, suggested the latter.

"Rachel, this is Lydia, all the way from England to meet you," Anne-Marie said, dispelling any doubt.

She welcomed them in, gushing a little over the honour of being involved in Lydia's enquiries, how surprised she'd been by Anne-Marie's call, wondering what she could do or say to help. She had tea or coffee ready to be served along with biscuits, all neatly arranged on a tray she brought through from the kitchen. As Rachel poured the first cup Lydia thought she detected a hint of a tremor in the hand holding the cup and saucer.

After a few minutes of small talk about Oxford and Cambridge and travelling, Anne-Marie said, by way of introducing the subject which had brought them to Rachel's house, "We had a fascinating day at the archives in Halifax yesterday, looking at all Mildred Tremain's papers. And we spent a day with Aunt Ameline in Chester."

"What can I tell you? I knew very little of my husband's family," Rachel said, sitting straight backed with her hands resting loosely in her lap. She feels the need to be on her best behaviour, thought Lydia, and she's scared to make a mistake or give a wrong answer.

"Simple things really," Lydia said gently, "especially about your son Peter. If all that we've found is true, then he might have a claim on the trust, as a beneficiary. I must emphasize there would be no guarantee that the claim would be upheld, it's quite likely that it wouldn't."

Just as she had with Ameline, Lydia explained how, helped by Anne-Marie, her researches had brought her to Nova Scotia, how her job was to identify possible claimants, not to make judgements. To be sure that Rachel was familiar with the family history, Lydia showed her an abbreviated version of her late husband's ancestry.

"I don't know where Peter is at the moment. He's not often in touch," Rachel said flatly, doing her best to disguise her feelings about her son.

"And the last you knew?"

"Thailand, I think. But that was a couple of years ago now."

"Did he write?"

"No, a phone call. He's not one to be close."

Like all loving mothers she wasn't blaming her son for his neglect, at least not publicly, not when talking to a stranger. She was understanding of him, explaining that being close was not his way, that he must be given his freedom to roam without her needs pulling him back.

As Lydia saw these things she saw through the placid exterior to someone acutely uncomfortable talking about her son, uncomfortable with herself. She felt herself to be in the spotlight and was doing her duty for as long as she must. She'd dressed the part and there could be no fault found with her performance, but her heart was not in it.

"I'm sure that's a great sadness for you," Lydia said with genuine sympathy. "I wonder, do you have Peter's birth certificate that I could look at? And maybe your husband's too? Robert, wasn't he?"

Rachel appeared a little taken aback, and looked to Anne-

Marie for some reassurance. Anne-Marie nodded her approval. Rachel retrieved a folder from a bureau with no searching, no wondering where she'd put it, she simply went straight to it. It was neatly labelled *Registrations*.

Lydia lifted the flap and saw within it the three familiar sections: births, marriages and deaths. Never in all her years of research had she been offered family information so tidily arranged for inspection.

Within births she found not only details of Peter, but of the whole family including Andrew, Peter's older brother who'd died aged twenty, Rachel herself, the boy's father, Robert, and his parents Kenneth and Margaret. All the marriages were there too, along with the deaths. Even William's death certificate, whose details were unaccountably missing from the online index. Everything Lydia could have asked for was right there in front of her.

"Thank you Rachel, this is wonderful, a real treasure trove for someone like me. It's all so ... organized."

"Everything needs to be in its place. For whenever it's wanted," Rachel said, dropping her gaze to her lap, embarrassed even by small praise. "My husband always ..."

Lydia glanced round the room and saw that everything was indeed in its place and there was nothing that could possibly be out of place, no magazines, no plants dropping dead foliage, no cluster of old pens on the bureau. Through the doorway to the kitchen she saw empty counters, a floor that shone from wall to wall.

Lydia set about photographing each of the certificates, conscious of Rachel unhappily watching her in the awkward silence. She may have agreed to Lydia seeing them, but she didn't much like it. As a distraction, Lydia thought, Anne-Marie asked her about her volunteer work at the local library and offered her own opinion on volunteering in general.

Lydia replaced all the documents exactly as they had been filed and handed the folder back to Rachel, who immediately replaced it in the bureau. They'd been in her house less than an hour and yet there seemed little else to say. Small talk about how long she'd lived there – nearly forty years – and the pros and cons of New Minas went only so far. A conversation about Peter seemed too stressful and Lydia feared that one about Andrew or her late husband might be even more so. And Anne-Marie's warning about Rachel's difficult life stood as a roadblock to every possible topic.

After a few more minutes and seeing no progress, Anne-Marie rescued her with, "Rachel, we really should be heading out soon. It was so kind of you to have us here today. I'm sure it's been really valuable for Lydia."

"Yes, amazing. I'm so grateful," echoed Lydia.

They drove away in silence for a few minutes until Anne-Marie said, "I'm sorry, I should have warned you. Rachel is a good soul really, but ..."

"That difficult life you mentioned, can you share it with me? If it's private that's fine, I don't need to know."

"He's gone now so it doesn't matter, but my brother was her biggest difficulty. Robert was a pig. He caused Rachel a great deal of pain. Physical pain too."

"Oh, I'm so sorry," was all Lydia could say.

"Poor Rachel could never do anything right, Robert was a bully his whole life. Rachel was never strong and he controlled her. Everything had to be perfect. He bullied the boys, too. I tried to speak to him, but he never took any notice of me. He was always on best behaviour when anyone else was around, but sometimes you could see the bruises. And if a visit got cancelled at short notice it was because one of them had something too bad to hide. I thought when Robert died Rachel might recover, learn to live her own life. She's a lot younger than me, but sometimes it's like she's waiting for him to come back through the door. She's told me some of it, but even now I don't think she's come to terms with it. She's still scared of him ten years later, still thinks he's watching her, still thinks he might come back and hit her."

"That's so terrible. The damage done can never be undone. You never heal from some things. Is that why Peter stays away?"

"I don't know, but the way it was, I think he blamed Rachel for not protecting him and Andrew, not standing up for them. I think he blames Rachel for letting Andrew die."

"Why? What happened?"

"I wasn't there but Andrew came home from school for Easter and was ill when he got home. Robert didn't believe him, or chose not to, and wouldn't get a doctor, said Andrew was lying. Andrew died a few days later. Meningitis. Peter left that week and so far as I know never went back to the house while his father was alive. He was only eighteen, I don't know where he went or what he did."

It was a bleak account of family life, very different from Lydia's own experience, but she could feel something of the pain and imagine the anguish. She wanted to ask Anne-Marie about her own childhood, wanted to ask if Robert learned his parenting from their father Kenneth, but she didn't.

ooo

"Do you think it's been worth coming?" Anne-Marie said once they'd ordered their food. The Henry House was quiet on a Sunday evening, despite Halifax being full of visitors.

"Oh yes, certainly. I'd like to stay longer but thanks to you and Ameline and Rachel's careful filing, I've gathered all the information I need and a lot more besides. And thank you for bringing the details of your brother Gilbert. We didn't talk much about him, were you close?"

"There were a few times we might've been, but him being that much older and living with his mother, we didn't share much when we were young. And he was grown up while I was still a child. There was never much to bring us together, and our father and his mother never forgave each other, they never spoke so far as I know. And neither of us had children to be the bridge between us. So no, we were never close. In fact now I think about it, I didn't know him at all."

"Families," sighed Lydia, "I'm not close to my brother either. Without our parents to draw us together, to be our centre of gravity, we drift further apart every year."

For a few moments they each reflected on their situations, on distant brothers and deceased parents, yet both with hundreds of virtual relatives populating their digital family trees.

"What'll you do tomorrow?"

"Play tourist. I'm taking a day off. I'll walk by the water again, maybe go on the old warship, the *Sackville* wasn't it? My uncle, who I loved dearly, crossed the Atlantic a few times during the war. He'd definitely go and see it, so I'll go for him. You're welcome to come with me if you like, I should have said that."

"I have an appointment. The dentist." Anne-Marie pulled a face which suggested it wasn't a simple check-up.

"What about Tuesday? My flight leaves late, we could go Tuesday, I could go to the archives again tomorrow."

They spoke a little more about their lives, opening up more easily for having spent so many days together. Anne-Marie talked of how she'd never had any ambition, not to be a wife or a mother, not to be a manager, not to travel and see the world nor any particular part of it, but that meeting Lydia had made her think she should do more than a couple of volunteer mornings serving coffee to old people at a day centre. She'd had what she now realised was an undemanding life, free from drama, mainly healthy and without money worries. Just spending time with Lydia – a most unlikely turn of events, she thought – had made her wonder if really it hadn't also been free of experience too.

"Come to England," Lydia said. "Come and see where I

live, come and see where your grandfather was born, where his grandparents brought him up. Come and see where he spent much of his youth in Wheadon St James. And see where your great-grandmother is buried. I could even show you a house she once lived in and the grand house where she spent half her life."

"A grand house was it?"

"The manor house? Yes, it's very grand."

As soon as she'd said it the image of St James Manor was in her head and she could see the great lawn with its magnificent horse chestnuts, the tennis court and the stables, the library and the kitchen with Georgina opening a bottle of wine for lunch. As these things filled her mind, she knew she should tell Anne-Marie all about them. She should tell her all that was at stake in the search for a beneficiary of the St James Trust.

"Anne-Marie," she began, "I must tell you something. First, everything I've told you about coming here, about the trust and so on, all that is absolutely true."

"But?"

"But there's more to it than that. First of all there's a title. A minor one, but a title none the less. And then there's the manor house, not to own but to be lived in, and yes, it's a very grand house indeed. Then there's all the money that goes with it. It's in trust but the beneficiaries do very well from that trust. It's a great deal of money."

Anne-Marie nodded. "I didn't think you'd come all this way if it wasn't a lot of money."

10

It wasn't as if she'd have been spending her own money, she could have taken a taxi from Heathrow right to The Old Rectory – easy, comfortable, business-like – and charged it to the trust. Instead she'd taken the bus, half motivated by economy and ecology, half by what? Some dim memory of puritan denial of luxury left over from her childhood? Next time, Lydia told herself as she waited jet-lagged in the drizzle at the Trumpington park-and-ride, next time she'd have a taxi all the way, not just the last couple of miles.

The house was almost as she'd left it, although the garden was greener for a week's rain after being scorched for much of the summer. The small change in the house was that Mrs Webb, Stephen's occasional housekeeper, had returned from her travels and baked and cleaned, leaving a chatty note about shepherd's pie and airing out bedrooms. Mrs Webb's and Lydia's paths rarely crossed and she was certainly a pleasant enough woman, but as with long-distance taxis, a housekeeper was something Lydia wasn't quite ready to accept as normal. Employing a servant – what else was she? – made Lydia uncomfortable, although she'd have been hard pressed to explain why. But a shepherd's pie for supper without having to lift a finger towards making it was something she could gratefully accept without causing herself too much discomfort.

Just as Nova Scotia had made all else fall away, so returning home exhausted from travel already made her time with Anne-Marie in Halifax seem like a dream, quicker to fade than the time to cross the Atlantic. And for what purpose had she flown those thousands of miles? Little more than to listen to stories and make copies of documents. And collect a DNA sample, she mustn't forget that, nor must she forget to deliver it to Charmaine Thibaud at the genetics laboratory. In fact, there were a dozen things she should attend to, first of which was to speak to her employer.

"The DNA will tell for sure," Lydia said after they'd exchanged the essential pleasantries on a video call, "but really I don't think there's much doubt. William Tremain survived the explosion and his descendants are alive and well in Nova Scotia. Or rather, two of them are. The whereabouts of the potentially most important one are unknown."

"Thank you so much, I knew you'd be right for this," Derek Ballard said with undisguised warmth.

"Can I ask you, Derek, if all this is confirmed, will it be enough for you to continue the trust or will you be completely satisfied there's no male heir?"

"I've been asking myself that question a lot more lately, in fact, since you started work. If you'd come up completely empty then I think I would have been satisfied. But this is different, it muddies the water. I'm inclined to think the trust will continue. I haven't spoken to counsel yet, but I'll need to."

"Have you mentioned this to Georgina Stoppes?"

"No, and I'd ask you not to either. For now it's only my speculation. Are you going to the manor house tomorrow?"

"Yes. She'll ask what I've found. I'll need to tell her that much at least."

"Of course, and I'll see you there, perhaps we can have lunch."

When he'd gone from the screen Lydia wondered what she might do in Derek's place, what would make her completely satisfied there was no natural heir. After all, she was the one who had the knowledge and the experience of researching family histories. Above all, she knew that in the twenty-first century she could never know everything there was to know about people's lives a hundred and more years ago. How could she be completely sure of anything from those times or, for that matter, from a year or a month ago? The answer was that she couldn't. The elusive Peter Tremain might not be alive, and even if he was, he might still not have a good claim or any claim at all.

The next thought caught her quite unawares.

If Peter Tremain's supposed existence were enough to cast a doubt on the extinction of the baronetcy – and therefore prevent the termination of the trust – then her work was done. Once a doubt was established, that one question alone could be enough to continue the trust. She might find another dozen illegitimate Stoppes offspring or ten distant cousins from a clandestine 19th century Stoppes marriage and it would make no difference. The trustees must either be completely satisfied or not. Degrees of dissatisfaction would be irrelevant.

Once the DNA results came in as expected it would be over. In fact anything more that she researched might well be a complete waste of time. Perhaps she should suspend her work immediately.

ooo

As she turned in through the gate on Thursday morning, St James Manor took Lydia by surprise. Over the weeks of burning summer it had become tired and brown, frayed at the edges like a once-favourite shirt, and familiarity had dulled its grandeur. Now, after a week's rain and her own absence, it was as magnificent as the day she'd first set eyes on it and it took her breath away. Once again the lawn was a perfect emerald carpet, the horse chestnuts a luxuriant backdrop, the drive a nut-brown sweep to the ivy and stone of the house itself. Under a perfect sky in a morning light more reminiscent of spring or autumn, every colour was saturated, every line and curve sharply defined.

She slowed and stopped, then stepped out to let herself be enfolded in the setting, become as one with it, swept up in its history of baronets and privilege, of church fêtes and wartime billets, of public families and private tragedies.

The images dissolved with the crunch of gravel behind her. She turned to see Gloria's car, its owner calling through the open window. "What's up? Anything wrong?"

Lydia shook her head. "Nothing. It's just so beautiful," she called back.

Her friendship with Gloria still sometimes surprised her. Perhaps in her quieter moments Gloria felt the same, puzzled how she'd fallen in with someone as buttoned-up and straightlaced as Lydia. Perhaps, just as Lydia was a little jealous of Gloria's lack of inhibition, Gloria may have envied something of Lydia's reserve. Perhaps they had each learned something from the other and were the better for it.

Georgina was waiting in the kitchen, full of questions and welcoming hugs like they were both family, offering coffee and toast while she heard all about Lydia's Nova Scotian adventure.

"Does it all amount to anything? Anything that'll change the outcome?"

"I've no idea, Georgina, but you can ask Derek Ballard. I think he's coming over later."

"Yes, he phoned. Late morning he said."

"Do you want me to carry on as we were?" Gloria asked, having said little since they'd arrived.

"Yes, I think so. We'll see what Derek thinks, but for now, yes, we should. I'll come with you."

They'd only been settled in the library a few minutes, Gloria dutifully entering details of household expenditure for 1956, while Lydia attempted to complete the report of her findings in Halifax, when Gloria said sharply, "The house, I need to talk about the house."

"What house? My house, the one in West Street?"

"Yes, the one in West Street, what other house is there?"

"Has something happened? Is there a problem?"

"No, nothing's happened, I just need to talk about it. We need to ... we need to make a proper arrangement. It's too ... casual."

Nothing may have happened, but something had changed, that much was obvious. Then Lydia realised that Gloria hadn't had a cigarette since they'd arrived. She could suddenly see it in her face, her complexion had changed, become softer. And if she was giving up then it explained her tetchy mood.

"Do you want to, er, go outside, talk about it in the garden?"

"And have a ciggy? Of course I want a ciggy! But ..."

"You've stopped! Fantastic. Brilliant. Well done."

"It's temporary, just temporary. We're saving up."

"For a house?"

"For a baby."

Lydia's mouth opened a little but no sound emerged. A baby. Of course, why not? What could be more logical than for Gloria to be pregnant? She was apparently happy with Eddie, was of an age when she'd probably started looking at her clock, they were both working and they had a place to live. The house! No wonder Gloria wanted to have a proper arrangement.

"Wow. That is marvellous," Lydia said without much warmth, still stunned by the news.

"Don't get too enthusiastic."

"No, sorry, I mean it really is wonderful, so long as you're both happy about it. I knew you looked different, I just didn't think ..."

"Didn't see me as a mother?"

"No, I mean yes, why not? Let me give you a hug."

After a few moments, Gloria disengaged herself.

"So, the house. If something happened to you I don't know

where we'd be. And you might change your mind and want it back at any moment. We need to get it sorted."

"Yes, of course, I see that. We will."

"Soon please. Now, where was I?" she said, turning back to her 1956 household accounts in an almost business-like fashion, which Lydia thought most un-Gloria. Changes were happening quickly.

It is the expectant mother who is supposed to be afflicted by baby-brain, not the mother's friends, but Lydia could settle to nothing for the rest of the morning. Gloria's news set in train a whole sequence of thoughts, each tumbling over the other to demand her attention. The house in West Street and how she might make a suitable arrangement led naturally to her own situation at The Old Rectory. What was her situation exactly? That was as casual as the way Gloria was living in her house in Osney. And hadn't she and Stephen spoken of changing their wills, but neither had made any move to do so? And then there was the question of children, not that she might still have any, but that she might still come to regret not having any. Which questions brought her to memories of past lives and the many dissatisfactions that came with them.

She had still not completed her report for Derek Ballard when the man himself arrived at the manor house. Having chatted briefly with Georgina, he came quietly through to the library, rousing Lydia from her distractions.

"You must be Gloria," he said, reaching out his hand. "Thank you for all your work on this, Lydia has told me a lot of good things about you."

Gloria accepted the compliment with a downward glance but without comment, where once she might have swelled with pride and come back with a smart response.

"Now," he said after a brief embrace with Lydia, "I want to hear all about Nova Scotia. Not just what you found, but what you think, maybe even what you didn't find."

They went to the garden where Lydia repeated all she'd previously told him, adding a few more personal details and thoughts of her own. When she stopped, the solicitor stood and paced back and forth a few times deep in thought.

"If the DNA comes out as we expect then it shouldn't change anything," he said.

"We still don't know if the DNA will come out at all. I'm taking the new samples to the lab tomorrow, I'm sure they'll have some indication by now. Dr Thibaud said she'd let me know if they came up blank."

"I'm meeting with counsel tomorrow, an initial opinion, nothing more. A specialist in such things. Who'd have known there would be a specialist? I suppose there's one for every occasion these days."

"Local?"

"No, no, too rarefied for that. London."

He sat down again on the bench beside Lydia and studied the patio slabs beneath his feet for a minute or so, then said, "What do you think? Is there something else yet to be found, some clinching telltale piece of evidence that will change everything?"

"You don't know what's under any stone until you look. But do I think there's a legitimate male heir from an as yet undiscovered line that can be traced back to the the first baronet? No, I don't. So it might all depend on what counsel's opinion is when you see them tomorrow. And then again in these days of equality what would a court think of a female claimant? Could a court overturn those years of male preference? Can a royal warrant be overturned?"

"Thank you, Lydia, that's not what I need to hear."

"And if you're looking for complications," Lydia persisted, "suppose Amanda Stoppes decided she wanted a sex change? She'd be a he and presumably qualify as a male heir."

"It would certainly be interesting. And expensive, for sure."

"With some obvious doubts and unanswered questions, I wondered if you'd like me to stop work, at least temporarily?"

"No, let's get the DNA results and hear what counsel has to say before we do that."

"Stephen's home at the end of next week, I'll be stepping back then for a couple of weeks anyway."

"Then we'll carry on with your work, at least until then. It'll be a good moment to take stock before we decide on the next steps."

The decision to postpone any change of course seemed to satisfy him and his mood brightened.

"So, how about lunch, Lydia? I'd enjoy the company," he asked, making no pretense that it would be a purely business meeting.

"Thank you, another day that would be lovely, but I have to catch up with Gloria. Why don't you ask Georgina? I'm sure she'd be delighted," Lydia answered without hesitation, and wondered later where the idea had come from.

ooo

Saturday brought Lydia a wave of exhaustion as her travels and lack of true recreation caught up with her. There hadn't been a single day since Stephen had last been home that she hadn't spent some part of it on the Stoppes project. And, when she wasn't actively doing something, a part of her was looking for clues, constantly trying to tease out some new meaning from dry records.

With the tiredness came its old companion depression, lurking in the shadows, waiting for an opportunity to take root. As she lay in bed letting the heaviness of her body pin her to the mattress, familiar demons gathered around her. The corners of the room grew dim, while beyond the window grey clouds chased a procession of showers across the land as if conspiring to cut off her only means of escape. Perhaps it would be better to stay as she was and succumb now, rather than in a week's time on the eve of Stephen's return.

Even if she could move her limbs and the day were welcoming there was nowhere to go, no Thames to wash her troubles away, no towpath to distract and absorb her. That friend, that constant companion, flowing so invitingly past her door in Osney, reminded her of more failure: thoughtlessly ignoring Gloria's concerns about the house and doing nothing about her will. So many good intentions, so much inaction. The room grew smaller and darker.

That notion of a wasted journey, of how little had truly been achieved by her travels, returned and morphed seamlessly into self-doubt and unworthiness. Hand in hand with unworthiness came an image of poor Rachel Tremain, standing at the door of her obsessively ordered home. Lydia's woes were as nothing to Rachel's, even if the physical abuse had stopped years previously. Rachel had been cursed with an unworthy life, never matching her husband's demands or expectations despite his violent encouragement. A decade later she had barely started to heal. What if she were installed at the manor house as the sixth baronet's mother? Mistress of the house and all that went with it? No, thought Lydia, it would not be a reward, it would not be compensation for a brutal marriage, it would be a burden Rachel would struggle to carry, a burden to grind her down further.

The light in the room had grown a little brighter.

The prospect of Peter Tremain becoming the sixth baronet was still a distant one. Apparently insurmountable barriers remained before that could happen, but idly drifting through the implications of such a thing reminded Lydia of how rarely she considered the effects of her work. Perhaps people's lives may not have been changed dramatically by her discoveries, not as they might be with the Stoppes baronetcy, but even a photo album finding a new home had some effect, it meant someone had a new view of their history.

And it changed Lydia too. Every one of her projects had taken her to new people and unfamiliar places. She was the richer for having done so. Wasn't Stephen among those new faces and experiences? And he had changed everything. Would the same be said for Rachel Tremain when the whole story was told? She couldn't know, nor could she feel responsibility for any gain or loss that might result.

From standing on the edge of her private abyss, Lydia had been pulled from the brink by a woman thousands of miles away, a woman she'd met just once. Proof, as if she needed any, of how lives can be touched in the most unexpected ways by the most unexpected people.

There was a sudden lightness in her limbs where minutes earlier there'd been nothing but gravity, nothing but a deep inertia. All thoughts of surrender evaporated as the day beckoned.

Her phone pinged the arrival of an email. Nigel Aylton, with a long message and attaching photos, both better dealt with on her laptop than the phone. A day without Stoppes was no longer possible.

Around midday, just late enough to allow Lydia to take a guilt-free bottle of Bousval from the summerhouse fridge, she settled to take stock. She'd see what Nigel had sent her, see if it threw any new light on her little painting of Prudence Mallingford or the St James Manor house. Then, if Stephen hadn't already called, she'd call him. Their habitual Friday chat hadn't happened and its absence nagged at her.

Nigel Aylton had been busy. He'd attached a dozen photos, all freshly made from previously unindexed images. The first was dated 15th May 1875 and Nigel had copied the note from the original glass slide: *Sir Clarence Stoppes, Bart. with his family and household at St James Manor House, Beds*. Lydia checked her notes. The baronetcy had been conferred in 1874 and the family had purchased the manor house and its estate in April 1875. The photos may have been commissioned to celebrate their taking up residence.

Even without identifying names it was easy to see who was family and who was household. Sir Clarence and Lady Stoppes were at the centre with their son Edwin standing between them while their two daughters, Mary and Sarah, stood one each side. To the left, Sir Clarence's side, were five men, three in working clothes, two better dressed, clearly the indoor servants. All stood at a slight distance to the baronet, presumably the distance indicated seniority within the household. The arrangement was mirrored on the right where six females of mixed ages stood awkwardly in caps and aprons.

Lydia imagined that the day had been seen as an important moment in Stoppes history, a moment to record, using the very latest technology, their ascent to both the baronetcy and to the landowning classes. Sir Clarence's virtues and service had been recognized, even if it was by his aristocrat father pulling levers in the background. Despite the odd misfortune, the Stoppes hadn't really looked back since.

What the photo also said was that at this important moment when the family and household were gathered, there was no mystery figure, no half-hidden face staring at the camera from the shadows. There was no suggestion of a complication. It was a photo that reflected exactly the entries in the family Bible, it made the same statement, announced the same confidence in the future. That was the same Bible where only a generation later the entries abruptly ended after the second baronet's marriage.

Apart from Edwin, the gangly fifteen-year-old at the very centre of the photograph, Lydia hadn't found even a hint of secret marriages or unrecorded offspring. Edwin's son William was the only blemish on the Stoppes' perfect record and even then he was hardly kept secret. Edwin had done exactly as his father had encouraged him to do, ensuring that both Elizabeth and their son were without difficulty in life. The more Lydia thought about the whole Stoppes saga the more she felt sure there was no possible candidate for the position of sixth baronet other than Peter Tremain, last heard of somewhere in Southeast Asia.

Nigel Aylton had written a long message regarding the set of photos he'd sent and suggested that he could print copies and give them to the Stoppes family. He also made clear he'd welcome the chance to visit the manor house himself and perhaps take photographs from the same positions as his great-great-great-grandfather Cedric had done. Lydia wrote a note of thanks and said she'd ask Georgina Stoppes about a visit.

As she poured a second glass of wine the sun broke through the scurrying clouds. She'd wait another five minutes and then call Stephen. But five turned into twenty and then a third glass and then an hour until she'd convinced herself that Stephen was ill, or worse, bored with their weekly chats. There was a slippery downward spiral just waiting at every turn. For once, she recognized it and quickly dialed so as to have no time for second thoughts.

He answered almost immediately.

"Two minds, one thought," he said. "I've been about to phone you for an hour. I'm in Havana having a day off. There's three of us come to town for a couple of nights, just to get away, sit in a restaurant, walk down a street. We're at a little boutique hotel in the old part of the city. It's really charming. Here, look, I'm still in bed." He panned the camera round the room, then to the balcony to show her a view of the roofs of old Havana. "We should come here. We should make a date and do it."

Stephen was more animated than she'd seen him for weeks. "Yes, we should," she said. Then after a slight pause, "I'm missing you, Stephen."

"Yes, I know, but only a week to go. It'll be the same as

last time, Paris then the hop to Heathrow. It could still be three weeks, but more likely two."

They chatted on about his return, what they might and might not do, where they might and might not go. None of it amounted to much, more a catalogue of the little things in life, things people do together when they enjoy each other's company.

"What about the Stoppes? Any news there?"

"Not really. I saw your Charmaine Thibaud yesterday. She was as competent as ever. I took the saliva samples from Anne-Marie and Ameline Tremain in Nova Scotia."

"Results soon, I imagine."

"She thought so. They'd had a problem with one sample but tried something different and it seemed to be OK. With luck it'll be next week, Friday perhaps."

"And you'll need to work on that, while I'm home," he said, a statement, not a question – Stephen's usual manner of speaking, something Lydia had noticed about him soon after they'd met.

The timing hadn't occurred to her, but Stephen was right. Yes, she said she'd be stepping back from the work at the manor, but the results of the DNA would need to be addressed. Not only that, but if they were as expected then it might mark the end of the whole project. She couldn't see Derek Ballard wanting her to dig around any further and finding Peter Tremain would be a job for someone else, someone with a different set of skills.

"Will you be in college at all?"

"Certainly, and I'll have to stay in touch with Paris. We'll fit in with each other. We know how to do that."

"Yes, we will. And I want to get something arranged about a will. I know we spoke about it but it's more urgent now. Gloria's having a baby and is anxious about the house in Osney and worried about something happening to me. Any thoughts? And who should I use?"

"Gloria? That's big news. Isn't it?"

"Oh yes, it's big. I'm, er, thinking of leaving her the house. What do you think?"

"It's always changeable. But if you want it done quickly then ask your friend Derek in Bedford. When we've thought about it a little more we might want something different, but if it's important to you both then get something done, even if the finer details aren't quite decided. Ask Derek how you can protect Gloria's position, you might not have to leave the house to her. And yes, I must change mine, too."

ooo

As had become her habit, Georgina Stoppes was waiting with coffee brewed and a dish of warm croissants when Lydia arrived on Tuesday morning. How easy it would be to let the project stretch out, to spend a couple of days at St James Manor every week, endlessly looking for possible baronets, endlessly trying to prove a negative while lapping up the hospitality and the life of luxury.

But, thought Lydia, it wouldn't be an honest life and it would be a life without purpose, apart from self-indulgence. It wasn't something she wanted, although she could well see how others might think she already led such a life, supported in luxury and paid to indulge her favourite pastime. And others might easily see how undeserving she was of such a life, but for once, on this Tuesday morning, the weed of unworthiness found no place to grow and strangle her brighter blooms.

"No Gloria today?" Georgina asked as they finished coffee.

"No, she's ... not feeling very bright today, she may be in tomorrow."

Gloria's pregnant state wasn't Lydia's news to tell and the brief text from the mother-to-be had not gone into any detail beyond *sick as a dog*.

"Derek Ballard's coming over later, isn't he? He wants to meet the photographer from the website."

"He did, but he's gone to London instead." That had been the second text Lydia had received before she left The Old Rectory.

"I didn't really understand what he wanted with the photography man anyway."

Lydia explained the connection via her own Mallingford portrait and Derek's family portrait to the painter-turned-photographer Cedric Aylton and from there to the website and Nigel Aylton.

"I had no idea," Georgina said. "It just shows we're all connected in some way or another."

After they'd considered this for a few moments, Lydia said, "Did you go somewhere local for lunch with Derek last week? I wondered what we might do with Nigel Aylton today."

"We went to The Hare at Little Nesbit. Not bad, but nothing special. And there's plenty here for the photography man. By the way, how long have you known Derek Ballard?"

"Not that long, we met when somebody I knew needed a solicitor urgently. He was very helpful, then he and his uncle helped out on another little mystery I was working on. Why do you ask?"

"Nothing really, I probably got the wrong impression. Let me just say he speaks very highly of you. Very highly. He did so when he first came and spoke to me about the trust after Chris died, said how good you were at what you do. But last week it felt like more than that."

"He's always been a complete gentleman with me, friendly, but business first," Lydia said, but for some reason her mind conjured up a moment when once, weeks ago now, Derek Ballard had stood close to her as they looked at a picture in his uncle's cottage. Had that been a moment of something other than business?

"Oh no," Georgina said, "it was nothing improper, he's very old-fashioned like that. Anyway, I shouldn't have said anything at all. I probably imagined it."

The two women had started well and their relationship had slowly edged towards a real friendship in the few weeks that they'd known each other. Now it edged a little further. Lydia should invite Georgina to visit The Old Rectory to return a little of the hospitality she'd found at the manor. One day soon, perhaps when it was all over.

The morning passed slowly while Lydia fiddled at this and that, unable to settle to a single strand and follow it through the archives. The idea that she wouldn't find anything of importance was so strong that it deterred her from looking.

Nigel Aylton arrived about noon, spilling his excitement around him as he brought an armful of albums and prints into the manor house. Lydia guessed he was maybe forty, but still with the exuberance of a teenager. He couldn't get enough of the house, couldn't say often enough how grateful he was to be invited, how excited he was to be where his ancestor Cedric had once been. It was one thing to stand in a street and view a public building just as Cedric had done, but quite another to come to a private house and walk where Cedric had walked – and speak with the descendants of those who Cedric had spoken with! As if that were not enough, Nigel was sure that Cedric would be just as excited and just as grateful as Nigel himself was.

"These are for you, Lady Georgina," he said, presenting her with a dozen pin-sharp prints, all beautifully mounted.

"Thank you so much, but no lords or ladies here please, Nigel. "

Together they poured over the images, each as fresh as the day they'd been made, each showing different aspects of the manor house. The most important was the family and household group that Lydia had seen before, but looking so much the better for being printed in a large format.

Having enthused over each photo, Nigel was keen to explore the garden and locate the exact positions from which they'd originally been made. At each location he carefully set up his tripod and took several shots using multiple exposures. When it came to reproducing the family and household, Lydia stood in for the domestic servants while Georgina played the whole family.

When even Nigel's enthusiasm had ebbed away a little he enquired wide-eyed about the portrait of Mistress Mallingford. "Did you, the painting, I mean, did you ...?"

"Yes, it's in the car," Lydia said.

He followed, almost running ahead of her in his excitement. Lydia had the framed picture wrapped in a large padded envelope. As she pulled it out to show the artist's great-great-great-grandson, he let out a little whoop and bounced up and down. In the bright sunshine it appeared a little drab, although the blue of Prudence Mallingford's dress retained something of its original verve. From Lydia's point of view the artist had done well to embrace photography and leave painting behind, for he'd had no great skill with the brush. Nigel, however, fell on it with delighted oohs and ahs.

"You know it's the only original I've ever seen, ever handled. The one on the website, the Crawford one, is in Australia."

"It's yours, keep it," Lydia said.

"No! I can't!" he squealed.

"I've tried to find a home for it with a Mallingford or some other descendant and failed, so I can't think of anyone better than a member of the artist's family. And not only that, but one who'll treasure it. Take it. And I'll make sure you see Derek Ballard's portrait of Sophia Cummins too. But I think he'll want to keep that one."

It was one of her more trivial re-unifications, but surely there'd never been one more important to the recipient. Mostly her jumble-sale photo albums, her auctioned bric-abrac or long-lost medals were welcomed with interest and genuine thanks, tinged with that slight puzzlement of why she bothered. Nothing she could remember had brought anything close to Nigel Aylton's joy.

ooo

No sooner had his secretary ushered Lydia into Derek Ballard's office than she buzzed through to interrupt them.

"Sorry. Important," he said.

Lydia sat silent, guessing that it might be a call concerning the Stoppes business, for if it had been anything else surely she'd have been asked to leave. Not that there was much to be gleaned from Derek's monosyllabic side of the conversation. Lydia still hadn't completely decided to ask about making a will. Georgina's comment had slightly unsettled her, enough to wonder if she should keep her personal affairs well away from her working life. But she did need to get it done, for Gloria's sake if not her own. Sitting there, watching the solicitor engrossed in the business at hand, jotting a note or two as he listened to the unknown caller, she found it hard to doubt his intentions. Surely he would have said something, made his feelings known if indeed he had such thoughts as Georgina had suggested. Too old, perhaps, too insecure, too risk averse, better to keep what he had.

"That was counsel I saw yesterday," Derek said, "The overall gist of her opinion is that any challenge to the inheritance of the title or of property would be very long, very expensive for all parties and with no guaranteed outcome for anybody. Some aspects have precedent, others apparently not. And as you probably realize, it wouldn't only involve the civil courts but also the College of Arms. It might even end up in the Supreme Court if there were points of law involved."

"So, something to be avoided if possible."

"Yes. Unfortunately I foresee another aspect to this. About winding up the trust."

"Because of what we've found about William Tremain?"

"Partly, but because of what you haven't found too. Let's say I was satisfied that there was no likely successful claimant to the baronetcy. Satisfied enough with your work, satisfied the trust had been diligent and comprehensive enough in its enquiries to wind up the trust. Then some time next year, next decade, someone comes along and disagrees, someone who has a claim. Wouldn't I do well to test the evidence, or lack of it, in front of a judge before winding up the trust, rather than hoping nobody rocks the boat in the years to come?"

"Is that what counsel has suggested?"

"Yes, they have," he said slowly, resting his elbows on the desk and pressing the palms of his hands together.

"So much easier if there definitely was a sixth baronet," Lydia said. The country lawyer nodded, half distracted in private thought. "I'm going to see Dr Thibaud at the lab in Cambridge tomorrow," she continued, "She has some results for me, not all, because she hasn't finished with the samples from Nova Scotia, but she thought I'd like to have the others. I'll call you as soon as I know anything."

"Oh, right. But bad timing, I thought it might be next week. I have a medical thing tomorrow, probably not back on duty until Tuesday, it depends how it goes."

"Nothing serious?"

"Cataract," he said, indicating his right eye. "A simple procedure, or so I'm told. But I'm not looking forward to it."

Briefly, Lydia considered what ailments of age might await her in later years. That slight suggestion of mortality reminded her of making a will.

"Have you time to help me make a will?" she asked a little tentatively, still not a hundred percent sure she wanted Derek to assist her. If he had no time it would spare her the decision.

"If it's straightforward, yes, of course. It's really a case of filling in the blanks on a standard form. Something more complex might take a little longer. For obvious reasons the wording should exactly represent your intentions and all contingencies."

"It seems simple to me. Something for my brother and my nieces, a property to a friend, the remainder to Stephen, my, er ..." again the slight stumble, "partner. Yes, my partner," she added emphatically as if to dispel any doubt – and to extinguish any flame that Derek might be secretly carrying.

"Any mortgages on the property? Is it rented out? Any particular considerations should any of the beneficiaries predecease you? Does Stephen have children?"

None of which Lydia had given the slightest thought to.

11

"Each sample has the same analysis and I've made a file for each one," Charmaine Thibaud said as she handed the paperwork to Lydia. "And I've put the digital version of all that on this memory stick. And on this stick," she pushed a second device along the table, "are the raw DNA files. There are four different formats for each sample in case you want to use them elsewhere. And if you need something else then let me know. I've done every different analysis we can do here. It should be enough for most purposes."

"That's fantastic, thank you so much."

"This final file is a summary, the relationships between the samples."

"Any big surprises?"

"I don't know what you were expecting. They're all related, I can tell you that."

"That's a relief!"

"I've ordered them into what seems to be the generational order according to the dates you gave me, although of course I can't tell which child was born first amongst siblings."

Lydia's eye was racing ahead of the commentary, down to where there appeared to be a disconnect in the generations. She bit her tongue and let Charmaine Thibaud continue.

"The people coded *ET*, *ME* and *SL* are the oldest. They are siblings who share common parents."

"That matches the record. They are Sir Edwin Stoppes, and his sisters Mary and Sarah. The codes are simply their initials, *ME* for Mary Eloise, *SL* for Sarah Lucy and so on."

Dr Thibaud wrote the names against the initials on her summary sheet.

"Next, there are children of two of those siblings. *GM* is the child, a son, of Edwin and *AR* is the son of Sarah."

"Good. That's Sir George, George Melville Stoppes, son of Edwin, and Albert, son of Sarah Lucy. What's next though?"

"Next are two grandchildren of Edwin. They're your *EC* and *CM*."

"That's Elizabeth and Charles, the children of Sir George, my *GM*, yes?"

"No, the father of these two is not present in the samples you gave me. The paternal grandfather is your Sir Edwin, certainly, and the father is related to *GM*, possibly a brother but more likely a cousin or half brother. Whoever the father is, they are not represented in the samples we processed. But all the samples belong to the same wider family."

"And the last two?" Lydia said uncertainly.

"Your *ChM* is the son of Charles, and so in turn *ET* is a great grandfather of *ChM*. And *AE* is the daughter of Elizabeth. They're cousins, they share the same unknown grandfather and are the great grandchildren of *ET*, your Sir Edwin."

"*ChM* is Sir Christopher Stoppes and *AE* is Ann Elizabeth Wykham, the daughter of Elizabeth Claire Stoppes," Lydia said mechanically, as if recalling something learned by rote but of little real interest. Her mind was racing over the possibilities of her having made a mistake in recording the samples, of there being an error in processing. Not that she wanted to challenge her host or the work of the laboratory.

"I take it this is not what you were expecting."

"No. Getting the samples analyzed was intended to provide us with a base line, a series of DNA readings from a series of known individuals. Their identity and genealogy was already known and recorded. The idea was that if another person declared themselves to be a member of the family there would be a mini DNA database from several generations for comparison. Something that would settle any argument."

"You do still have that."

"Yes, and thank you, I didn't say that properly, but thank you so much."

Lydia considered the information in silence for a few moments, unsure how best to ask the burning question.

Charmaine Thibaud rescued her. "You're wondering what to do with the unexpected results. I'm certain there's no mistake in the analysis of each sample. I'm certain there's no mistake in attributing the relationships. There's always a remote possibility of this or that, a one in many millions chance of a duplication, but with a family group like this I think you can discount that completely. Which leaves two questions, I suppose. Did we label the samples correctly when we put them in the sample containers? And did you label the freezer bags correctly when you transferred them from wherever they were?"

"Both transfers were double checked, Georgina Stoppes checked the freezer bags with me and you and I made your sample boxes. I watched you take each one, split it into two parts, record them and label them. We held the labels against the freezer bags and checked the details matched. We scanned your labels and they brought up the correct information."

"We did."

"There's a third possibility, perhaps. The teeth were in little memento boxes, some ornate, one gold, one silver and so on. Inside they had the names of the children whose teeth they were and little cameo photos, the kind you get in a locket. One of those boxes could have been accidentally swapped for a different child's teeth, or wrongly labelled."

Even as she said it, the idea struck Lydia as ridiculous. How would such an accident occur? And if it were intentional then who would have done such a thing, and to what purpose? To fool people checking the DNA a hundred years later into thinking the lineage was incomplete?

"I'll have the other two results next week. I hoped it would be today, but something urgent came up."

"Thank you, they will be interesting. I can tell you now I'm expecting one more grandchild for Sir Edwin Stoppes. If not then I've made a lot of mistakes."

On the bus home, halfway back to Trumpington, Lydia recognized the house of Laurence Durham, the colleague of Stephen's who Lydia had previously helped. The story might have rested on wills, but it too had been a question of paternity, unsatisfactory in some ways, but it was what had first brought Lydia and Derek Ballard together. Now, unexpectedly, there was a question of paternity in the hitherto unblemished Stoppes' record.

But there was more to it than that, she suddenly realised. If Charles, the fourth baronet, was not the son of George, the third baronet, then Charles shouldn't have been a baronet at all. And if that were the case then Sir Christopher should not have been the fifth. What proofs were needed when inheriting a baronetcy, not perhaps today, but back in 1972 when Charles inherited the title and the estate? Not much more than a birth certificate she guessed, and certainly not forensic DNA sequences.

She would need to speak to Derek Ballard immediately, or at least as soon as she'd ordered her own thoughts. The DNA revelation about Sir Charles' parentage would be crucial to Derek's role as trustee of the St James Trust. But a moment later she remembered he was not available, he was having eye surgery, which would leave her alone with her dilemma until after the weekend.

By the time Lydia had walked the mile or so from the bus to The Old Rectory her thoughts had shifted from George not being the father of Charles to who might be. A brother, a half brother or even a cousin were Charmaine Thibaud's suggestions – more than suggestions, the DNA was very clear. A half brother was possible, but the only known half brother,

William, had been in Nova Scotia since 1917 and a number of people were certain that he'd never returned to England. In addition there were two cousins, Valentine who died in a mining accident in Canada, which was the reason William and George had travelled there, and Albert Morrisey, Sir Edwin's sister Sarah's son, missing presumed dead at Ypres in 1915.

A full brother for George was also possible, but the idea of such a person being utterly absent from the official and family records and yet having grown to adulthood and fathered George's children was totally incredible.

As Sir Edwin had shown himself willing to acknowledge and support his illegitimate son William and William's mother, it seemed unlikely that he would have completely ignored another son conceived in similar circumstances. Unless he was ignorant of the child's existence. A man might father a child and be wholly unaware of the fact. And yet how could such a child have remained so connected to the family that he could become the father of George's children and still remain invisible to the world? It was as unlikely as George having an unseen brother.

All of which left a sickening lump, heavy in Lydia's stomach: somewhere, somehow, she had made a huge mistake, perhaps a mistake of omission, but a mistake for sure. The easiest to make would have been to have somehow missed a tenth, or even eleventh, ornate little box of baby teeth in a nursery drawer, or to have simply recorded the contents incorrectly. That might change everything.

How thoroughly had she searched the nursery? How overcome with the beauty of the little boxes had she been? And how dazzled by the potential of their contents? She would return to the manor house on Friday after checking with Georgina. For now her head was still spinning with possibilities, and besides, she'd already drunk most of the large glass of Bousval she'd poured the moment she'd got home.

ooo

"Coffee? Croissant?" Georgina asked.

"No, thank you, not this morning. I want to check something. Did you put the little boxes the teeth were in back in the nursery?"

"No, they're in the drawing room, in the little writing desk. I'll get them. Something wrong?"

"I've made a mistake somewhere and have to check back."

Georgina returned with a blue velvet draw-string bag that reminded Lydia of the one in which her brother had kept his marbles as a child. Inside, the precious boxes were each wrapped in tissue paper. Georgina spread them out on the counter and together she and Lydia unwrapped them.

"So what are you looking for?"

"Just the names, just to be sure that I recorded them correctly."

One by one they opened each box and checked Lydia's list against the contents. The two matched perfectly.

"Have you had the DNA results? Is that it? Is there anything I should know?" Georgina said with the same note of anxiety as when Lydia had reported Felicity's DNA match to Anne-Marie.

"No, it's nothing at all to do with Sir Christopher. And I haven't told Derek Ballard yet, he's not available until next week."

The weight of responsibility for overlooking something so important and obvious bore down on her so much that Lydia felt her mouth begin to twist as tears welled in her eyes. Too late she blinked them back, Georgina had seen her distress.

"What is it, what's wrong?"

"Somehow I've missed something, I've probably wasted all this time and effort. According to the DNA from the teeth, Sir

Charles and Elizabeth," Lydia pulled the two trinket boxes from the group on the table, "are not the son and daughter of Sir George." She pulled the third baronet's box to join the other two. The childhood faces of all three gazed back at them.

"And Chris …?" Georgina asked, holding the fifth baronet's box gently in her palm.

"Sir Christopher is Sir Charles' son. No problem there."

Together they sat and stared at the three generations of Stoppes, until Georgina said slowly, "So how did Charles inherit from his father if he wasn't his father?"

Lydia looked at her and nodded, "Exactly. None of it makes any sense. I must have missed something. So, can I go back to the nursery and look again? Maybe I was too preoccupied by finding these little treasures I never looked any further."

"I'll come with you."

In the nursery the two women divided their labours. Georgina began with the floor-to-ceiling cupboard where Lydia had found the badges and spent shells, while Lydia returned to the drawers in the dressing table. In a few minutes they'd both found nothing of interest and moved on to the other furniture, then to the nanny's room. There was no missed item, certainly no extra box of baby teeth that might magically explain the mystery of the Stoppes succession.

"What next? Is there anywhere else you haven't looked?" Georgina gently pressed.

Lydia thought for a moment. She had certainly not been through every drawer and cupboard in the house and could still see no good reason to do so. Only one place came to mind, and that was an unopened trunk in the attic, the locked one of the three.

"We'll break it open if we have to," Georgina announced as she led the way up the narrow stairs.

It wasn't necessary. With a little more force than Lydia had previously applied to the catch, the latch released. They thought at first the trunk was full of blankets, but the blankets turned out to be uniforms, Sir George's and his wife Miriam's they guessed. The khaki was that of a captain, or so Lydia thought. She didn't recognize the WAAF insignia, but guessed at a junior officer of some kind. Lady Miriam Stoppes would hardly have been anything less.

All of which was certainly interesting and on another day might have led to all sorts of enquiries, but it didn't answer the urgent question. Lydia vaguely wondered if, after so many decades, there might still be strands of the owner's DNA lurking in the fabric and what new light such knowledge might throw on the family's history. But she had enough to deal with without adding fresh complications.

"It doesn't have to be something you've missed, does it?"

"Thank you, Georgina. That's kind of you, but there must be some trace of this, somewhere there must be a clue. Or an awful lot of lies that've fooled me. And, I suppose, fooled a lot of others."

ooo

A combination of a cancelled flight and motorway congestion meant it was gone eight before Stephen arrived home. Having prepared herself to welcome him hours earlier, Lydia had filled the wait by sitting idly in the summerhouse fretting and drinking more wine than she intended, her excitement a little diminished by each new message of further delay.

They were both too jaded to properly appreciate their reunion, as if the effort of finally achieving it was barely offset by the pleasure of the moment. After the sudden crisis of the Stoppes DNA Lydia had wanted him to be home more than ever, to share those troubles and to be wrapped in his easy company. He was her confidant, he was the one to whom she could admit her failures, he was her sounding board for fanciful ideas, he was that calm other viewpoint which had so often brought perspective to her puzzles.

Now he was too weary for her to ask and she was too distracted to help with his burdens. It was, Lydia saw in a moment of clarity, no way to live, no way to nurture their relationship. Another six months of it and they would not so much fall out of love as drift apart and be lucky to find a paddle to rescue themselves. They did not have the half a lifetime of sharing and intimacy that might have sustained them through the leaner times.

Tomorrow she should say as much, but for now she said, "Shower and bed. I'll bring up a bottle. No Cuba and no Stoppes. But you can tell me about Havana and the hotel where we're going to stay."

Which he did until they both fell asleep and dreamed their separate dreams.

Morning brought refreshment for them both and a quiet start, each of them still a little preoccupied with their other lives. As Lydia wrestled with how to broach the subject of putting a limit on the time they spent apart, Stephen caught her unawares and said, "Can you see an end to the Stoppes business yet?"

"I think so. What about Cuba?"

"Possibly, although there might be a few trips for a while yet. But this phase is nearly over. We don't have a brief to explore further, even if we wanted to."

"Do you want to?"

"I've recommended a detailed survey of a much bigger area. It's being discussed. They'll want the answers from this excavation before they'll risk opening up another. And there are minefields to be removed before anyone can even think of a survey, never mind putting a spade in the ground."

"Actual minefields? That explode? You never said about minefields."

"That's how they found our first body, removing a

minefield. They took them all out before we started. But there are more, nearby."

Minefields and mass graves are items on the TV news, not things that touch you personally across the breakfast table. Lydia wondered how it was that her world had changed so completely in so short a time.

After a pause she said quietly, "You asked about the Stoppes business."

"Yes. I miss you, I miss us. We're not giving ourselves a chance. Coming home I thought a lot about how we might continue to do what we enjoy doing but see more of each other. I'm not ready to retire, I want to carry on at college and sometimes take up other opportunities. I'm sure you want to carry on with your work, I certainly want you to. But these last few months have been too much, too separate, for us. Certainly too much for me."

So, even without speaking, they had both sensed the malaise creeping into their lives. But where Lydia had struggled for the right words, hadn't even known how to start the conversation, Stephen had it all thought out, summed up and distilled to the essence of the problem.

"We have to finish what we're doing now."

"Oh yes," he nodded, "But that should be manageable. This next spell should be my last long trip. I was hoping you'd be able to come for a while too."

"I will, I hope. My time with the Stoppes may be coming to an end, and not the end I'd hoped for. Maybe this is not the right moment, but I really would like to talk about a problem that's come up. I think I've got things wrong, maybe it was always too big a thing, too important a thing. This is not just finding a home for a photo album or a couple of medals. There's a title and a great deal of money at stake here. I think I may have let people down, I think I'm out of my depth."

For once, Lydia's sense of incompetence was not accompanied by cruel self-loathing. Instead it felt like a realistic assessment, not something to be proud of but something she might nonetheless live with.

"I doubt it. You usually end up being right, even when you're sure you've got it wrong. Is it what Charmaine Thibaud was working on? And since whatever it is appeared, you've checked everything you've done? Yes, of course you have."

"I have, but more likely it's something I haven't done. And remember it all started off as trying to prove a negative anyway."

"Tell me."

So Lydia told Stephen of the DNA results and how they couldn't fit with anything she'd found, which meant she'd missed something, something very important, or the results were wrong and on balance she thought it was more likely to be her omission than Dr Charmaine Thibaud's mistake.

"With these readings I've no idea what it does to the trust or even the Baronetcy of St James," she concluded.

"You haven't told Derek Ballard yet?"

"No, this only happened on Thursday. He's had eye surgery, cataract removal, he may be back tomorrow."

"Even the competent Charmaine Thibaud is not infallible, and I'll look at the details later, but from what you say, it would be almost impossible for an error to come up with the actual father being a cousin or half brother."

"Which leaves my error."

"Well, yes it does, but the laboratory was dealing with a fixed and known set of data. You've been dealing with a huge and undefined set of data and with no way of knowing if you have included all the relevant items. Hardly an error unless it was right there in front of you. And even then ..."

"But where can I look now? I've exhausted the records, there's nothing in the family papers. The records might be wrong, there are plenty of errors in the registers, but for there to be nothing in the photo albums, no reference in the journals or accounts, no trace at all, that's too much."

"You say there were two cousins as well as the other son William?"

"Yes. Valentine, dead in a mine in Manitoba in 1917, the other, Albert, lost at Ypres in 1915."

"Then look there. Missing in action and reported dead in a mine accident isn't conclusive. Either could have survived."

"Agreed, but Albert's teeth were one of the samples, so he'd have been identified as the missing father. And how would Valentine have become the father of Charles and Elizabeth?"

"Who came back from Canada in the 1920s? Could it have been Valentine, swapping places with George? People have been known to do such things."

"The family would have known, he'd have been found out. And why would he?"

"Maybe they did know, maybe they wanted it that way, maybe having a baronet in the family was important. And maybe the money was important. People have been murdered for less, a lot less. I've seen it."

Which struck Lydia as providing a quite different slant on things. Was a family conspiracy to lie about the inheritance and the title remotely possible? It wouldn't be the first time Lydia had discovered criminal intent, but the Stoppes?

"I've never even considered it. Do you really think it's likely? It would change everything."

"I've no idea how likely, but it's possible. A lot more work for you, I'm sure. But I'm just playing devil's advocate here. And from what you say, everything's changed already."

ooo

Lydia had barely sent the message on Tuesday morning, *Call when you can, Stoppes developments, likely important*, before Derek Ballard was calling her back.

"What's happened?"

She told him.

"Let me get this right, the DNA says that Sir George, third baronet, is not the father of Sir Charles, fourth baronet?"

"Yes. But Sir Charles is the grandson of Sir Edwin."

"Based on the teeth you found."

"Yes."

"And Sir Charles' real father was likely a cousin of Sir George?"

"Or a brother or half brother."

The solicitor was silent for a few moments while he scribbled out a crude family diagram, rehearsing the relationships in a low whisper as he did so. When he was done he said, "Could the teeth be wrong?"

"They could. The question then is how and why would someone have mislabelled the little boxes. I can't make any sense of it. But the bottom line is I may have made a huge mistake somewhere or missed something."

"No, Lydia, the bottom line may be more profound than that. The succession and the inheritance may be flawed. I daren't even think about the implications of that. Unravelling that might keep several lawyers busy for years. I wouldn't begin to guess at what cost. Suppose for a moment that you haven't missed anything, haven't made this great mistake. What then? Who could be a candidate for the real father of Sir Charles?"

"Four theoretical possibilities. William Tremain, who never left Nova Scotia, Albert missing in action at Ypres but ruled out because the DNA from his teeth would have identified him as the father, Valentine dead in a mine accident in 1917, and fourth, an unknown, unrecorded, cousin or brother of the person whose teeth were labelled as being Sir George's."

"And your instinct is which?"

"They all seem impossible, which takes me back to it being

my mistake. Even if the mistake is in not finding that fourth person."

Again they fell silent until Derek said, "What next?"

"I thought I'd concentrate on Valentine and see if there is any hint of him surviving his supposed death. And tomorrow, or sometime this week, Dr Thibaud is due to tidy up the last couple of DNA samples, the ones I brought back from Nova Scotia. I'll go and see her then. Does that sound all right?"

"Yes, do that. I think I must make another call to Elaine Perryman, she's the barrister I've been sounding out about this business."

Lydia hesitated over adding, a little tentatively, "You remember Stephen's home on leave? I'm not doing the Stoppes full time for the next couple of weeks."

"Ah, yes, thank you for reminding me."

"How's your eye? did it all go OK?"

"Yes, thank you. A transformation. I'll get the other one done in a few weeks. But I can't drive for a day or two. Can you come to me if necessary?"

While Lydia had been talking to Derek Ballard, Stephen had slipped away to the study. When she found him he too was busy on the phone. As she came in he wrote *Paris* on his notepad and turned it towards her. They were both still at work, but at least they were under the same roof.

In the summerhouse she began her search for Valentine Charles Valence, the second baronet's nephew by his sister Mary. His birth was undisputed, recorded quite properly in 1884. Lydia's own notes had his journey to Canada as being on the *RMS Virginian* in 1909. She checked again and found the same information. Then she looked at everything she'd found about The Mary Mine, but where previously she was searching for a reference to George Stoppes in that connection, now it was Valentine who was the focus.

The history of the mine was superficial at best, and gave no details of personnel. A vague reference to production difficulties *towards the end of the first war* gave no details. There was no mention of Valentine in the available mine records, nor any she could find in death notices or newspapers. The provincial vital statistics site with its clunky search engine offered nothing better. No deaths recorded with a surname Valence for the whole year and a single Valentine – surname unknown and not in the same district as the mine – in December 1916. Yet as a partner or stakeholder in the mine, Valentine surely would have been an important enough figure to warrant careful recording of his death and the circumstances surrounding it.

All Lydia had to go on was Valentine's mother telling her brother Edwin that she'd been told her son was dead in an accident. She hadn't even known if he'd been given a *decent Christian burial.* If George had written with any details after he had arrived in Manitoba, he would most likely have written directly to Valentine's mother, his Aunt Mary, for there was no such letter in the Stoppes archives.

All of which left Lydia exactly where she had been a couple of hours previously, and, short of travelling to Manitoba to study the provincial archives, there was no further avenue of enquiry open to her.

When Stephen came to the summerhouse he brought coffee and the envelope of DNA reports that Charmaine Thibaud had prepared. He sat leafing through them, making no sign or sound to indicate his approval or otherwise. When he'd finished he put them aside and said, "I'm not expert enough to be sure, but it seems to me that Dr Thibaud has done an extremely thorough job with your Stoppes teeth. Every action recorded, every analysis delivered, even the Y-chromosome and the mitochondrial. I don't suppose she gets to do all the tests on each individual sample very often."

"I'm planning to see her later in the week, could we go together?"

"We could, and take that river trip we promised ourselves."

"I keep forgetting we're on holiday."

"But it's hard to switch off and do nothing. Especially when the rest of the world doesn't want us to stop. Did you get anywhere with your puzzle?"

"Not without going off to the wilds of Canada."

They sat in comfortable silence for a few minutes until Stephen asked, "How's your friend Gloria getting on?"

At the mention of Gloria's name, Lydia felt the ground move beneath her. Five days since she'd given Gloria a single thought. Five days in which her good intentions of finding a suitable tenancy contract had come to nothing. Her shortcomings as a landlord were as nothing compared to her deficiencies as a friend.

"Oooh," she moaned. "I don't know how she is, I should have been in touch. I should have done something about the tenancy. And a will, I need to make a will. Can you help me arrange it? Do you have a solicitor in Cambridge?"

"Not Derek Ballard then."

Lydia paused. Why not Derek?

"Not if we're doing it together. Are we? It doesn't matter really, I have to get something done, I promised."

Something about the conjunction of a solicitor and a promise took Lydia immediately back to a thought she'd first had only a couple of weeks into Stoppes enquiry, when she'd seen Robert Ballard's work diary from 1953, ... *he was set on it. He'd made a promise and would keep it.* And a short time later, ... *refused any alteration or advice.* The trust itself remained the biggest clue to what lay behind it, now this latest DNA contradiction underlined the fact.

If George had known that Charles and Elizabeth were not his children – and why shouldn't he? – that might account for the peculiar wording of the trust, the wording resisted by his own lawyer. And Sir George had, at least in part, created the trust as the result of a promise, most likely a promise made to someone who also knew the truth. Who more than his wife Miriam would know that he wasn't the father?

"Have you thought of something? Something important?" Stephen said, interrupting her reasoning.

"Sorry, yes. Let me make a note."

Quickly Lydia scribbled *Who was the promise made to? And when? Trust made in 1953.*

"Sorry, where were we? Oh yes, making wills. What do you think? Are we ready to do that? It feels as if we've had a trial separation rather than a trial living together."

"Maybe being apart has told us more about what we really want than being together."

"You're right. I have no doubts. Can we arrange something, something that works for us both? And for Jacqueline, of course. I only have my brother and nieces."

A little later when they'd made an appointment with a solicitor, Lydia texted Gloria: *How's the sick dog? Legals on house this week. Let's meet in Oxford soon.*

ooo

They had plenty of time before Charmaine Thibaud was expecting them, time in which they might get a sandwich and find a spot by the river to enjoy the sunshine, time which they might spend at the new exhibition at the Fitzwilliam, time to do a hundred things. But what they chose to do was visit a travel agent and book flights to Havana for Lydia. She would follow the same route as Stephen, via Paris, and travel in five weeks' time, three or just possibly two weeks after he'd returned to the exhumation site near Guantanamo. She'd stay for ten days, mainly in the temporary quarters with Stephen, but with a weekend at the little hotel in Havana that he'd so enjoyed.

It was a moment to commit, a moment to know what would be most important, regardless of what might be happening with Derek Ballard and the Stoppes or with Gloria and the house in Osney.

The Stoppes enquiry would have gone as far as she could take it by then, of that Lydia was quite sure. After all, wasn't it almost done now, even if the greatest puzzle remained. And if she was mistaken then the next step would simply have to wait until she returned. Hadn't Derek Ballard said it might keep several lawyers busy for years? A couple of weeks more wouldn't make much difference.

And Gloria's concerns over security would be settled soon. It had been simplicity itself to have a tenancy agreement drawn up, even if the legal assistant had questioned the minuscule rent. Lydia had settled on a token amount since it appeared that a rent of nothing meant there was no tenancy at all. With no tenancy there'd be none of the security that Gloria was seeking.

They'd also made their wills, or rather, they'd decided what should be in them and would sign them in a few days. Stephen had made only one change to his previous, which was to leave Lydia some money and the opportunity to live at The Old Rectory for as long as she wished. Only after Lydia's death would his daughter Jacqueline fully inherit her childhood home.

Completing these tasks had left them both slightly euphoric, as if great things had been achieved, hence the moment to commit and the booking of flights.

As previously, Charmaine Thibaud was waiting at the entrance, expecting to smooth Lydia's way to the laboratory.

"Oh, Professor Kellaway," she said, a slight deference clear in her voice. "I had no idea you'd be here today. In fact, I'd heard that you were away on a project with the UN."

"I am, but I'm on leave, so here I am. I hope that's not inconvenient."

"Not at all, we're delighted to see you."

Lydia had forgotten how much respect Stephen attracted

from his peers and colleagues. There'd been a time when she'd also been a little in awe of him, a time when his titles and learning made her own skills feel trivial. Now she saw a little of that in the esteemed Doctor of Genetics who was welcoming them.

The two academics occupied the walk to the lab with a discussion about the new equipment and the possibilities which it opened up. Lydia trailed in their wake, not knowledgeable enough to contribute nor fully understand, but pleased that she could at least follow the conversation and gain something from it. Her reading on DNA and genetics over the previous few weeks had not been time entirely wasted.

"Now, Lydia, these two saliva samples," Charmaine said as they settled at her table. "I've produced reports in the same format as the other subjects, and I've re-drawn the summary of the family group." She pushed the reports and their accompanying thumb drives across to Lydia. "You'll be pleased to know you were right about your Edwin Tremain gaining a grandchild. The first sample, you marked it Ameline, is not only the granddaughter of Edwin and therefore a cousin to Charles and Elizabeth, but also the daughter of your *GM* or George, the one who wasn't the father of Charles and Elizabeth. Does that fill in a big gap in this family?"

Lydia was silent as she studied the revised summary. It simply could not be that Ameline was George's daughter. George was at The Mary Mine when she was born; her father was William, for whom there were no samples, no baby teeth in a jewelled keepsake box.

Stephen reached carefully across and took the details from Lydia, studied them briefly and then returned them. He knew enough to understand the fresh contradiction that Charmaine Thibaud's work had introduced to the equation.

"And the other one?" Lydia said hoarsely. "That's Anne-

Marie. Her great-grandfather is Edwin, yes? And her grandfather is George too?"

"Exactly so. Of course as the relationships get more distant there's more chance of anomalies, but with a fairly close family group like this we can have great confidence even over a few more generations."

The finer points of likelihood and degrees of uncertainty all had their place, but for Lydia and for Derek Ballard, for the trust and the Stoppes themselves, the nuances were irrelevant. The family tree needed to be redrawn. The Stoppes were not who they thought they were. Almost, but not quite.

"Thank you so much Dr Thibaud, Charmaine, you've been brilliant," Lydia said, recovering herself. "The work you've done, it might have implications for the family, for all manner of things. One day someone might want you to swear to the truth of it. Or do it again and swear to the truth of that."

"I'm sure I could do that," she said, glancing briefly at Stephen.

ooo

"These should be kept somewhere safe," Stephen said, holding the nine flimsy freezer bags each containing a small forensic sample box.

"Where's best? I don't want them in the fridge for ever and a day."

"No, they need somewhere special, forensic storage. I know someone who will know the right place. Will you tell Derek? There'll be a fee of some kind."

"Yes, I'll let him know, then it'll be up to him."

Arranging special storage for the Stoppes' baby teeth was the least of the things Lydia should be telling Derek Ballard. The simple facts from the DNA analysis needed telling above all else, but Lydia held back. The first thing Derek would ask would be what she thought, and at that moment she was still shocked by the revelation.

"If the person the world thought was William, was actually George, does that mean that the George here in England was actually William?"

"Only yesterday the George here in England might really have been Valentine."

"I can't call Derek again and tell him it's all changed."

But she would have to at some point. And at some point soon, Lydia knew that.

"It would seem logical that if the man in Nova Scotia was really George, then the man in England was William. If not, then there was a third person involved in the swapping, which seems even less likely," Stephen suggested.

"It certainly messes up the baronetcy. The Nova Scotia family should have inherited. Peter Tremain is not just a possible claimant with a doubtful chance, he's the next in line and should have been all along. How's that going to play out?"

"Very slowly, I should think," Stephen said dryly.

"You know, this all rests on two baby teeth put in a box more than a century ago. Could it be that the teeth were swapped and the people were not? I can't see a single reason that such a thing might happen, and if it did where's William's little trinket box? And aside from a bizarre accidental switching, where's the motivation? Until the discovery of DNA what possible reason would there have been?"

"Your William in Nova Scotia lost his memory didn't he?"

"Yes, and there is documentary evidence of that. His nurse's journals still exist in the archives."

"Maybe he remembered being the wrong person."

"Because that's what his paper's said?"

"Short version: he picked up the wrong jacket, took a big bang on the head, lost everything until his doctor or nurse told him he was William. Possible."

"Yes," Lydia said slowly, "possible, but too short. At first he was reported as dead."

"OK."

"But he was reported dead by George. George Stoppes wrote to his parents and told them William was dead. George told the first-aid station where he was taken and pronounced dead that the dead man was his half brother William Tremain. It wasn't that the dead man just happened to have put on the wrong jacket. He had William's papers in his pocket, he was reported as being William by George. George went to Manitoba. George came back to England and became the third baronet."

"But George wasn't George, was he?"

"Not if we are to believe the teeth."

"I want to say that the teeth don't lie and, of course, they don't. It is safe to accept that the Nova Scotia people, Ameline was it, and Anne-Marie? It is safe to accept that they are direct descendants from the owner of the teeth. Whether they are George's teeth is another question."

"So," Lydia mused, "do we believe the teeth's label or do we believe the writer of letters who signed himself *your affectionate son George Melville*? In fact, who continued signing himself George for the rest of his life."

"A lie repeated doesn't make a second or third lie. Neither does it make it make it any truer. The teeth were labelled as they were for more than a hundred years, but the years don't make it a truer label. In weighing the evidence it should simply be a question of whether the teeth were correctly labelled or was the man calling himself George telling the truth."

"And those two facts are mutually exclusive, aren't they?"

"Yes, apparently. If they were the true George's teeth then he became William."

"Who would have put those babies' teeth in their little treasure boxes? Surely only a mother. Or a nanny on instructions from a mother. It would be hard to make a mistake with just a single child in the household losing his milk teeth. And I keep coming back to motive and finding none."

The afternoon drifted away in an unsatisfactory cloud of indecision. Although Lydia's only true interest in the Stoppes family history was to present the facts, or their alternatives, to Derek Ballard, she was keen to be sure of her own interpretation of those facts. And mixed up with her interpretation were the implications for the living Stoppes family, both at the St James Manor and in Nova Scotia. And, for that matter, in a bar somewhere in Thailand or Cambodia.

Unable to resolve any of the questions, she finally texted Derek Ballard: *Beginning to look like 3rd bt was actually William while George lived in ns as William. Implications for trust? Huge?*

Within a few moments he called her.

"Is this why he created the trust in the way he did? Because he knew very well there could be another line of succession?" he said, with little in the way of a greeting.

"Perhaps," Lydia answered as calmly as she could, "although at one point he certainly thought his brother was dead. Something must have put a doubt in his mind."

Even as she said the words Lydia remembered two things. First that the third baronet had made the trust partly because of a promise he had made to someone, someone who must have known the truth. And second that there was something that could have sown such a doubt: a letter from Kenneth Tremain in 1943 referring to his father William who'd lost his memory.

"Ooh, I know what that was," she said, and told him. "Of course he knew there might be another line, the real George would've had no need to create such a strange trust. The real

George would have had no doubts. And I can guess who that promise was made to, but I want to check my dates."

"This is getting very messy. I can't even begin to imagine the fallout from this."

"Yes. Sorry," she said, even though it was no fault of hers.

They were silent for a few moments before Derek said, almost as an aside, "Elaine Perryman, the barrister, asked if I had the original Letters Patent, the Grant of Baronetcy, she thought it would be useful to see. I don't have it, as you know, but didn't you say you'd seen it in London?"

"In the family deposit box. I can ask Georgina to get it or she and I could go there together. But I can tell you where there's a copy of the standard, the template, if you like, that all the grants were copied from. Look online for *A History of the Baronetage* by Pixley."

By the time Lydia had finished with Derek Ballard, Stephen had moved into the garden. He'd put a couple of glasses and a cool bottle of Prosecco in the summerhouse while he inspected his garden and all that had grown since he'd last seen it.

"We haven't had much time to enjoy this place," he said when she joined him. "We should make more, make that part of the changes we spoke of, not just travelling and bucket-listing."

For a few minutes she let the day and the garden consume her, let the Stoppes and their mysteries slip away. Stephen's gentle company was addictive, more than she remembered. Perhaps it was simply that she was more addicted, absence, as ever, making the heart grow fonder. But he was also her intimate, her honest opinion and partner in delving into ancient history – and the Stoppes would not be denied.

"I was thinking about William and George, about how those few moments in Halifax in 1917 must have been for them. One minute a clear path ahead, for them both. The next, completely without warning, everything changed. They were only two among thousands, who knows what miseries and changes befell all the others, we can only guess, but we know how it changed for our two. I wondered about the actual moment of the explosion and the minutes that followed. What really happened to them? Was it just as George said? And if it wasn't George doing the saying, if it was a lie, if it was William who'd become George, what should we believe and what should we not?"

"You're believing the teeth, not the letter writer."

"I think I am," she said quietly.

"The moment he told the people at the first-aid post that the injured man was William Tremain, the moment he showed them William's papers, there was no going back. There was no saying, 'oh, sorry, no, I got that wrong, I'm William and this is really George.' He was utterly committed from that moment on. For ever."

"That would have been quite a leap to make on the spur of the moment."

"To immediately see the possibilities and seize the opportunity? Yes, that needed very clear thinking from someone who a few seconds earlier had been almost blown apart."

12

Lydia sifted through her notes until she found the entry she was looking for. Elizabeth Calbain died December 5th 1952, just one month before Sir George, or William as he probably was, approached his solicitor about setting up the trust.

For a long time Lydia had considered Miriam, the third baronet's wife, as the most likely person to have been made the promise that prompted the setting up of the trust. Now, with William apparently having taken George's name and place at the manor house, there was a better candidate: his mother, Elizabeth Calbain. A mother surely knows her own son, even if he has been away for ten years or more, even if he has sprouted a beard and been injured in an explosion.

More than that, in 1943 Elizabeth Calbain had received a letter from Kenneth Tremain asking for information about his father William, a father Elizabeth must have known was not her son. And in knowing it was not William, she must have known that it was almost certainly George. Yet no matter how great the wrong that had been done, she did not denounce her son. Instead, she extracted a promise from him that he would do his best to ensure George's children and grandchildren did not lose their inheritance completely.

"It wasn't a wholehearted repentance though, was it?" Stephen suggested.

"Because?"

"He knew the facts, he could have let them be known, instead of hiding behind ifs and maybes," Stephen said, a little more harshly that he might usually have spoken.

"That might have deprived his own children of their position and privilege. And those children were also his mother's grandchildren. Maybe she didn't want the record set too straight. I suppose above all else you are loyal to your own children, regardless of their sins. Imagine if you found that Jacqueline had committed some fraud or deception."

He thought for a moment or two before saying, "You're right. More than that, I would hope she got away with it, hope she avoided any kind of retribution. But I would like to think I'd tell her she was wrong and tell her she should make some kind of reparation."

"Yes, you would. Maybe this was Elizabeth Calbain's feeling too. There's nobody else who'd have known the truth. As you said, there was no going back. Poor George in Halifax might not have known who he was, but William certainly did. Without that promise to his mother he might have done nothing and nobody would ever have been the wiser."

As the afternoon grew cool and a shower threatened, they retreated to the comfort of the drawing room. Lydia tried reading her new book but couldn't get started, the Stoppes and their history, particularly George and William, were too much of a distraction.

"Stephen," she said after a long silence, "what did you mean earlier when you said how it needed very clear thinking when William passed George's body off as his own?"

"It may have been a sudden impulsive decision, seizing what he saw as an opportunity to take his younger brother's better position in life. It may have been just that, but to do it he must surely have at least considered the idea previously. If you've never thought of such a thing, I don't think it comes to you at such moments. I think the first thought is always the welfare of your brother. Or your friend, I don't think it needs to be a close relative. But the first instinct is not 'what can I get out of this?'"

"Maybe it wasn't his first thought. After all, he did go looking for help. Maybe he only had the idea when he thought that George was dead."

"He *said* he went looking for help."

"Why wouldn't ...?"

Lydia answered her own question before she'd even finished it. One big lie. Locked in, no going back. Everything that followed was fashioned to support that one big lie. She didn't want to ask the next question, she hadn't given it enough thought herself. Her imagination was working overtime as possibilities whirled through her head. If William had made the big lie about who was who, had he made an even bigger lie about what exactly happened? In the chaos and confusion of the biggest explosion the world had ever known, anything was possible. He might get away with anything.

"When you said about it needing some very clear thinking, were you also suggesting ... something else, something more sinister?"

"Suggesting, no. But wondering, yes."

"That he might have ... I don't want to even think it ... he might have made George's injuries worse, might have attacked him?"

"Might have tried to kill him?"

"Yes. Were you wondering that?"

"I was. It was the idea that William must have previously considered taking George's place. It seemed to me to lead on quite naturally to William doing something about it, not just seeing an opportunity." After a moment, suddenly tired, he added, "I've seen too many dead people recently."

"I'm sorry, it's not fair of me. I'm just preoccupied. I'll stop. Shall we eat out tonight?"

"And talk about what over our meal?" he asked gently. "Something trivial while you're thinking about George and William? No, we'll eat here. Please, carry on with what you were saying."

She hesitated before continuing, "You'd think maybe that if William had an idea to kill George and take his place that he might have done so long before they got to Halifax. From all I've read and found, nobody spoke of any animosity between them. Their father packed them off to Canada without any reservations and their aunt thought it a good idea, even said how they'd compliment each other, what one couldn't do the other would."

"Do you know what she meant by that?"

"It's a guess really, but William had some disability in his leg I think, and George's shoulder was hurt at school in a shooting accident. The headmaster wrote to his father about it."

As Lydia recalled the details of the grovelling letter almost begging Sir Edwin to not take the matter any further, a fresh picture of the scene in the school shooting range sprang to her mind. William Tremain was also present at this near-death experience. She'd found no other account of the incident, no follow-up apportioning blame, nothing to suggest any ill-intention from William or the other cadet present at the time. But George was badly injured. Being shot in the shoulder, even with a training rifle, was very close to being shot in the head, very close to being killed.

Stephen nodded in agreement when she told him the details. "A trial run, perhaps, if you've a cynical turn of mind. Or completely unconnected, simply an accident with a gun when unsupervised young men fool around. He'd certainly not be the first person to be shot by a gun thought to be empty. Nor the first to be shot by someone claiming it was an accident."

"It must have been hard growing up with a younger brother, an official child while you were always semi-official, known for what you were but unacknowledged. And watching your little brother getting preference at every turn, being groomed to be the next baronet. And if you were disabled as well ..."

"Was that an accident, too?"

"Maybe, I didn't find anything like that, but it seems he used a cane."

"Did anything else happen to the young George? Falling off a horse, an almost-drowning, a cricket bat accidentally connecting with his skull?"

"There was something, but I don't remember exactly, something else at school. It must have been in a letter. And William ran up a big medical bill at school himself."

"Do you know who the doctor was? He might've been important, there could be a record of his specialisms. It seems there's a record of practically everything."

It took Lydia a while to find the reference, deep in Gloria's files rather than her own as she'd remembered it. The attending physician and sender of large bills was Sir Bernard Rothwell. Stephen was right, there was a record, more than a record, a short biography at the Royal College of Physicians which showed that he had a special interest in Heine–Medin disease or infantile paralysis, both later known as poliomyelitis.

It wasn't proof, but it was certainly an indication of why William might have walked with a cane. Polio in the early 1900s was a fearful affliction, with death a distinct possibility. William may have got away lightly with only an impaired leg. Which, Lydia reminded herself, was very easy for her to think, less easy for a fit boy of eleven to think when his football and cricket were taken away from him. All the more galling to watch his younger brother grow into the sporting life while he was relegated to the sidelines.

Lydia showed Sir Bernard's brief biography to Stephen.

"Not only is there a record of practically everything, that's always been the case, but now it's an instantly accessible record."

"Have you been using records to fill in the background to your victims? Finding context for their lives? And their deaths too, I suppose."

"Sadly, no. We are entirely limited to facts that we can extract from the bodies and the ground they were in. Likely or certain cause of death, age, gender, likely date of death. Calibre of bullet, number of bullets, entry points, exit points, clothing and labels, personal possessions. And don't forget DNA and the condition of their teeth. I could go on, the list of facts we can obtain is almost endless. But speculation on who might have pulled the trigger, or why, or relating the deaths to any other event is all for others to draw conclusions. When I say deaths, they were all murders and not even official, judicial, murders. They were killed for their beliefs or their willingness to fight for them or to keep them quiet. Some may simply have been in the wrong place at the wrong time – a father taken from a son's house, a brother hiding at his sister's. Maybe a few old scores were settled too, who would know now?

"I can say that to you, but I cannot say that in any report. None of our people – we've begun to call them our people – were dumped with a signed confession from their killers in their pockets. And we're not so foolish that we think our people were innocent, we know they may have also killed in their time and in similar fashion to their own deaths."

It was a bleak assessment of every aspect of his grisly work.

"Old scores? I suppose it must happen. When fortunes change and the tide turns, old scores get settled. We're so pampered and protected, we forget how truly ugly war is, how quickly civilised values disappear."

"It is a thin veneer at best."

When they'd had their supper and begun to think about the end of their day, Lydia sat scrolling through photographs on her phone. She had accumulated hundreds from the Stoppes enquiry, many duplicated to be sure she had a readable record, and she had already forgotten the significance of some. But she had deleted none, so she was fairly sure she would have taken a photograph of a letter from George's house-master at Snaresby College. It meant enlarging and reading the first few words of each letter she'd photographed, but at length she found it.

Sir Edwin

I write to inform you that your son George, for whom I have the privilege of caring, has recently been confined to the sick-bay with a case of chickenpox. I am informed that it is a mild case and he remains in good spirits. You should be aware, however, of an incident which occurred last night during which the recently installed gas fire leaked noxious gasses which permeated the area. Your son was found nauseous and light-headed after the alarm was raised and you will be pleased to know that he has quickly recovered, although he does remain under Matron Queasly's close supervision. You will also be happy to hear that William Tremain is allowed to visit each day as he is known to have previously been infected with George's ailment.

When she'd read it twice and wondered at the proximity of William to another moment of danger to George, Lydia passed her phone to Stephen.

"At the very least William must have realised that George could have died. At the very worst he could have opened the gas tap."

ooo

Georgina placed the pale blue box with the faded script and red wax on the library table.

"And I've bought a fire-proof safe to keep it in," she said.

She'd fetched the box and its precious contents from the bank in Fleet Street the previous day. Now she and Lydia were going to completely unfold the stiff vellum and make copies of it, both photographic and a transcription. Aided by a copy of the standard document from *A History of the*

Baronetage, Lydia was expecting the process to be quite straightforward. It was after all, simply a matter of looking at the obscure Gothic handwriting, using the plain English version to interpret it, then making as sure as possible that the plain version represented a fair interpretation of the Gothic version. Doing it in tandem with Georgina should ensure accuracy and bring two minds to bear on any difficult passages. And if they couldn't resolve some discrepancy then it might be for more learned minds than theirs to interpret.

It was not an easy balance between being gently respectful of the old document and the need to press it flat to read and photograph it. The complication of the Great Seal of England, attached by a cord to the bottom of the sheet, required especially careful handling. But as they worked, the vellum began to bend to their will more easily, assisted by some heavyweight volumes from the library shelves. After ten minutes or so the sheet was face down, revealing the brief inscription on the reverse – and apparently none the worse for the process.

The wording amounted to little more than a wrapper for the whole, noting the date of the warrant and that it had been duly recorded at the College of Arms in a manner *for correcting and preventing abuses of the Order of Baronets*. Lydia wondered if such abuse included impersonating your half brother. Having transcribed and photographed the words they turned the document right-side up and replaced the book weights along the edges.

It was a very grand document in every sense of the word. The first line with its engraved portrait of the great queen overlaying the illuminated V of Victoria was something to behold. Everything else on the page, and presumably the world, was subservient to *Victoria by the Grace of God*.

When Lydia had meticulously photographed the whole document they set about making the transcription. With the template to guide them the first few lines were easy enough.

One or two words might have fooled them if it weren't for that, but otherwise it was straightforward. At the first gap in the standard text, where the new baronet's name should be inserted, the Stoppes warrant correctly had *Clarence Charles Tremain Stoppes of St James in our city of Westminster*. The name was repeated as simply *Clarence Stoppes* no less than three times in the following lines. There could hardly be any doubt over who was being granted a baronetcy.

The deviation from the standard came shortly afterwards. Where the template indicated *and the heirs male of his body lawfully begotten and to be begotten*, the Stoppes warrant had something different. One word. No matter how much they tried to fit the letters to be *lawfully* they stubbornly refused to comply.

Georgina had the bright idea of looking for other occurrences of the same shaped letter and then seeing how that letter appeared on the template. After a little time they had assembled sufficient letters to make a stab at the tiresome word.

"Howsoever!" Georgina said triumphantly, and once she'd said so then it became obvious.

"*And the heirs male of his body howsoever begotten and to be begotten*," Lydia read aloud.

"*Howsoever begotten*. I don't think they had test-tube babies in mind when they wrote that. Would that mean illegitimate sons could also inherit the title?"

"Yes, I think so, especially when you consider the standard was *lawfully begotten*. But it may need a lawyer to decide that."

"You need a lawyer to decide anything. But does it make any real difference? I mean, of course there's a difference, but will it really make any difference? It's fascinating, I'm thoroughly enjoying it all, but it seems somehow irrelevant, academic, not something that will touch me or Amanda or Felicity."

"If it means what we think, then it makes a huge difference. And again, it makes no difference at all. I think there likely is a sixth baronet, I think it will take a lot of sorting out. I don't think the trust will be wound up anytime soon, and that's probably all that would really affect life here. But that's not for me to say or even guess," Lydia added hastily.

"Shall we do the rest and see what other surprises there are?"

Which they did, and found none. The three further places where Clarence's name were inserted were all completed correctly. The whole document, apart from that one word, was exactly as the template suggested it should be.

As they sat in the kitchen contemplating their discovery over a glass of wine, a buzz of questions swarmed in Lydia's head. Foremost amongst these was, who knew?

"Did Sir Christopher ever say anything about the succession to the baronetcy? Anything that might suggest he knew about the wording?"

"No, now and again he would tease the girls about how they couldn't inherit. Otherwise no. I don't think I ever heard the question discussed. It was assumed, it didn't need discussion. Unless it was a family secret, so secret that everyone forgot about it."

"I can't imagine what Derek Ballard will say. I seem to be telling him something different every day. I keep thinking about the last time we saw the Letters Patent at the bank, and how it was too difficult to read and I said I'd do it later because I was sure they were all the same."

"You weren't to know."

"No, but I should have checked. A lot of stuff might have been cut short if I had."

"If you hadn't done all that you have then we might never have seen it. Nobody would have been any the wiser and the assumption would have continued. I would never have thought to check. I didn't even know it existed."

Georgina went to top up their glasses but Lydia stopped her. "I have to drive home."

"You can always stay here. You know you'd be welcome."

"I know, thank you, but Stephen is home. We haven't seen much of each other. You know how it is."

"Yes," said Georgina after a slight hesitation, "I know how it is."

ooo

Derek Ballard stooped a little to embrace Lydia as she greeted him.

"Thank you for coming over, and welcome to The Old Rectory," she said.

"I'm glad to come, it's very good of you to make time to see me. I haven't forgotten that Stephen is home."

"Except that he isn't, he's in college this afternoon."

Lydia led the way through to the terrace where afternoon tea was waiting for them. Mrs Webb had been in the house that morning and found little to occupy her time, so she'd filled the freezer and made scones.

"I hope you don't have any more surprises for me today," Derek said as they settled in the sunshine. "I think Elaine Perryman is beginning to be a little weary of my daily calls, although it turned out that yesterday's has provided a great talking point, even what might pass for excitement in a barrister's sober world."

"Because of the Stoppes baronetcy?"

"Indeed, yes. Apparently it answered a long-standing question of succession. There was known to have been only one example of what is called The Bastard's Remainder, and that was way back in the 1600s. It had been rumoured for years that there was a second, but to which baronetcy it was attached was unknown. More properly it is called a Special Remainder, but I rather like The Bastard's Remainder."

"Remainder?"

"The terms of the succession."

"So William was the rightful third baronet after all. That one word *howsoever* really does change everything."

"So it seems. I must stress this is purely based on counsel's opinion. To be absolutely certain we will probably have to wait until the succession is tested in the College of Arms, or even some higher court. Did you have any idea this was on the cards?"

"No, not at all, but I should have guessed there was something. The first baronet, Sir Clarence, wrote to his son when William was born. He shared his own illegitimacy and spoke well of his father, urging Edwin to do likewise and take care of his new son. I was looking at that letter earlier. It spoke of the baronetcy being a unique honour given to the family. It might have been unique to the family but there's nothing unique about a baronetcy, although it didn't strike me when I read it. Now I think he meant it as a reference to the terms of succession."

"He must have pulled some strings to have that variation included. Elaine wondered if he'd been offered something more, a barony perhaps and was bargained down to a baronetcy in exchange for his Special Remainder. My question is why keep it secret, or at least, why not tell his son about it?"

"Maybe he did, or maybe Sir Clarence thought the Letters Patent would be enough. And then again, Sir Edwin thought that William was dead, so he had no reason to mention any special terms of the succession. After William, George was the rightful successor."

As they ate their scones and drank their tea, the Stoppes, their millions and their titles, the manor house and its estates, all stepped back a little, as if knowing their time in the spotlight was drawing to close. It wasn't quite finished but the outcome was clear. After a few minutes Derek Ballard said as much.

"Lydia, can you complete all this, give me a final report, and a final account too?"

"The report's all but done. I take it the trust will not be wound up yet?"

"No, definitely not. I knew as much but the advice from counsel is quite firm. There is good reason to think that there is a successor to the title. The only people who could possibly object are also beneficiaries of the trust as it stands. I think they'll be quite content that it continues."

"Have you told Georgina yet?"

"Not at great length, but I spoke to her this morning and told her the trust would continue, nothing will change for her or Felicity and Amanda."

"I like Georgina, I think we may become friends after this. Better friends, I should say. She hasn't adjusted to life without her dear Chris."

"It's a very big house for one person, even if you have family visiting. But I suppose when it's been your home for more than forty years you wouldn't be in any hurry to leave."

"It's more the absence of Sir Christopher than anything else. I think they were very close. In a funny way I think my being there, the whole investigation, has been good for her. She's got to know more about his family than she ever knew before. She's even found things in her own house she didn't know were there. Will you give her a copy of the report and all my notes?"

"I wasn't going to, but I can, if you like. No reason not to. Or you could, that may be better."

"Yes, I'll do that. What about Peter Tremain, will you make any effort to locate him?"

"That's not yet decided. It seems that the process of succeeding to a title has changed over the years and Peter

Tremain's claim is complicated to say the least. Perhaps not on paper, perhaps not to you or me, but to prove the claim might require a case to be brought. That way there'd be no comeback from anybody."

"You'll need the teeth, and I need them out of the fridge," Lydia said, and proceeded to tell Derek about the specialist storage for forensic specimens.

"Will you write to Peter's mother?"

"Yes, we'll do that. If she hears from him it might start the ball rolling."

Around them the afternoon grew calmer, the little gusts and eddies from the heat of the day dying down to nothing. Lydia wondered if Derek had something else to say, an unmentioned topic he was hesitating over. Georgina's comment about how highly he thought of her came back, along with the moment at his uncle's cottage, a moment of physical closeness while they studied a painting. Suddenly she wished for Stephen to be home. His arrival would surely mark the end of Derek's visit, while his absence invited him to stay.

"Come and look at the rest of the garden," Lydia said, needing movement instead of being pinned to her chair.

They walked slowly round, as Lydia babbled about flowers and fruit of which she knew next to nothing. Derek smiled and nodded in all the right places until they reached the summerhouse, where Lydia explained she'd done so much of her work on the Stoppes.

"I should say, Lydia, you were exactly the right person for all this. It was an impossible job in many ways, but you've been an enormous help. I know the family think so. And Gloria's a gem, too. Thank her will you, please? I hope you're not sorry you took it on."

"Of course not," she said, relieved at what he hadn't said. "It's been brilliant. I wish I'd, well, done better, been a little quicker on the uptake in some places."

Then he said, "There's something else I want to ask you, too," and her stomach did a little flip.

ooo

They'd planned to spend the day on the river, a lazy summer cruise for four or five hours with lunch served on board. It was something they'd promised themselves since Lydia first came to The Old Rectory, long before she'd taken up residence there. But their plans were thwarted by the weather. The lunch and the cruise could still have been had, but only with everything battened down to keep out the wind and driving rain.

They had three days before Stephen would be whisked away to Heathrow, Paris and Havana, three more days of their trial living together before their trial separation resumed. But this leaving would be a little different to his previous departures. The separation had done its work, reinforced the sharing of their lives, underlined the importance of spending those shared lives as often as possible in a shared space.

Now Thursday was washed out, but they adjusted quickly and went to the new exhibition at The Fitzwilliam for a couple of hours before lunch in college, in the Armoury, that very private dining room perched in a corner overlooking Second Court. They were the only diners.

"What do you think, in the end?" Stephen said as they finished their rosemary braised lamb.

"About William and George? There's no getting away from one fact, William took George's place and passed George's supposedly dead body off as being his. That cannot have been an accident, or a clerical error. Is it conceivable that William himself was concussed, confused, couldn't tell dream from reality and thought he was George? I wish it was, but for them both to wake up not knowing who they were? What are the chances? No, sorry, he simply lied."

"For obvious reasons."

"Yes, for obvious reasons," Lydia agreed regretfully.

"And the other stuff with the shooting and the gas fire and who knows what else?"

"I think he wanted to see what he could get away with, wanted to test the limits. Maybe he wanted to damage his brother too, give him a disability to match his own."

A college servant, his lush silver-grey hair matching his butler's apron, appeared noiselessly to remove their empty plates before gliding away to the unseen kitchens. A minute or two later he returned with profiteroles perfectly arranged in triangular pyramids.

"It's a horrible irony that William should have done all that he did to take something that was already his. The repercussions, not just then, but down the years and still echoing today, were huge," Stephen said.

"If he'd have known about the special remainder, his whole life might have been different. He'd have grown up with quite different values and a different outlook. He wouldn't have lived a lie for more than half his life. And he wouldn't have created the St James Trust."

"If and if and if ... the consequences are unknowable. If George hadn't been shot he might have been fit enough to go to Flanders instead of Canada. In which case he might never have returned. There'd be no Halifax family, William might never have travelled alone, you would never have heard of the Stoppes and the baronetcy might have died out many years ago."

"Everything different. Everything."

A squall of rain briefly splattered across the leaded glass of the window overlooking the quad below, pulling them from an imagined past to present reality.

"How did you leave it with Derek Ballard? Is it done?"

"Yes, it's done. Or as done as it's going to be. He has

everything I can give him. Even my invoice, which I felt bad about."

"So that's that."

"Not quite, I'd like to keep up with Georgina, I think you'd like her very much. When your work in Cuba is over I think we should have her over."

"Of course."

"There's something else, too," Lydia said, "I didn't mention it last night, I don't know why, but Derek Ballard asked if I'd like to have a look at another project, something quite different. He has a friend or a client, I'm not really sure which, maybe both, who wants to find out what medals her grandfather was entitled to from his war service. I said it would have to wait, but I'd have a look at it."

ooo

Lydia had parked as she'd done previously, a little away from her house in West Street. Then, instead of walking to the door and knocking, she'd taken the towpath to the lock and then on towards Grandpont, beside the slow summer river. At seven she'd been too early for any but the most determined of joggers and a handful of college and hotel staff cycling to their duties. And at seven it was still three hours before Gloria was expecting her.

Once in the city she'd breakfasted in the quiet busyness of the Covered Market, indulging herself with the egg and bacon of her memories. It didn't disappoint. As the food on her plate had disappeared she'd eaten more and more slowly, stretching out the time to savour each minute and mouthful.

Then it had been back to the river, a little busier than earlier. For a few minutes she paused opposite the marina, promising herself that she would continue to return to the Thames in Oxford for as long as she was able, regardless of whether or not she still owned the house in West Street. And when she was not able, she'd return in her mind, reliving such mornings as this.

In her bag was the paperwork for Gloria and Eddie to sign, the essential agreement to give them the security they deserved. It would mean security for their child too, when it was born. Not that Gloria was going to sign before making further objections about wanting to pay her way and not relying on handouts. Her complaints had bounced back and forth by email and text over the previous few days as Lydia had stood her ground. It was either the token rent or Lydia would give them enough for a deposit on their own house, Gloria could take her pick of the lesser of two evils. And should Lydia die while they were still her tenants, they would inherit the house anyway. But, to avoid more argument, she hadn't mentioned this detail to Gloria. If it happened then she wouldn't be around to argue the point.

By the time she stood in front of her door in West Street it was almost ten.

Acknowledgements

As any writer will agree, creating a story such as *Old Wrongs* may be a solitary task but it can never be achieved without the help of others. That help comes in all forms, from the simple encouragement of friends and family to the huge contribution made by a first reader and an editor. My first reader and tireless editor is Grace Keating, to whom I'm eternally grateful for her wisdom and insight.

Sometimes the help is specific and solicited. For *Old Wrongs* I had to learn about the Baronetcy, its history, and its processes; about DNA analysis to a much deeper level than may be apparent from the story; about real-world locations, like Hoares Bank, where I chose the Stoppes family to have their London account. All these topics required the help of experts.

For knowledge of the Baronetcy, I am most grateful to three people in particular. First to Sarah Rawlings, secretary to the Standing Council of the Baronetcy, for her time and patience in answering my many questions without complaint. Second, to Grant Bavister of the College of Arms for his detail responses to my queries and for pointing me to other valuable resources. And last, but by no means least, to Sir Charles Knowles of Lovell Hill, 7th Baronet, for remembering an old friend from back in the day and for happily exploring his own heritage, thereby furnishing me with details I might never otherwise have found.

For my new knowledge of DNA and the processes involved in analysis, I am particularly grateful to Dr Sue Pope of Principal Forensic Services who went far beyond answering my questions by offering insight into the Stoppes family relationships as I proposed them. Any errors that may be detected in Old Wrongs are all my own, *not* Dr Pope's.

For reasons of security, none of the details of the bank in Fleet Street are quite as I have described them. However, it was the true sense of the place, so important in any story, that I wished to capture. For helping me achieve that, my grateful thanks go to Pamela Hunter, Archivist at C Hoare & Co, who so generously gave of her time and knowledge.

So many contributions, other than my own, have gone into making *Old Wrongs*. Thank you all.

David Wiseman
Annapolis Royal, NS
December 2022

About the author

DJ Wiseman was born and educated in Essex, UK. Having lived on the South Coast and in Bristol, he settled in Oxfordshire in 1973. In recent years he's lived in Canada, where he's now a resident of Nova Scotia.

Lifelong interests include travel, maps, reading and photography. For more than twenty-five years he's had a passionate interest in genealogy, discovering branches of his family scattered round the globe.

His writing, both short and long, has been recognised and enjoyed by readers and critics alike on both sides of the Atlantic. He continues to work on ideas for future projects.

Other novels
A Habit of Dying *2010*
The Subtle Thief of Youth *2012*
The Death Of Tommy Quick And Other Lies *2016*
Casa Rosa *2019*

By The Same Author

A Habit Of Dying

Amongst the old photo albums Lydia Silverstream discovers a disturbing journal, the key to one puzzle but an enigma in itself. In her attempts to re-unite the family albums with their rightful owner, Lydia travels the country from Oxford to Essex, Cumbria to Sussex. As the story of the blighted family is pieced together from the fragments of history, the tantalizing journal with its deeper, darker secrets comes to dominate both past and present.

"A well crafted, intriguing and enjoyable tale."
– *Oxford Journal*

"A well written, well paced piece of puzzle-solving that will please family history buffs and fans of old-fashioned detective stories alike." – *Daily Info Oxford*

"There's a great deal to enjoy here, believable characters with a great plot twist near the end."
– *FH Book of the Month*

By The Same Author

The Subtle Thief Of Youth

The aftermath of a summer storm reveals the grotesque secret hidden for years. As mud and water cascade through Whyncombe St Giles and Germans, they uncover the remains of Melanie Staples, a schoolgirl lost for over a decade. As a second girl goes missing on the same day resources are stretched and we glimpse the darker side of Cotswold life as the great and the good close ranks.

"An intriguing and original mystery – DJ Wiseman has a real gift for creating and telling a strong and carefully crafted story." – *Helen Ward, Oxford Info*

"As surely as the deluge strips away the landscape of the parish, the secrets of the villagers are peeled back to reveal the raw truth of the past. A beautifully layered tale."
– *Simon Humphreys, author*

By The Same Author

The Death Of Tommy Quick And Other Lies

Old certainties prove to be anything but as genealogy sleuth Lydia Silverstream responds to a dying man's plea. Her work, her home, her stuttering relationship, even her skills as a researcher, all the familiar patterns are disrupted, leaving her with more challenges than ever. And why won't a mother tell her son who his father is? It all goes to show, as always, there's so much more to a family's history than certificates would have you believe.

"This is a wonderful book. I greatly enjoyed A Habit of Dying, the first book to feature Lydia Silverstream, but the follow-up, The Death of Tommy Quick and Other Lies, is astonishingly good!" – *Peter Calver, Lost Cousins*

By The Same Author

Casa Rosa

After a bachelor life which included many of the usual vices, Harry Rose retires to his island paradise on the Pacific coast of Central America. A chance encounter leads him to employ baby Gabriela's young mother, Estefania, as his live-in housekeeper, a temporary arrangement that lasts until Gabriela is six, when her mother leaves her in Harry's care for a couple of nights. Her mother has done this before, Harry is fond of Gabriela, he treats her well and Gabriela loves him. But this time Estefania does not return. Days turn to weeks and months until Gabriela is almost eight, when their idyll is shattered by accusations of abuse and of murdering the missing mother.

"I found I had to ration myself – I could easily have read this novel in a single sitting. But that would have been like drinking Chateau Lafite from the bottle – to get the most from this wonderful novel take small sips and roll them around in your mind." – *Peter Calver, Lost Cousins*